HEREDITY

JENNY DAVIDSON

SOFT SKULL PRESS

Heredity
isbn: 1-887128-79-4

First Edition

Book Design: DAVID JANIK WITH ANN BENOIT
Editorial: RICHARD NASH

Distributed by Publishers Group West
1 800 788 3123 | WWW.PGW.COM

Printed in Canada

Soft Skull Press
71 Bond Street
Brooklyn, NY 11217
WWW.SOFTSKULL.COM

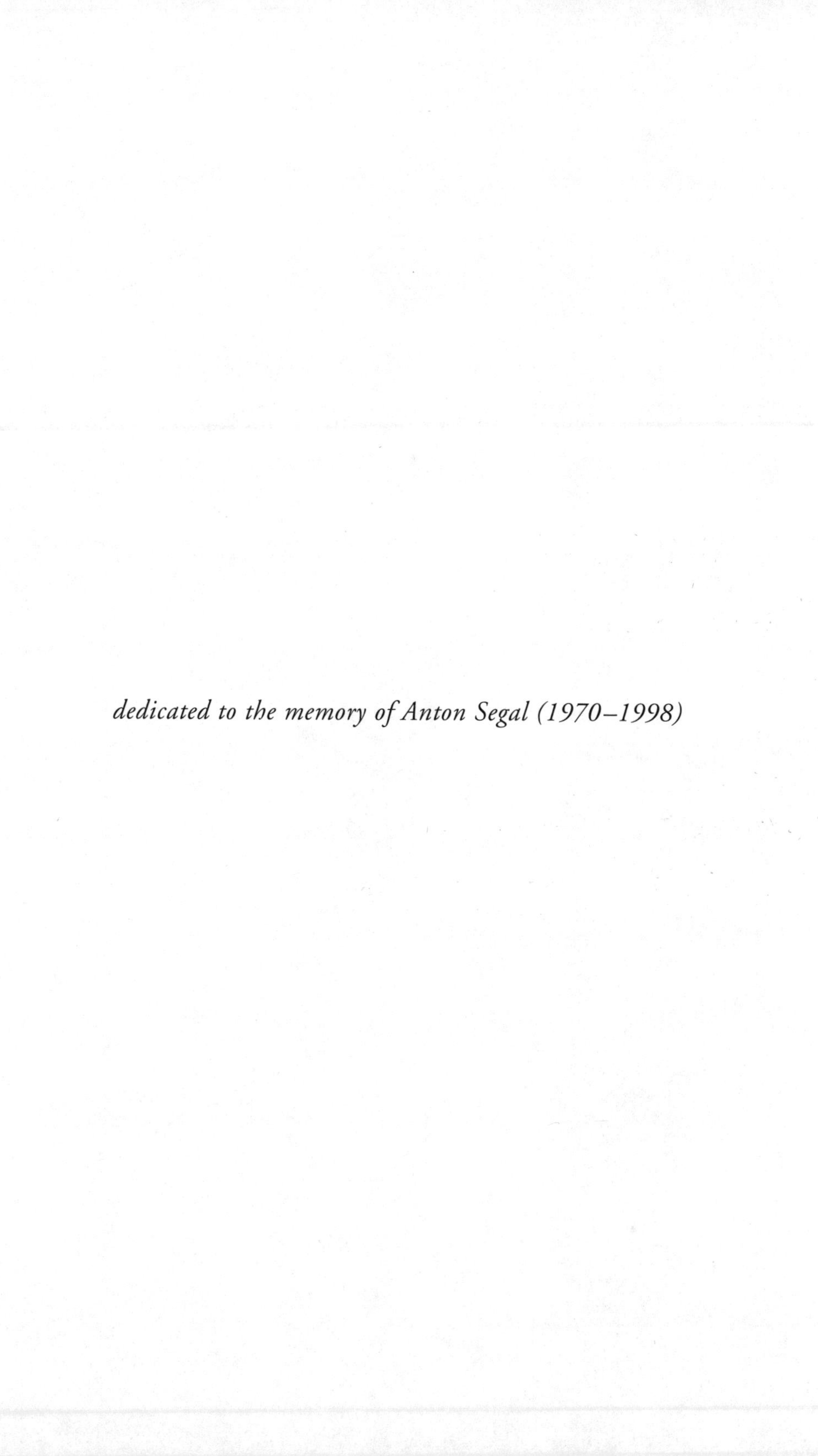

dedicated to the memory of Anton Segal (1970–1998)

I hang up the phone one afternoon in early June and consider my options. I can kill myself. I can kill my father. Or I can simply disappear and move someplace nobody will even think of looking. If I flee the East Coast, I can get by in Austin or Albuquerque in some low-profile line of work (bike messenger, grill cook, egg donor). Eggs could mean big money, but who would want them, minus the Ivy League credentials?

I throw myself down on the bed and start thinking hard. The phone rings. I pick it up and hear the voice of an old friend, now editor of a budget travel guide series.

"Our London researcher just came down with hepatitis," she says. "We need a replacement. Are you interested?"

Two days later I fly from JFK to Heathrow. I pick up a bottle of duty-free and a copy of *Jurassic Park* in the terminal and spend the flight reading and drinking Scotch. The plane lands at dawn and I haul down my carry-on from the overhead compartment. After passing through miles of corridors, I show my passport to an official and walk out of customs without opening my bag.

I take the underground to Earl's Court, the train full of early-morning commuters who look as jet-lagged and hung over as I feel. It's gray and rainy outside the station and I walk quickly to a dreary Australian-owned hotel I've used before. I pay for a room and sleep all through the day and evening, waking only to stumble down the hallway and pee in a toilet that reeks of Lysol and vomit. I fall back into bed and sleep again till morning. I check out without consuming the pallid fried egg, the fatty strip of bacon, the lukewarm tea and leathery toast the dining room serves in the name of English breakfast.

The first agency I visit lets furnished rooms near Russell Square. I pay down eight weeks' rent in American Express traveler's checks, sign a short-term lease and take the set of keys they hand me.

I spend the following week trudging round the grim parts of London that house bed-and-breakfasts. I double-check the address, I climb the stairs, I ring the bell at reception, I speak to the manager. I request prices for single, double, off-season rooms, explaining that my father may come to visit—with or without his wife—at some unspecified future date. Asking to look at a room, I inspect the premises closely, examining the mattress, lifting the toilet seat, inspecting the shower curtain for mildew. I fend off the sexual advances of several hotel proprietors. The smell of bacon lingers in these neighborhoods.

When I finish with accommodations, I lower my standards. I am not paid enough to eat in the restaurants I am supposed to review. I jot down a special or two from the menu posted in the window—smoked-salmon frittata (£8.95), lamb vindaloo (£5.35), sweet and savory crepes (£3.50-7)—and lean up against the glass, peering past lace curtains to examine the decor. For reasons of legal liability, I note the date and time of each visit before moving to the next location.

I write up my copy in irregular batches, pasting up the text with an old gluestick and inventing lavishly when my notes prove inadequate. I correct each entry in red, blue or green felt-tip and fill the margins with neat annotations. When I finish, I xerox each page at a copy-shop near the university and mail my editor the originals from the post office opposite the Russell Square tube station.

When I finish Food, I move on to Museums. I visit the Victoria and Albert, the National Portrait Gallery, the London Dungeon, the Imperial War Museum, the Museum of the Moving Image. In one of the out-of-date guidebooks from which I sometimes plagiarize, I find a description of the Hunterian Museum, a collection of medical curiosities acquired by the great eighteenth-century surgeon John Hunter. I learn that the museum may be viewed by appointment only at the Royal College of Surgeons in Lincolns Inn Fields.

One morning towards the end of the month I phone the curator of the Hunterian Museum. The telephone in the foyer of my building does not accept coins, and I buy a phonecard at the corner newsagent before I call. I haven't talked on the phone for two weeks.

The curator answers after the tenth ring, just when I'm about to hang up and write the whole thing off.

I tell her that I'm a medical student visiting from America and that I'd like to see the collection.

She invites me to come round the next morning at ten.

I note the time in the empty pages of my appointment book.

◉

Brushing my teeth at the sink the next morning, I consider what to wear. I want to make a good impression. My usual jeans and cardigan will not suffice. The other options are limited. I settle on a short wool skirt and black ribbed turtleneck, pulling on several different pairs of cotton tights before finding any without holes. I twist my hair and pin it up, then apply lipstick before the small mirror over the sink.

The Royal College of Surgeons stands only five minutes from my bleak walk-up. Crossing the threshold of the museum, I find myself surrounded by glass jars of alcohol-pickled specimens, articulated skeletons and prints of anatomical curiosities. The curator sits in an office at the end of the long vaulted gallery, phone to her ear. I watch her speak silently behind the glass for a few minutes until she ends the call and rises to greet me.

"Would you like a cup of tea?" she asks.

"No," I say.

I want to get down to business.

"Don't be overwhelmed by the mass of detail," the curator tells me as she spoons condensed milk from a sticky tin into her instant coffee. "There's always a method to Hunter's madness. He designed the collection to highlight the constant changes in the structure of living things. Just as individual animals modify their behavior to protect themselves in everyday life, so species adapt to make sure that their genetic material—Hunter won't have called it that, of course—will be passed on intact to subsequent generations. He spent over £70,000 acquiring the anatomical specimens you see here, you know; it's an astonishing collection, even by today's standards."

Especially by today's standards, I think.

The curator hands me a pamphlet guide to the collection.

"Take as long as you fancy to look about," she adds. "It's lovely to see somebody so young, we don't get many visitors from America these days."

The curator returns to her office and I begin to wander along the cases lining the main gallery.

First I examine the highly specialized tongues of the chameleon and the woodpecker, the luminous organs of the torpedo and the electric eel, the sound-producing mechanism of the cicada. I look at mutilated and partially regenerated lizard tails and at preserved fetuses from a variety of species: Cape ant-eater, kangaroo, walrus, armadillo.

A series of dissections illustrate the operation of the pancreas in the rattlesnake, the goose and the elephant. Though it is strange to think that I share a gland with the rattlesnake, the label reminds me that we are both vertebrates.

I observe carefully the cross-section of a nine-pound tumor of the parotid gland, removed over a century ago from the neck of a thirty-seven-year-old rigger. I scrutinize a large cyst full of wool and fatty matter taken from an otherwise healthy sheep.

The next case contains the preserved body of a female Surinam toad. In cells below the skin of her back, her eggs incubate before emerging as young toads. The eggs remain visible beneath the skin.

Skeletons abound. Pride of place is reserved for the assembled bones of Charles Byrne, the eight-foot "Irish Giant"; Charles Freeman, the "American Giant"; and Caroline Crachami, the "Sicilian Dwarf." They stand together in a large glass case at the center of the gallery. Caroline Crachami is tiny, her skull no larger than a cat's. A placard informs me that her skeleton is just over nineteen inches high.

I look at holes puncturing the jejunum of Lieutenant Colonel Thomas, struck in a duel by a bullet that passed below his ribs and all the way through his body, reappearing below the skin of his back; at the skull of a Bengali child to which is attached a second skull, an imperfectly formed twin whose neck ends in a massive tumor; at five female quintuplets, three of them stillborn, the other two surviving only a short time after birth. Even anatomy can express tragedy.

After finishing with the first floor, I climb the stairs to the upper gallery. I stop first at Case 73, which contains the bones of the infamous William Corder, hanged in 1828 for the murder of Maria Marten in the Old Red Barn. A small notice informs me that the museum owns an account of Corder's trial bound in leather tanned from his own skin. Unfortunately the book is no longer on display.

I move to the next set of bones. I now face the articulated skeleton of Jonathan Wild, identified as eighteenth-century Britain's most notorious thief-taker. Wild set up an office for the recovery of lost and stolen property, but he wasn't exactly legal: he supervised gangs of thieves, giving them pitifully small sums to hand over the goods they'd stolen, then selling the things back to their rightful owners at something approaching their real value. If a highwayman or pickpocket rebelled and refused to comply, the thief-taker arrested him and handed him over to the real officers of the law, who would see the offender tried and hanged. More than a hundred men and women died as a direct result of Wild's betrayals, and people rejoiced in the streets the day Wild himself was hanged for receiving stolen goods.

Jonathan Wild is my height, 5'7" or so. A catalog number has been stenciled on his forehead and the back part of his skull has been sawed off. His forehead is broad and low, his face square, his brow strongly marked. He has a wide chin. There are a few teeth in the upper jaw and only one in the lower, but according to the pamphlet the curator gave me they are all free from decay and almost a full complement of teeth remained in his jaw when he died.

I find Jonathan Wild sexy. I check him out for a while, stirring only when the curator wanders towards me. I thank her for her help and head for the exit.

Walking downstairs, I rifle through my bag for a pen. A man moving too quickly across the wide vestibule bumps into me and knocks the bag from my hands. Its contents spill out onto the tiles.

I kneel to pick them up.

He bends down to help.

As I gather keys, lighter, lipstick, I look up into the stranger's face. I recognize him at once.

"Gideon Streetcar," I say.

He looks at me, polite, English, bemused.

"Sorry," he says. "Have we met?"

And as I look at him his face breaks into a smile.

"Good god," he says, standing and brushing off the pin-striped knees of his trousers. "It's Dr. Mann's daughter. I'm terribly sorry, I'm afraid I've forgotten your Christian name."

"Elizabeth," I say. "Elizabeth Mann."

We shake hands, his eyes resting on my face.

"Are you free for lunch?" he asks. "I'd love to hear what your father's up to these days. I think of him often, you know."

"You're not the only one," I say.

And we walk out together into the open space of Lincolns Inn Fields.

◉

Gideon raises his glass.

"To the beautiful Elizabeth," he says.

I resent this English glibness.

"To the distinguished Gideon," I say.

He takes my compliment at face value. We're sitting across a table in an upscale *trattoria* in Gray's Inn Road, where the waitress has greeted Gideon by name and brought us a bottle of white wine and another of Pellegrino.

"What are you doing in London?" he asks.

I mention the name of the travel guide that employs me.

"Wonderful, wonderful," he says. "You should have called, Miranda and I would've been delighted to have you stay with us."

I am not surprised that Gideon's married. He lives in Hampstead with his wife Miranda, a thirty-four-year-old interior designer whose clients include several top models, a newspaper magnate and the French fighter-pilot author of a recent surprise bestseller.

I have never liked the name Miranda.

"How's your father?" Gideon asks.

"As far as I know," I say, "he's fine."

"I enjoyed his piece last month in the *New England Journal of Medicine*," Gideon says. "He's very eloquent on the trauma of infertility." He pronounces the word 'trauma' the English way, so that the first syllable rhymes with 'cow.'

"He's just been appointed head of OB-GYN at Yale-New Haven," I say.

"What a coup," Gideon says. "That fellowship to the States was an extraordinary piece of luck for me, you know. I could never have set up shop over here without his backing. I assume the cult of Dr. Mann carries on as strong as ever?"

"I heard that one of his patients gave him a Mercedes last year," I say. "To thank him for what he'd done for her."

"A Mercedes?"

"S-class," I say. "Silver exterior."

Gideon whistles and shakes his head.

"Extraordinary fellow," he says. "Those hands . . . a privilege to see them at work. Any yen to join the medical fraternity yourself?"

"I think not," I say.

"I dare say you'll come round to it. I remember your father used to rave about the trophies you carried home from the state science fair."

The biology projects I conducted under my father's supervision still give me nightmares, but I do not mention this to Gideon, who pours me another glass of wine and calls the waitress over to our table.

"We'll start with the portobello mushrooms," he says. "Grilled rack of lamb to follow, with broccoli, baby carrots and a few new potatoes."

The waitress takes away the menu, which neither of us has opened.

"I've lost track of how old you are," he continues. "Twenty-one? Twenty-two?"

"Twenty-five," I say.

"No," he exclaims. "God, water under the bridge, what?"

At fifteen, I was desperately in love with Gideon. I don't like him much now. I do not like English men, I do not like doctors and I do not like men who order for me in restaurants. For a moment I panic. If I stand up and leave before the food comes, what will Gideon think?

Before I can do anything rash, the waitress arrives with the appetizer. The starter, as they say in England. The word 'starter' irritates me and I frown as it comes to mind.

"Have one," Gideon says, pushing the plate of mushrooms towards me. "They're absolutely delicious."

"I hate mushrooms," I say.

I find his look of disappointment extremely gratifying.

I drink another glass of wine and watch Gideon eat the mushrooms. He transfers each one to his plate and cuts it into tidy quarters. With his knife, he balances each portion on top of the fork in his left hand, then carries the fork carefully to his mouth.

I am attracted by the precision of his greed.

Mushrooms consumed, Gideon mops up the juices from his plate with a piece of bread. Then he wipes his mouth neatly with a napkin and lays his knife and fork together in the position of six o'clock.

We finish the first bottle of wine as the lamb arrives and the waitress fetches another from the racks behind the bar.

Gideon carves several delicate chops and spoons vegetables onto my plate.

He offers mint sauce.

"No, thanks," I say.

I hate mint sauce.

I eat several mouthfuls of lamb, chewing carefully and swallowing without enthusiasm. The wine has killed my appetite.

Gideon eats alternate bites of meat and vegetable, allowing himself in turn a morsel of lamb, a slice of carrot, half a new potato and a floret of broccoli. After finishing each chop, he grasps the bone between thumb and forefinger and gnaws on it, crunching down and sucking out the marrow.

"What are you doing this afternoon?" Gideon asks.

"Nothing much," I say.

"You must come round after lunch for a drink at my office in Doughty Street. For once I've got an hour free; I was supposed to go down with Miranda last night to her parents' place in Kent, but I thought I'd tie up some loose ends in town today and take the train later this afternoon. Do come back with me, I think you'll appreciate my little collection of nineteenth-century surgical instruments."

I snicker, remembering the mad twin gynecologists played by Jeremy Irons in *Dead Ringers*. Gideon bears an unnerving resemblance to Jeremy Irons, though he is considerably younger and possibly better-looking.

He finishes his food and stands.

"If you'll excuse me for a moment," he says. "I'm just off to wash my hands."

He strides to the back of the restaurant and I tip the last of the wine into my glass. I realize that if I go with Gideon now there's a good chance we'll fuck when we get to his office.

When Gideon returns, he pays the check.

"We'll have espresso and grappa back at my place," he says.

He says the last four words in a fake American accent. Is this his standard seduction line, or does he save it for American visitors?

He holds open the door of the restaurant and I brush up against him, half by accident. Outside, we stop and look at each other.

Gideon draws a deep breath.

"Let's get a move on," he says, resting his hand for a moment on the top of my thigh.

As we walk along the crowded pavement, Gideon points out famous buildings. Doughty Street turns out to be an elegant row of late Georgian houses.

"Charles Dickens lived at No. 48," Gideon says. "I'm just next door. I share the premises with four colleagues, we've each got a separate suite but we went in together on a state-of-the-art operating facility: all the latest equipment, surgical nurses and lab technicians and so on. We don't deal exclusively with fertility problems, of course, though that's where the money seems to be these days. I'm also at University College Hospital three mornings a week, and our endocrinologist consults at Great Ormond Street."

The door of the house has recently been painted bright red. I trail my hand along the railing by the shallow steps leading to the front door, my fingers picking up a sheen of grime.

Gideon holds the door open and guides me up the broad flight of stairs to his first-floor suite. The waiting-room has a high ceiling, tall windows and gorgeous moldings. The seats are elegant but comfortable-looking and the dark red Turkish carpet screams money.

The receptionist sits at a Chippendale desk in the corner of the room. Mrs. Beardsley is stocky and middle-aged, her short hair tinted streaky blond. She wears a baby-blue silk twinset and pearls. She rises as we enter the room and Gideon performs brief introductions. She looks suitably impressed when my father's name is mentioned; she has met him several times, she tells me, and each time he remembers her name—empathy, one of the seven habits of highly effective people—and asks after her daughter.

I'm tempted to point out that it's a cheap memory trick, and that he probably uses a mnemonic to peg her name to the bleached whiskers on her chin. Beard, Beardsley. But this hostility would be misdirected. I say nothing.

"I've typed up the notes on yesterday's patients," she tells Gideon. "Everything's set for next week. Your wife called to say that she'll meet you off the 3:20 at Tunbridge Wells."

"Thanks so much, Mrs. Beardsley," Gideon says.

"Would you mind terribly if I left now? I promised Agatha I'd stop by for an hour this afternoon to see the baby. Agatha's my daughter," she adds, turning towards me. "It's all thanks to Dr. Streetcar that I've got such a lovely granddaughter, they tried for ages to have a baby and she'd given up hope, really, but the good doctor came to the rescue."

Tears well up in her eyes and Gideon looks embarrassed. He lifts her jacket off the hatstand and helps her into it, patting the secretary on the back as she knots a diamond-checked scarf around her throat.

"Nice to meet you, dear," she says. "Have a lovely weekend in the country, Dr. Streetcar."

She waves to us both as she leaves.

Gideon shuts the door behind her.

The anteroom opens into a spacious consulting room. I check out the examining table. The room's appointments are at once luxurious and clinical: *Star Trek* meets "Not tonight, Josephine."

Gideon opens another door and ushers me into the small office at the back of the house, closing the door behind us. The walls are lined with woodcuts by the sixteenth-century anatomist Vesalius. Venetian blinds let in the light through a row of windows facing the alley. Gideon pulls a cord to close the slats.

I step up to the case of instruments at the side of the room and look curiously through the glass. Finding the switch at the side of the case, I flick it up and suddenly the objects are lit from below. Gideon stands behind me, identifying syringes, lancets, trepans.

I notice a speculum identical to the modern ones in the room behind us.

"I totally get off on this morbid medical stuff," I say.

I feel the warmth of Gideon's breath on the back of my neck.

"Elizabeth," he says.

I lean forward over the case. He exhales loudly.

"Slide your hand underneath my skirt," I say.

He groans.

I feel his hand between my legs.

"Pull down my panties," I say.

He follows my instructions. I reach behind and stroke his inner thigh. He groans again and inhales. Less charitably, you could say he wheezes; the pocket of his trousers bulges with an asthma inhaler which he now pulls out, sucking and puffing several times before he stuffs the thing back into his pocket.

"Push my skirt up," I tell him. "Unbutton your pants and take out your cock."

He fumbles with his fly. He's breathing faster and more steadily, and so am I. He's got his cock in his left hand and he reaches his other hand round the front of my crotch and up between my legs. My pussy's hot and wet and I lean forward as he takes me from behind. He fucks me hard and within a minute or two I'm ready to come. I'm panting and I cry out just as he comes inside of me. His pants have fallen to his ankles, the buckle of his belt jangling as he moves back and forth.

We stay locked together for a minute, like wolves on the Discovery Channel unable to detach after they copulate. Then I pull away from him and drag my tights and underpants back up my legs. My hair's fallen down and I twist it back into a loose knot, fixing it with a clip.

"What about that drink?" Gideon asks.

He retrieves his self-possession as he does up his fly, then opens a cabinet and takes out a bottle and two shot glasses.

"Good idea," I say. I'm already completely trashed.

Hands steady, Gideon pours two double shots of grappa. We clink glasses and toss back our shots, me coughing as I swallow.

Gideon looks at his watch, a gold Rolex he exposes by shooting his wrist out from the cuff.

"I've got to dash," he says. "I'd love to see you again soon."

"I'll call you next week," I say.

He scribbles his cellular number on the back of a business card and hands it to me.

"Can I have your number?" he asks.

"I don't have a phone," I say.

I write down my address for him and tell him what he must know already: that the postal system works more efficiently in London than in New York.

"Just give me a minute or two and we'll walk out together," he says.

He washes his hands at the sink, scrubbing his nails with a brush and drying his hands carefully on a clean towel he then drops into a hamper beside the sink. His suitcase stands ready-packed beside a bulging leather briefcase and a laptop. He picks up his bags and shepherds me out of the office, locking the doors behind him.

Outside on the street, he hails a taxi.

"Can I drop you somewhere?" he asks.

"I'd rather walk," I say.

He gets into the cab and as it pulls away, I turn and head home.

◉

At seven o'clock on Wednesday evening the intercom buzzes and my heart begins to race. Nobody visits me here.

I push the talk button. "Who is it?" I ask.

A faint and tinny voice comes from the wall panel. It's Gideon.

I buzz him in.

I live up four flights of stairs. I have time to straighten the bedclothes and dump the remains of yesterday's takeout kebab in the trash before Gideon knocks.

I open the door.

Gideon stands there. He is laden with carrier bags, bottles, flowers.

I wrinkle my nose at him.

"Aren't you going to ask me in?" he says.

He drops the things he's brought on the floor and glances around the room. It looks better than usual in the late-afternoon light. A desk by the window. A single bed. A chest of drawers. A sink, a gas ring, a miniature fridge. I've taken down the tacky Impressionist reproductions from the walls and stowed them at the back of the closet. Nothing here belongs to me. Nothing reflects my personality in any way.

"Come here," Gideon says.

I go to him and we kiss. I press my body against his. He runs his hands over my hair and face.

"You're so pretty," he mutters.

I pull away from him and pick up the pack of cigarettes on the desk by the window. I pull one out and trawl through the top drawer for matches.

"Don't you want to see what I've brought?" he says.

"All right," I say, lighting my cigarette.

"First," he says, "a mobile phone."

He takes a cellphone out of a plastic bag.

"Service courtesy of BT," he says. "All the information's in the leaflet and I've already activated the line."

Cigarette hanging from my lower lip, I open the box and pull out the plastic and styrofoam packing. I flick the phone on, then off again. There's nobody I need to call.

"Now, what have we here?" Gideon continues. "Ah, a bottle of champagne."

"I don't have any glasses," I say.

He pulls out two champagne flutes and hands them to me.

"You can't say I don't come prepared," he says.

He twists the wire off the top of the bottle and eases out the cork with his thumbs. It pops and the wine spills out over the lip of the bottle. I catch it in the glasses and give him one.

"Cheers," I say.

We drink.

The taste of champagne lifts my spirits. I give Gideon a grudging smile. In fact, I am moderately happy to see him.

When I finish my cigarette, I take the extravagant bouquet of flowers and rummage in the cabinet above the sink for something to put them in. I find an empty marmalade jar, fill it with water and stick the flowers into it.

I put the flowers by the window.

"Lovely," says Gideon ironically. "I like your touch."

"You're probably used to the Martha Stewart kind of thing at home," I say.

He ignores my nasty emphasis and ferries the other bags to the counter by the sink. He takes out pâté, brie, olives, focaccia, cherries.

"Hungry?" he asks.

"Not yet," I say.

I take his hand and lead him over to the bed. We set our glasses down on the floor and begin to kiss.

Gideon unbuttons my shirt and pulls it off. He sighs when he sees the black lace bra I'm wearing underneath. He nuzzles my breasts with his lips before unfastening the bra and pushing me back onto the bed.

He undoes the buttons on the fly of my jeans and I wriggle out of them.

"I want you to go down on me," I say.

He tugs my panties down my legs and buries his head in my crotch. His fingers explore the scores along the inside of my thigh. Then he moves back up to the faded white crosshatching above my collarbone.

"What's this?" he asks.

"Nothing," I say casually, though my heart's pounding.

Events progress.

"Should we use a condom?" Gideon says.

He's lying on his back and I'm about to lower myself onto his cock.

"Did you know that in the seventeenth century the Marquis de Sévigny once tried a condom of gold-beater's skin?" I say. "He called it an armor against enjoyment and a spider's web against danger."

"I take it that's a no?"

Some time later I raise myself on my elbows to look at him.

"Sex makes me hungry," I say. "It's just as well you brought all that food."

◉

Dahlia. A genus of composite plants, natives of Mexico, introduced into Europe in 1789 and commonly cultivated in gardens. 'Blue dahlia': something impossible or unattainable (no blue variety of the dahlia having been produced by cultivation).

—*Oxford English Dictionary*

On Thursday afternoon I visit the indoor fashion bazaar in Brick Lane in the East End. As I half-heartedly paw over a pile of tiny cashmere sweaters—I don't know the designer's name, but all purchases are cash-only and they're undoubtedly beyond the budget of my travel guide's conjectural readers—someone calls out the name Elizabeth. I don't look up. I'm sure there are half-a-dozen other Elizabeths within earshot, in addition to the Emmas, Felicitys, Georginas and so on you find in upscale English settings. Then I feel a hand on my shoulder. I turn and see my old friend Dahlia.

Dahlia has sleek hair, prematurely gray and perfectly matched to the fur collar of the charcoal mohair overcoat she wears during winters in New York. A wave of homesickness engulfs me at the thought of that coat. Even a typical English summer isn't cold enough for her to break out the fur. In the here and now, she's wearing a sleeveless dress in yellow piqué cotton and bright red sneakers.

"All tat," she says, dismissing the clothes in front of us with a wave of her hand. The woman manning the stall glares at us and I am relieved when Dahlia drags me along the way, following the usual mutual expressions of surprise and delight, to a small coffee-bar. After wrangling with the waiter about whether it's possible to have her cappuccino made with skim milk—he says not, she insists, he finally gives in but I wouldn't put money on the low fat content of the drink that ultimately arrives—she turns to me and pats my hand.

"How's tricks, then?" she asks.

Dahlia is the child of an Israeli father and an English mother. She spent equal parts of her childhood in Jerusalem, South London and New Jersey, and her upbringing has left her with a bizarre accent, lots of mangled idioms and a repertoire of brilliant but obscurely expressed insights into favorite topics: couture, adultery, psychoanalysis, the phenomenon she describes as "the weak sadistic

American father." In spite of her inability to say anything in plain language, she is the very successful features editor at a London-based fashion magazine.

At first I don't know what to say. Dahlia has had her usual effect on me. I feel like a third-grader who's been taken under the wing of a particularly popular and aggressive eighth-grader: you're thrilled that she's taking an interest and grateful for her protection but there's always the lurking fear that she'll drop you for reasons as mysterious as those that drew her to you in the first place.

She takes my silence as an invitation. "You are sleeping with your father again, then?" she says.

I choke on my coffee. "Obviously I've never had sex with my father," I say.

"Who is he, then? A married man? A doctor?"

Dahlia has an uncanny ability to make bricks out of straw, a talent that verges on the psychic. She can tell from my face that she's on the money. "I thought so," she says with satisfaction. "Tell me about this man who is so very much like your father."

I give her a brief account of the last week's doings. I'm not afraid of shocking her, having heard the year before (at great length) the tale of Dahlia's ill-fated affair with a married person of unspecific gender. Due to her idiosyncratic syntax and highly abstract vocabulary, Dahlia's conversation is always enigmatic—Jane Austen as rewritten by Lacan.

"The law of the narrative," she says now.

I've never had a clue what Dahlia means by this phrase, one of her favorites, but in the context of our conversation it seems all too suggestive.

"You are acting out in your own person your relationship with your father," she adds when I don't respond.

"Gideon's not my father," I object now.

Dahlia shrugs. "What is your father doing these days?"

I am forced to admit that I do not know, that I have not spoken to him since before I left New York, that he has no idea where I am.

"We know what he's doing," says Dahlia now. "Your father is sleeping with his daughter."

"What do you mean by that?"

"How old is your stepmother?"

I count backwards. When he married her, she was twenty-five, seven years older than me. Now she must be thirty-two.

"How old are you now?"

"Twenty-five."

For Dahlia this is proof enough. "The case rests," she says.

"You mean you rest your case?"

"But what about this man, this Gideon?" she says, brushing off my irrelevant correction. "What is in it for him?"

I stop to think about it. "He wants to be my father's son?" I guess.

Dahlia shakes her head. "What did I say before? You're not listening. He wants to be Dr. Mann," she says. "He wants to fuck Dr. Mann's daughter. This is very bad."

Nobody else has Dahlia's knack for producing a purely psychological atmosphere of emergency. With Dahlia, though, it's crucial not to show any signs of fear, or her predatory nature will kick in.

"And when are you going to medical school?" she says.

Now I've had enough. I feel like I've just been beaten up. "I've got to go now," I say, standing up and digging in my bag for a few pounds to cover my share of the check.

"The funeral is not mine," says Dahlia. She gives me her business card. "Call me," she says.

I clutch the card in my hand as I walk away. At home I throw it in the trash, then panic and dig through the bin in order to find it again. Finally I stick it in the corner of the mirror over the sink.

◉

"Your father is really something. I never met another American who could do the *Times* crossword in less than twenty minutes," Gideon says with admiration.

Uneasily I think of Dahlia's speculations. Gideon and I are sitting across from each other in a small dark Soho restaurant. It's a week since we met, and we're in the early stages of what would seem to be a full-blown affair. We even have a date for the weekend: Gideon's taking me with him to an English country auction.

"Oh, everything my father tries, he does better than everyone else," I say to Gideon. I'm not boasting. Gideon's so eager to do the work of mythologizing that there's no need to take it on myself, but my father's resume is a laundry-list of embarrassing extracurriculars. The eighteenth-century landmark "cottage" in Woodbridge, the penthouse pied-à-terre in New York, the house on the Cape. Hitting the same tennis shot hour after hour with one of those stupid machines and earning the ability to make Billie Jean King sweat at the charity tournament. Running a six-minute mile. Running marathons. Running super-marathons where men (and a few women) trek fifty or sixty miles through the desert, stringy thighs all rock-solid in bright blue supplex shorts. Not to mention collecting the finest wines and the most precious stones and the rarest stamps and the earliest first editions.

"Mind you," Gideon adds, "I wouldn't want to cross him. I remember him raking me over the coals one day when I couldn't get the sperm to 'take,' as it were. I thought he was going to tell me to bend over and drop my pants so that he could strap me. A chastening experience."

"All doctors are assholes," I say.

"Present company excepted, I hope," says Gideon.

I shrug.

"Oh," I say, "think what you like."

Gideon laughs. He refuses to take me seriously.

"Surely you're being a little hard, now," he says, "on a group of respectable professional men."

He's slurping oysters out of their shells and discarding the detritus in a bowl by his plate. I don't like oysters. Sucking down an oyster is pretty much like swallowing a big expensive mouthful of cum.

"Not always men," I say.

"I suppose I've got to concede that one."

"Not always so respectable, either," I add.

"Oh?"

"Think about organ donation," I say. "Those transplant guys have shit for ethics."

Now I've pushed the right button. Gideon bristles and sits up a little straighter in his seat. "The popular prejudice against organ donation," he says, "is nothing but superstitious bunk."

"What happens when a rich and ruthless patient wants a liver or a pair of corneas, wants them really badly?" I ask. "You think the doctors won't help him out?"

"It's all regulated these days," says Gideon. "I don't mean to abandon the ethical question, but it's surely moot: every decision is hedged about with restrictions."

"Regulation may protect doctors against their worse selves," I say, "but it doesn't solve everything. What about those babies who were kidnapped in Guatemala and killed for their kidneys? It's body-snatching all over again."

"You read too many thrillers," Gideon says.

This may be true. I don't know whether children are actually kidnapped in Guatemala so that their kidneys can be sold on the black market. My wallet also contains a signed organ donor card, but I do not mention this to Gideon.

"Forget about organs," I say now. "Doctors are scamming across the board. What about the whole fertility thing? Assisted reproduction, and all that?"

"Why the hostile tone?"

"You treat rich women," I say, "women who'll pay anything to conceive a child."

Gideon becomes defensive.

"I treat other women too," he says, "women who aren't rich. Every woman has the right to have a child of her own."

"The right?" I say.

"The right to pass on her genetic material to her offspring, to perpetuate the family line in her descendants. I simply help women—and men, too, for that matter—to do so. The pull of heredity, you know. It's a strong force."

"Heredity is overrated," I say. I'm goading Gideon now, to see how far he'll go.

"How can you say that? Do you know how many live births I've made possible? Do you know how many babies have been born because of me?"

"How many?" I say.

Gideon stops. "I don't actually know how many," he admits. "We're almost into triple digits, though. Enough that I've lost count."

"Quite a boast," I say. "It must give you a huge rush, being the modern equivalent of an emperor with a seraglio of child-bearing women."

"They're not my children in that sense," Gideon says irritably, "and I might add that I don't think you're treating this topic with the gravity it deserves. Half my family died in the camps. You think I'd be willing to raise a child who doesn't carry my genes? I can't afford to. Generations of dead Jews, all depending on me to propagate. I'd do anything for a child of my own. Anything."

Gideon sounds entirely in earnest. I've heard this line all my life. My father's family got out of Germany in 1937. All his aunts and uncles and cousins died in the Holocaust. He had no siblings and I am now the sole legatee of the Mann genes. I pour myself another glass of wine in order to avoid speculating about why Gideon doesn't yet have a child of his own.

"What about genetic screening?" I say, taking a new line. "Can it really be a good idea to let people think they're entitled to improve the species when they reproduce? It smacks of eugenics."

Gideon brushes off the objection. "Once you've got the embryos, how can you resist doing genetic diagnosis before you implant them?" He's passionate now, in the evangelical mode. The best salesmen always believe their own pitches. "We can prevent people from passing on the genes that cause cystic fibrosis, Tay-Sachs, sickle-cell anemia, Huntington, all kinds of metabolic disorders. Have you ever seen a child with Tay-Sachs? It's gruesome and there's not a hell of a lot you can do to arrest the progress of the disease. Would you choose to bear a child who was a carrier, knowing what might lie in that child's reproductive future? Of course not. No sensible human being would dream of it."

"That's no excuse," I say. I'm inexplicably angry, and I will say anything now to make Gideon feel bad. "I still don't see where you draw the line between selecting for better embryos and outright discrimination. The Nazis would have gone crazy for this technology—that's why they've banned it in Germany, they're way more sensitive than we are to the ethical implications. Assisted reproduction gives parents and doctors complete control over who gets born and who never sees the light of day."

"Complete control—that's absurdly hyperbolic," Gideon says patiently, as to a stubborn child. "It's not a problem for philosophers. It's a problem for doctors, and I can assure you that we always bear the Hippocratic oath in mind."

"You're being willfully naive about the consequences," I say. By now I'm pretty much mad with rage, possibly out of proportion to the subject at hand. "What about the time when Linus Pauling suggested that the government should tattoo the foreheads of people with one copy of a recessive disease-causing gene—Huntington's or sickle-cell anemia—so that they couldn't accidentally have children with another person who carried the same gene?"

"Oh, but he was completely mad, wasn't he?" Gideon says dismissively. "Went around recommending mega-doses of Vitamin C, regardless of liver failure and other dire side-effects? That was ages ago, anyway. Nobody takes him seriously these days."

"But they did for a long time," I say, "because he was Linus Pauling and he'd won the Nobel Prize."

Gideon knows that Linus Pauling's not worth defending. He backs off. "There aren't too many chaps like that around, anyway, thank god," he says.

"No?" I say, casting about for more ammunition. "What about Robert Graham and the Nobel Sperm Bank?"

"It was only malicious detractors who called his enterprise that," Gideon says, outraged. "It's the Repository for Germinal Choice. And I'd like to know what's wrong with supplying sperm from men with genius-level IQs to well-adjusted married women with IQs in the 140-plus range?"

"More power to him," I say, "but if you were a well-adjusted and highly intelligent married woman, would you buy sperm from an outfit like that?"

Gideon concedes the point with reluctance.

"And what about that guy in Virginia," I continue, "the infertility doctor who used his own sperm to make his patients pregnant? Ninety children and counting. . . ."

"Give it up, Elizabeth," Gideon says. "We're talking here about women who are desperate to have babies. What about you? What if you couldn't have a child of your own without my help, or the help of someone like me?"

"I don't know," I say slowly. "I don't know what I'd do."

"You'd like to do everything by yourself," Gideon says, cheerful again now he's made his case.

"That's true," I say.

"Of course, even doctors can't do everything," Gideon adds. "But we can do a hell of a lot."

"I know," I say.

"Have another drink," says Gideon.

When the next round comes, he makes a toast. "To assisted reproduction," he says, holding up his glass.

I refuse to drink and he starts laughing. "To Saturday, then," he says.

"To Saturday," I agree.

◉

I wake up on Saturday morning only minutes before Gideon's due to pick me up. There's just enough time to brush my teeth in the sink, throw on some clothes and run downstairs to meet him.

"Bedroom hair," he says approvingly, ruffling it with his hand.

I take a brush from my bag and bend down with my head between my knees to give my hair a few brisk strokes.

"Not safe," Gideon says. "Put on your seat-belt, for god's sake."

The novelty of driving down the motorway in the left-hand passenger seat of Gideon's SUV quickly wears off. We stop for breakfast at a fast-food restaurant called the Little Chef (inferior to McDonald's, I decide, though Gideon disagrees) and then head on towards Warwickshire. It seems like an awfully long way to go for an auction, but I'm not complaining. I fall asleep after a while, waking up to find us off the motorway and driving along a small country road.

"Two more miles," Gideon says. He reaches over and brushes the hair out of my face. I smile at him. I'm too sleepy to tease him by pretending to be resentful. Sneaking a quick look behind us, he checks that the road is clear. He leans across and kisses my cheek.

We park in a field and trudge through what seems like at least a mile's worth of rutted mud before we come upon the house. It is a small, perfectly crafted Palladian mansion, the walls a gorgeous pale yellow under the sun's dim rays. Unlike most of England's country houses, this one has stayed out of the hands of the National Trust. The auction will be held outside; we've missed the first session, but the lots that Gideon's interested in aren't coming up until lunchtime. Tea is being served under a red-and-white striped tent about a hundred yards from the auction block, and Gideon and I amble towards it.

The crowd's distinctly prosperous: lots of weathered middle-aged couples in well-worn Barbours and weirdly expensive-looking Wellington boots. Under the awning, we find trestle tables and chairs, old-fashioned tea urns and a lavish spread of cakes and doughnuts. The setting induces in me a fit of greed. There are no drinks in sight (it's barely eleven o'clock in the morning) and I put a jam doughnut onto a thick brown china plate.

"I love English doughnuts," I confess to Gideon as we wait in line.

"You don't prefer American ones?" Gideon asks. "I thought you were down on everything English."

"Doughnuts are the exception that proves the rule," I say. "They're perfect here: granulated sugar instead of powdered, proper deep-frying, real strawberry jam instead of that generic red jelly."

Gideon shudders. "That word always reminds me of the contraceptive sort," he says. "Never could face it when they served jelly at school. Can't believe people really eat the stuff. So you're a doughnut snob, is that it?"

The tea-lady slops a cup of dark orange milky stuff onto my tray—I've stopped asking for tea without milk, the English brain can't process this request—and Gideon pays for our teas at the register at the end of the counter.

We take a place at one of the long tables. As soon as I'm sitting down, I grasp the doughnut between my thumb and forefingers and take a huge bite. It's even better than I imagined. Gideon starts laughing.

"Sometimes you're surprisingly easy to please," he says. As his eyes roam over the people near us, though, he freezes. "Oh, shit," he says. "Elizabeth?"

"What?" I say. The lump of doughnut in my stomach turns to lead.

Before he can answer, he's standing to shake hands with a man who's just appeared behind me, a salt-and-pepper Mephistopheles in tweed.

"Streetcar," the man says, pumping Gideon's hand and looking me up and down.

"John," says Gideon, visibly pulling himself together.

While I don't pretend to have mastered the protocol that governs the British male use of first and last names, it's clear that if these two were chimpanzees, Gideon would be dropping to the ground and adopting a posture of submission.

John claps Gideon on the back. "So what have you got your eye on this afternoon?" he asks.

Gideon stammers a brief, largely incomprehensible answer.

"What's that?" John says again.

"Well, lot 173 and the next few looked interesting," Gideon admits.

John chuckles. "Only fair to let a man know what he's up against," he says. "A chap I met last week in Sussex tipped me off that 176 is the one to go for; can't vouch for it, mind you. And who's this?"

"A new friend," Gideon says, turning to me with a look of appeal. "We actually hadn't introduced ourselves yet, sorry. . . ."

"Oh, you've just met? Funny, I had the impression you knew each other quite well."

As John's eyes linger with faint distaste on my striped Adidas running pants, I make a snap decision to play dumb.

"Hi," I say, "I'm Elizabeth. I'm, like, so excited to be meeting all these real English people. I'm just over here on vacation, and I can't believe how nice everybody's being—all my friends who've spent time in Britain told me that the

English are total snobs."

John winces, not so much at the content of my assertion as at my use of the words 'like' and 'total.' My strategy's worked. He's now written me off as a ridiculous American chick, and I can assume that any suspicions about my presence here in Gideon's company have been laid to rest.

"I'm so psyched to see a real English country auction," I continue, laying it on thick because guys like this expect from Americans nothing but bad manners and abuse of the spoken language. "I hope I'm not imposing, but would you guys mind if I tagged along while you're bidding? I'm afraid I'll blow my nose or something and end up buying some incredibly expensive thing I don't want."

A fastidious expression crosses John's patrician face. There's clearly nothing he'd like less than to have me trailing around after him all afternoon. "Gideon, I trust you'll do the honours for our little American friend? I've got other fish to fry, I'm afraid."

"I'd be delighted to explain things to you as we go along," he says formally. "I'll look forward to seeing you later, John."

The Englishman leaves us as abruptly as he appeared. Gideon's hand shakes as he picks up his cup of tea. "What on earth possessed you to sound so bloody idiotic?" he says.

I explain my tactics.

"I don't think he suspected anything," he admits with grudging approval.

"Who was he?"

"Miranda's father."

"Oh, fuck," I say.

"No, no, I'm sure he won't make anything of it," Gideon says. "He's the sort of English country gentleman who still refers to Americans as colonials. I'm more worried, to tell the truth, about whether he'll snap up the lots I want."

I'm not sure whether to be relieved or offended.

"He's the most single-minded collector I've ever met," Gideon continues, "and I've known quite a few. He often outbids me; he may wish me well in general, but when it comes to collecting, it's a point of pride with him to get whatever he wants."

I have a burning desire to help Gideon outmaneuver his evil father-in-law, but unfortunately I don't have a negotiating bone in my body and I can't see how I'll be able to help. The time passes quickly. Gideon mulls over possible bidding strategies without arriving at any conclusions. I've never seen him so indecisive.

Once the bidding starts, the auctioneer's patter is so fast and so arcane that I literally can't understand a word of it. We're seated on narrow folding chairs in rows before a podium. There's a bit of rain but that's not going to put off the serious bidders. The money changing hands seems excessive, especially considering that nobody really knows what's in these boxes. No advance viewing allowed. It's what they call an "eclectic collector" sale: antiquarian books, manuscripts, ephemera, autographs, maps, postcards, miscellaneous collectibles, all sealed in boxes with only the most general of descriptions. An unusual format, but one that appeals to the inner gambler: there's a chance of getting something really good for much less money than usual, and meanwhile the auction house is able to unload a lot of crap.

The three boxes in which Gideon is most interested are numbered 173, 175 and 176. I can't help feeling that John named the last box only to throw Gideon off the track, but Gideon insists there's a chance it's an elaborate double-bluff. All three are labeled "medical collections," without making it clear whether it's print and manuscript material or the actual instruments that make a collector like Gideon drool.

As we reach the low 160s, I feel Gideon tense beside me. John is seated on the other side of the aisle. They're careful not to look at each other.

Lots 169 to 172 are early twentieth-century medical paraphernalia, in which neither of the men has much interest. The ones that follow are all eighteenth-century. The lure is that there's something really valuable inside one of these sealed boxes. The risk, of course, is that there's nothing at all remarkable: you bid as far up as you dare.

Lot 173 is knocked down to John, after a heated round of bidding, for well over a thousand pounds.

Lot 174 is sold to a mousy-looking woman bidding for a small museum in Newcastle.

With Lot 175, the bidding goes out of control. Gideon's broken out in a cold sweat. He and John are raising by hundred-pound increments. Even the auctioneer looks surprised. Neither man is willing to pull out, but it's Gideon once again who loses his nerve.

"I can't spend more than two thousand pounds on something that might be worth only half that, can I?" he whispers to me.

I shrug. I refuse to take responsibility for the consequences of his decision.

The lot goes to John.

Now Lot 176 is under the hammer. "Damn it," Gideon says suddenly, "I've got to get this one." The bidding hits three thousand pounds before I've even figured out where it started. A minute later Gideon's the proud owner of Lot 176, a box scarcely bigger than his laptop computer.

We have to wait out the rest of the bidding before we can go and claim the goods. Finally they wind things up and we make our way over to the tables behind the auctioneer. John and Gideon home in on their lots and face off over the boxes.

Gideon's inexplicably nervous. I can tell he's still all keyed up.

John eyes him speculatively. "Well, old chap, you got yours and I got mine," he says. "Can't wait to see whether we got what we wanted. Now, if you're having second thoughts, I might be open to a little negotiation."

Gideon hems and haws. He's clearly second-guessing himself.

"What do you say? Fancy a bet?"

It's a fatal challenge. In the end, they decide to flip a coin. Heads, and John gets to trade one of his boxes for Gideon's precious Lot 176. Tails, and Gideon gets to buy one of John's boxes for what he's just paid for it.

The possibility of gaining an extra box proves impossible for Gideon to resist. He's already regretting having pulled out of the bidding so soon. Next thing I know, we're watching John flip a pre-war gold sovereign, a lucky piece he carries in his pocket.

Heads.

"Bad luck, old chap," says John, sweeping down on the box and tearing it open. "Care to choose which of mine you'll take instead?"

Gideon's already cursing himself. He can tell from John's behavior that Lot 176 was indeed something special. The auction-house man must have tipped him off to it. "I'll have 175, I suppose," he says with resignation.

"Shall we open the boxes, then?" John suggests.

I stand by as they examine the contents of each box in order.

John's first box is a small treasure-trove. Lot 173 turns out to be an early nineteenth-century wooden case. John opens the clasp at the side and lifts the lid of the box to reveal a bone-handled amputation saw and all the kit that goes along with it: several scalpels, sturdy needles and rolls of cat-gut, etc. I know I'm imagining it, but I catch a faint whiff of blood and disinfectant.

"Very nice," Gideon says. He pulls out his inhaler and takes a few puffs.

Lot 175, Gideon's consolation prize, is a dud. It's a small box, full of nothing but papers. Gideon leafs through quickly, exclaiming with the disgust when it becomes clear that the water-damaged manuscript inside has no evident medical connection and that the printed pamphlets and news clippings that accompany it are equally devoid of interest.

"Might be worth something, I suppose," says John. "Take it along to that fellow in Brook Street and see what you can get."

Gideon grits his teeth.

The last box is the heaviest. "Will you do the honors, Gideon?" John asks. "After all, it belonged to you for a few minutes."

All I really know at this point is that John's a complete sadist. He's playing with poor Gideon, who opens the box now with a trembling hand. And what's inside is pure gold. It's an apothecary's portable pill-making outfit, a beautiful little piece of machinery—a press with pill-molds all in different sizes, tiny metal tools to tamp down the ground powders, vials of pigment, a miniature file that looks like something out of a doll's prison—in a lacquered box with a silver handle.

John crows with delight. "Streetcar, now I forgive you for marrying my daughter," he says, slapping Gideon on the back. Gideon looks like he's just been hit by a truck. He can't believe he let this one slip.

"Miranda's going to murder me when she hears about this," Gideon tells me as John strides off with his new possessions.

Our drive back to London is not particularly pleasant. Gideon won't stop berating himself for letting the box go. Finally I get sick of trying to shore up his confidence.

"OK," I say, "you suck. You're easily manipulated and you don't know what you want. You take stupid risks. And your father-in-law's a major asshole. Satisfied?"

Gideon makes no answer.

When we reach London, I don't even suggest that we have a drink. Gideon pulls over in front of my apartment building and leans across to kiss me. "Sorry I've been such dire company," he says.

"Don't be silly," I say. "I know it was a crushing disappointment. But I had a nice day anyway."

"It's good of you to say so," Gideon mutters, looking thoroughly unconvinced. He kicks the box sitting by my feet on the passenger side. "I never want to lay eyes on that damn thing again."

"You still haven't checked out the manuscript," I point out. "It might turn out to be a real find."

"I'm not fucking interested in manuscripts," Gideon says. He sounds so much like a little boy that I can't help laughing, and after a minute Gideon joins in.

"I still can't believe I let that wanker trick me out of it," he says as I open the passenger door. "I should know better by now, Miranda's told me enough stories about how he operates."

"I could always give you a blow job right here in the car to cheer you up," I say.

He's clearly tempted, but it's a busy Saturday afternoon and the traffic wardens are out in force. Even if we didn't get nabbed for public indecency, the odds are good that Gideon would get a ticket for double-parking.

Instead we kiss. Afterwards, he perks up. "Look, Elizabeth, you don't want this stuff, do you?"

"Me?" I say, looking at the box on the floor. "What would I do with it?"

"You're the one who's always poking around museums and libraries," he says. "It would make me feel better, really, if you wanted to take it home with you and have a look. I don't think I can bear to have it under my own roof!"

"Are you sure?" I say. I find it hard to believe that he doesn't have even the slightest urge to examine the box's contents more closely.

"That's settled, then," Gideon says, handing it to me. "You can let me know if it looks interesting, and meanwhile let's just pretend none of this ever happened."

Upstairs, I make a cup of tea and sit down at the desk by the window, the box before me. As soon as I start to look into it, my hands start shaking. The newspaper clippings and pamphlets that Gideon found so boring are all about Jonathan Wild, the sexy eighteenth-century organized crime guy whose skeleton I saw at the Hunterian Museum the day I met Gideon.

In addition to the printed material—all rare, all well-preserved—the box contains a bundle of manuscript. Sheets of paper have been sewn into loose signatures, six or seven separate little books tied together with a faded pink ribbon. I am disappointed to find that all but one of the little booklets have been so badly damaged by water that they are virtually unreadable. The pages adhere to each other, and only a few isolated words on the front of each wad of paper are legible. I come back to the pages at the top of the pile, though, with an acute sense of anticipation. When I read the first lines at the top of the page, my jaw drops. I prop my feet up and as the tea grows cold, I begin to decipher the words on the page in front of me.

Revenge is a dish best served cold. I left the house this morning, my maid at my side—she doesn't know yet I haven't the money to pay her wages, but the household has been turned so thoroughly topsy-turvy these last weeks that I'm only surprised she hasn't already given notice—and walked about the city till I found myself before the booksellers' stalls hard by St. Paul's. I purchased half-a-dozen pamphlets and brought them home to read. The absurd tales they tell about the man who was my husband! I have half a mind to go and ask for my money back. A greater satisfaction awaits, however. I mean to write with my own pen the secret history of my life with my husband, Thief-Taker General of Great Britain and Ireland, the late illustrious Mr. Jonathan Wild. As to the truth of what I write, I refer you to the public record, which omits much of the matter I have unfolded, and gets many things wrong besides, but which will back me up, I believe, in many minute particulars, and must give credence to my story.

Mr. Wild died a week ago on the gallows at Tyburn. There, I have said it now, and I hope never to have as great a disgrace visited upon me again, having had one husband already go out of the world by the steps and the string. It was a very great injustice that they hanged Mr. Wild, but I have never been one to cry over spilt milk. Now I must look to my own, and I mean to get myself well out of this place: yesterday I booked my passage on the *Honour*, sailing for Maryland this Friday week. The bailiffs say that I must think about removing tomorrow, or the day after at the very latest, and I mean to set up house in the Americas. I have heard that a gentlewoman can live well there on ten pounds a year; in this way, I will preserve my stock and live only upon the income, applying myself to a sober life and industrious management. Wild is a common name enough, and nobody need know who Mary Wild was once married to, no, nor the origins of my husband-to-be. For I do not mean to go alone.

I was bred and born within the walls of Newgate Prison, where my own mother perished not three weeks after being brought to bed with me, having previously pleaded her belly to save herself from Jack Ketch. It was not the hangman but the fever that took her, though, and my aunt Spurling, whose husband was the prison turn-key, took me into her own home the very same day she laid her sister to rest in the cold ground. As an orphan I was eligible for the charity-school in my uncle's home parish, and there I learned to read and write, to curtsey and say my catechism, to sew and do plainwork and cast accounts and write a neat hand. After I finished at school, I served with my aunt in the taproom of the Lodge at Newgate, where the greatest evil of our situation was that we must put up with my vile uncle Spurling and his daily offences against nature and decency. "It's as natural for a turn-key to dote on women as for a hound to love horseflesh," my aunt would say in her cups, but my uncle came to grief in the end when he forced his attentions—all unwanted—on a prisoner, a coiner called Jane Housden whose acknowledged lover William Johnson was also due to stand trial for counterfeiting.

When the case came on in the sessions-house of the Old Bailey in September of the year 1713, it was Mr. Spurling himself who ushered Mrs. Housden into the dock. I could not see properly from where I sat, but I heard the woman's lover call out her name, Mrs. Housden turning her head to find him in the throng before the court. She seemed then to plead with my uncle, but while he kept dragging her forward, the lover Johnson pushed past the constable at the gate and threw himself after her towards the dock. Mr. Spurling pushed the man back, and a minute later my uncle lay dying on the ground, Johnson brandishing his pistol and Mrs. Housden screaming "Kill the bastard!" as the officers of the court struggled to keep her quiet.

They prised the bullet out afterwards from his head, and my aunt kept it as a memento; when in liquor she used to bring out the enamel pillbox in which she kept it and show the fatal slug to favored visitors. The court sentenced the two lovers to death, though they seemed wholly insensible to the enormity of their crime, and they were hanged in the sessions-yard. Johnson's body was afterwards hung up in chains at Holloway, and my aunt and I used to visit there every year on the anniversary of my uncle's death.

My aunt stayed on after as tap-woman in the Lodge, and I to assist her. Mrs. Spurling was a good-natured creature enough when the mood took her, but more often she cursed and slapped me when I made her uncomfortable. Mind you, I learned from her the thrifty ways that would stand me in such good stead later on, when I was charged with running Mr. Wild's household and determined upon stopping the abuses of his domestics. We sold gin for a penny a quartern—we called it geneva, or strip-me-naked—gin was cheaper than beer, and as the signs at the lowest houses had it, "Drunk for a penny, dead drunk for twopence." When in funds, we also served brandy, punch and laudanum, though it was hard enough to get by in the months after Mr. Spurling's death.

I make no complaint about those who kept company in the Lodge. There were always gentlemen among the rascals, and anyone who affronted me was liable to find himself retching in the corner after getting a fist in the gut. It was the filthy squalor of the Lodge that I hated, and I resolved at last to take matters into my own hands. A long look around the room was enough to make your skin crawl. On the broken table, a bible and spectacles, a quartern pot full of gin, stone bottles, a bowl of plaster and a pipe of tobacco; a pint coffee-pot in the rusty grate; in the chimney corner a green earthen chamber-pot (never emptied till it was full to the very brim), besides chipped china dishes, a patch-box and syringe and pills for the speedy cure of a violent gonorrhea; on the shelves, where only my aunt and I could reach them, a rusty grenadier's bayonet, musket and cartouche box and an old headdresser's block, besides all the mess from years of hard drinking.

"We lose a mint of money by your bad housewifery," said I to my aunt one morning, and I began to toss this litter into a heap in the corner ready to take out to the street to be burned.

Though my aunt looked on with horror, she was too lazy to stir from her place by the fire and whack me with the wooden spoon she kept to stir the punch. "I'll send you to Bridewell if you keep this up," she muttered. "The house of correction is the only place for you: I'll be damned if you don't spend the rest of your days knocking hemp with a beetle and being whipped once a week in the stocks—and you know that Mr. Hemings the whipper strikes home at every stroke."

I scoffed at her threats and tossed a broken teacup across the room, where it hit the wall with a round crash. The sound of the china breaking was more than Mrs. Spurling could stomach. She rolled off her seat and lumbered towards me.

"I don't jest, little madam," says she, "I'll not have you any longer under my roof, you ungrateful hussy, rolling your pretty eyes at my customers, drinking with all the riffraff in Newgate, pretending you're above the rest of us and making my life a misery. For your dead mother's sake, I'll let you lodge with me a while longer, but having you underfoot day and night is more than a woman can bear. You'll have to go out to service, that's to say if anyone's fool enough to give you a place."

I had no character, of course, so the intelligence office would not help me, and though there was a very great shortage of domestic servants about that time, I tried a score of households in the more respectable parts of town without any luck. I wore out the leather of my shoes looking, and a very wearisome business it was too. At the end of the third day's searching, I began to fear I'd have to swallow my pride and return to Mrs. Spurling on my knees, begging I might stay in her employ.

And so it was that I found myself at the Office for the Recovery of Lost and Stolen Property. The house was next to the Cooper's Arms on the west side of the Little Old Bailey, intimate to Newgate and Christ's Hospital, a few minutes' walk south from Smithfield's abattoirs, just west of Holborn Bridge and Fleet Market. It was particularly convenient, of course, to the sessions-house at the Old Bailey, where Mr. Wild spent a great deal of his time.

It was a grander place than many I'd set foot in, yet after I had knocked at the door and been admitted to the parlor where Mr. Wild did his business, I found the house in singular disarray. The fittings were top-class, and no expense had been spared on furnishings, curtains and the like, yet though new, everything was already marred and marked and thick-covered with dust. The candle-sockets were full of grease, and the maid gave the door such a clap when she left me as shook the whole room.

Half-a-dozen men stood about the parlor, all bellowing at the tops of their lungs. Tankards of ale sat on the table, leaving rings on the dull surface of a piece of furniture worth more than we saw in a year at the Lodge. Sitting on the sofa was a man I knew at once. William Riddlesden's peculiar expertise was counterfeiting bank-bills and forging assignments on the Exchequer; after he'd taken part in the notorious break-ins to the Banqueting House in Whitehall and the Bishop of Norwich's house in King Street, he'd landed up in Newgate about the time of my uncle's death. All the world knew that Mr. Wild had saved him that time from the condemned hold, persuading the judge to pardon Riddlesden on the condition that he transport himself within six months. He did not stay in America long, of course, and when he returned to London, he became a very useful assistant to Mr. Wild, who held over his head (should he disobey the great man's orders) the threat of imprisonment, conviction—for returning from transportation before his time—and death.

At that moment, however, Riddlesden's history was far from my thoughts. "Will Riddlesden," says I, "you must take off that shirt at once, for it is drenched in blood; moreover, you are staining the upholstery on the sofa."

When he complained about the cold, I let Riddlesden put back on his coat while I examined the shirt. In addition to the bloodstains (several large patches and a fine spray that would be difficult to get out—I'd have to bleach it before it would come clean), it was badly torn in several places. I pulled out my housewife—another legacy of the charity-school days, I suppose, for my aunt never had such a thing about her person—and threaded a needle with white cotton, then stuck it through my sleeve while I felt the cloth.

A small dark man came up to me then, no taller than myself, well dressed and with the trace of an accent. "Let us take this fellow out of the front room," says he, "in case a client should meanwhile pay us a visit. I am Abraham Mendez Ceixes, by the way, Mr. Wild's chief assistant."

In the kitchen, while we waited for the boy to fetch some clean cold water, I was relieved to learn that the blood had not come from one of Mr. Wild's men, but from the violent criminal they had apprehended that morning, the last to be captured of five blackguards responsible for the vicious murder of Mrs. Knap. The fact had been much talked over at Newgate, and we had all speculated as to when and how the sinners would be punished. Mrs. Knap was a widow gentlewoman who took a fancy to see the play one night at Sadler's Wells; her son escorted her safely thence, but coming back to town around ten at night, five footpads attacked them in Jockey Fields, blowing out their link and tearing Mr. Knap's hat and wig from his head. The son was knocked down, and the mother crying out, one of the party fired a pistol and the rogues fled. Mr. Knap went at once for help, but when he lighted his link again and returned to assist his mother, he'd found her dead on the ground.

The hue and cry went up at once, and Mr. Wild had before long apprehended four of the five murderers. Will White, Jack Chapman and Tom Thurland were hanged at Tyburn on the 8th of June, 1716, while Isaac Rag had saved his own skin by turning evidence and impeaching not just his three colleagues in the Knap fact but nineteen other men he'd worked with. Mr. Wild had received rewards for each of these captures, but he needed still to lay hands on the fifth man, Timothy Dun, the villain they happened to have taken that very morning.

"How did Mr. Wild discover Dun's whereabouts?" I asked Mendez as I dipped the shirt in cold water and scoured the bloodstains with salt. He had followed us into the butler's pantry and stood watching as I labored over the shirt. Riddlesden sat on a stool by the sink with a pot of ale in his hand, trying to catch a sight of my bubbies whenever the handkerchief slipped down my bosom.

"Oh, Dun sent his wife to this house to get intelligence of whether Mr. Wild still sought him, and I followed her away again to his lodgings. She tried to put me off the scent—when I followed her to Blackfriars, she took water and crossed to the Falcon, then crossed again to Whitefriars, whereupon she walked at a fast clip to Temple Bar. I followed her to Westminster, and she took the boat thence to Lambeth. Dusk had fallen by then, and she thought she'd lost me. I kept at a safe distance, following her to a mean lodging in Maid Lane near the Bankside in Southwark, and marked the door with chalk so that we could find it in the morning. We went back at dawn to take him."

I scrubbed the shirt with renewed vigor as Mendez recounted the rest of the story. Dun lodged up two pairs of stairs; Mendez waited in the alley at the back of the house, while Riddlesden accompanied Mr. Wild up the stairs. They hammered on Dun's door, but he'd heard them coming and climbed meanwhile out the back window onto the roof of the pantry, about eight feet off the ground. Mendez saw Dun upon the tiles and fired a pistol, wounding him in the shoulder. Dun rolled down into the yard, by which time Riddlesden and Mr. Wild had joined them behind the house. Finding Dun lying on his back on the ground,

Riddlesden fired a round of small shot directly in Dun's face (thus the fine spray of blood, I thought; the larger patches must have come when he helped Dun into the coach).

"You should have seen him crying out for mercy," Riddlesden boasted as I cleaned out a nasty gash across his collarbone and bound it with lint, "his face torn all to pieces with shot, his ankle broken from the fall."

Mendez made a face and said that the important thing was they'd brought Mrs. Knap's last murderer to justice, which would earn Mr. Wild a reward from the government of forty pounds at least, and more if Mr. Knap showed himself a good son and made his proper compliments to the man who'd captured the last of his mother's killers.

Once I had got out the worst of the stains and sewed up several long rents, leaving the rest of the damage for the laundry-maid to repair, I had a word with the kitchen-maid. The cook was passed out dead drunk on a settee by the fire, but I saw in a flash what the kitchen could be under proper management.

Mendez soon came back for me. "Mr. Wild will see you now," says he; "show him a proper respect, by the bye, for he is a very great man."

"I am told I must take you on at once," says Mr. Wild, I standing at last before him, "so that my men's linen will no longer disgrace me."

I looked at my feet and did not know what to say (an uncommon occurrence, I can assure you). Mr. Wild was a man of great authority in his way, a dark stocky fellow with strong features and a Staffordshire accent thick as treacle. While his confidential manner tempted me to answer in kind, I knew he'd take it amiss if I gave him any cheek.

"I am a dab hand with the needle," says I at last, "in addition to cooking, cleaning and serving at table; if you take me on, you'll not regret it."

"You are no doubt a paragon of the virtues," says Mr. Wild. "Any other skills?"

"I have a way with flesh wounds and fevers," says I, "and have been known to mend what the surgeons cannot."

I was not fibbing here, for at Newgate I had often been called in to see men who hadn't the dibs for a more established practitioner, and I had in my own possession a surgical kit belonging to a barber who'd died on the gallows.

"Come here," says he then, and I approached him, thinking he might want a kiss and by no means averse to the prospect. In truth, I could hardly take my eyes off the man, and I thought I'd need little persuading to consent even to my own ruin.

Before I knew it, though, Mr. Wild had spun me around and thrown his left arm over my mouth, his other hand holding a knife to my throat. He'd moved so quick I saw only the flash of the blade, though I could feel it cold against my skin.

"The surgeons sent you, did they not?" says he. "Tell me the truth. They made you their agent, a young maid like yourself being unlikely to rouse my suspicions. You cleaned Riddlesden's wound: don't tell me you don't know what you're about. They have sent you to keep watch over me while I live, and to make sure they hear first when I die."

I felt the blood pound in my veins, in truth hardly knowing what to say to this extraordinary charge. "I know naught of these surgeons," says I.

He put the knife to my breastbone and slashed sharply through the top part of my bodice, which fell open about my chest. I put my shaking hands to the cloth and held it close about me.

"Swear you are not here to plot against me," he said, fumbling with his own hand for a Bible and forcing it into my own. "Swear you will not prevent my body from resting in peace below ground when the day of my death shall come. We have a kind of property in our own bodies. Every man should have the right, after he dies, to know that his carcass will molder decently in the grave. It is an abomination to cut men up in public and display them to view like so many curiosities."

My voice unsteady, I swore before God that I was innocent of any intrigue.

He must have believed me, for he let me go then. As I fell trembling into the chair before the desk, he began to clean his nails with the point of his knife.

"Mendez!" he called.

Mendez came running, having been waiting outside the door till my audience with Mr. Wild should be over. "Take the girl away," says Mr. Wild, "and make sure she comes tomorrow in better cloth."

The two men looked at me then, and me naked practically to the waist. It was all I could do not to cry.

Outside I said to Mendez, "It is not what you think."

"When it comes to Mr. Wild," said Mendez, "it is hard to know what to think. Be assured I'll say nothing to the others."

He gave me two gold broad pieces for clothes, and told me to come again the next morning and I'd be put to work.

You'd think I'd have known better, after this start, than to join the man's household. No such thing, though I well remembered the feel of the knife at my throat. I came the next day, and I swore never to give Mr. Wild any reason to question my loyalty.

◉

I'm glad to know I'm not the only one who has a problem with doctors.

Jonathan Wild did not want to be dissected.

He took every possible precaution to make sure he'd stay buried.

To no avail.

When I'm not fucking Gideon or checking the opening hours and admission fees at the Tower of London and other major tourist attractions, I'm at the British Library reading about anatomy. While I have tried to pull apart the pages of the next section of Mary Wild's narrative, each time I introduce a letter-opener between the sheets the corners of the paper start to crumble away in my hand. I don't have the expertise to do this myself, and I've made an appointment with a curator at the British Museum to get some advice on dealing with the manuscript without causing any more damage.

Meanwhile I'm out to discover as much as I can about how Jonathan Wild ended up in the hands of the anatomists. Specific details are few and far between, but the history of dissection makes some sense of Wild's exhumation.

In the sixteenth century, Henry VIII granted the Companies of Barbers and Surgeons the official right to dissect the bodies of four hanged felons each year. Right away the surgeons complained that this was not enough. The seventeenth-century surgeon William Harvey had so much trouble getting hold of cadavers that he had to dissect the bodies of his father and his sister. Charles II added the bodies of two more felons to the annual grant, but the shortage continued and the illegal trade in bodies grew.

Wild was hanged at Tyburn in 1725. Afterwards, his widow (the author of the memoir now in my possession) paid for a coach and horses to carry his body to a public house called the Cardigan's Head. The mob hated Wild so much that they tried to intercept the coach, seize the body and give it to the surgeons for dissection. Wild's men spread a rumor that the coach belonged to the surgeons themselves and as a result the crowds let it by. At two the next morning, Wild's body was safely interred at St. Pancras Church-yard beside that of his previous wife.

I'm shocked to learn that the woman's name was Elizabeth Mann. The odds against my having her name must be staggering.

Three days later, Wild's body was dug up by grave-robbers who paid somebody off to discover the location. The widow's efforts had failed to protect him.

They left the empty coffin at the end of Fig Lane near Kentish Town and transferred Wild's body to a hearse-and-six. A pile of skin, flesh and entrails was found the next week on Whitehall Shore; the surgeon who testified at the inquest identified the material as the remains of a dissected body, probably Wild's. The coroner ordered the remains interred in a burying ground for the poor.

The skeleton passed through the hands of a succession of surgeons. At the start of the nineteenth century, Dr. Frederick Fowler of Windsor bought Wild's bones with his practice, and in 1847, he donated the skeleton to the Royal College of Surgeons, along with the original coffin plate.

Before Fowler sent the bones to the museum, he detached Wild's skull. Without naming the original owner, he delivered it to the well-known phrenologist Deville in the Strand. Deville returned the skull to Fowler with a certificate of character, published by the *Weekly Dispatch* on 22 March 1840, which I find without any trouble in the microfiche room of the local public library:

> This is the skull of an individual possessing some useful faculties for mechanical operation, going about and comprehending things readily; but he is a singular character, with a large portion of brain in the region of propensities. And under disappointment of his own importance, pecuniary difficulties, or intoxication, he would be very likely to commit a crime. He would be fond of offspring or children, but not a kind parent, as the mandate must be obeyed. He would be the associate of a female, and probably be a married man, but liable to jealousy, being a doubter of the integrity of others towards himself; and while in this state of feeling, if aroused, he would be liable to do injury to those so offending him, and, if opposed, murder might be the result of such an organization.

Dissection was commonly viewed as the most brutal punishment the law could inflict. In 1752 Parliament allowed judges sentencing felons on capital counts the right to substitute dissection for gibbeting in chains. Only the most unpopular criminals were sentenced to be cut up. Nothing matched the public dread of being anatomized (though even my own major reservations about the medical profession do not persuade me that having your body treated in tar, enclosed in an iron frame and suspended in the air above the scene of the crime should necessarily be preferable to going post mortem under the surgeon's knife).

It wasn't just felons who were liable to illegal exhumation. No grave was secure. When Laurence Sterne died, the author of *Tristram Shandy* was buried in the church-yard at St. George's, Hanover Square. His body was stolen the same night and turned up two days later on a slab in Cambridge. Only when one of his old students recognized it was the body re-interred.

Many more surgeons now learned anatomy by cutting up the bodies of the dead. John Hunter's brother William insisted that anatomical dissection was the basis of surgery: "It informs the Head," he wrote, "guides the Hand and familiarizes the heart to a kind of necessary Inhumanity."

In 1765, John Hunter opened a private anatomy school at his house in Great Windmill Street. As in the Parisian schools, each student had his own corpse to work on. You can guess where the bodies came from. In spite of the Crown's annual gift, eight cadavers do not go very far towards satisfying the needs of a nation of doctors. All the private schools of anatomy obtained bodies illegally. The poorest medical students often paid tuition in corpses rather than coin.

It's a strange fact that the courts at this time did not consider exhumation a theft. Bodies were not real property and could thus be neither owned nor stolen. Grave-robbers were careful to leave woolen shrouds and grave-clothes behind in the coffin to avoid prosecution for theft.

All the anatomists coveted the bones of Charles Byrne, the eight-foot Irish giant who astonished audiences by lighting his pipe from a street-lamp. He begged in his will to be buried at sea in a lead coffin. His wish went unfulfilled. When word got out that Byrne was ill, John Hunter put his man Howison to watch Byrne's house. At last Byrne died and the next day the undertaker's men left the house with the coffin. As the coffin weighed a great deal, they understandably stopped at the pub for a drink. Here Howison approached them and offered them fifty pounds for Byrne's body. They laughed in his face and asked for five hundred, and Howison promised them whatever they wanted.

Howison smuggled the corpse into Hunter's house. He and Hunter pushed it into a boiler and cooked it until the flesh separated from the bones. And Byrne's skeleton still stands in the center of the gallery at the Hunterian Museum.

Five hundred pounds was more expensive than most, but by the 1790s, increased demand and limited supply caused the price of corpses to soar. A standard adult's body cost two guineas and a crown, a child's six shillings for the first foot and ninepence per inch thereafter.

A posse of grave-robbers would go at night with wooden shovels and a dark lantern to new graves, where the digging was easy and the bodies fresh. They laid down a canvas to collect the displaced earth, dug a hole at the head of the grave all the way down to the coffin, and inserted hooks or crow-bars under the coffin's lid. Once they had heaped sacking over the hole to muffle the sound of cracking wood, the remaining earth acted as a counter-weight, exerting pressure to snap the lid. Then they hoisted the body out with ropes and checked that it was fresh enough to sell.

(As the Jews buried early, their cemeteries often yielded the best subjects. I make a note to tell my father about this—it's the kind of thing that interests him—when I speak to him next.)

The next step was to strip the corpse and throw the grave-clothes back into the ground, then truss up the body and put it in a sack. The resurrection-men transported bodies to their destinations compressed into crates, stored in hay or sawdust, roped up like hams, sewn into canvas, packed in chests, barrels and hampers. Bodies were salted, pickled or injected with preservatives to stop them from smelling.

Grave-robbers dared not wear their working clothes—stained with mud and clay—during the daylight hours lest they excite the attentions of the mob. In 1795, three men were found carrying five bodies in sacks from the burial ground at Lambeth. The men who were arrested told the judge who tried them that they served eight surgeons and an articulator of skeletons. The relatives of those who had been buried at Lambeth now appeared and demanded the right to dig for their friends. They forced their way past the parish officers into the graveyard and began to tear up the ground like madmen. They found many empty coffins.

It's clear who deserves the blame. Those dead people didn't want to be cut up. The bereaved didn't want it to happen either. The grave-robbers had to make a living somehow. Say what you like: it's the doctors you can't forgive.

People tried to thwart the body-snatchers. The relatives of the dead did everything they could to protect them. They placed small sticks, stones, shells and flowers over the graves to betray any signs of disturbance. Prudent grave-robbers took the trouble to replace these tokens before they left.

The rich had their coffins soldered shut before they were buried. They bought special patent coffins whose spring-latches prevented the lids from being levered open. They constructed cast-iron vaults along the same principles. Those with less money fastened iron straps or metal bands to their coffins with screws that could not be withdrawn. Other bodies safely putrefied above ground in a dead-house.

Still, there's only so much you can do. Think about this: one surgeon bought a graveyard himself, charged customers for plots, then took the bodies up again and sold them to his pupils.

◉

Gideon and I develop a routine.

I work most days in the library at the British Museum.

At half-past twelve I step out of the library into the women's bathroom and call Gideon on my cellphone.

"Let's meet for lunch," he says.

"All right," I say. "Steps of the museum in half an hour?"

Twenty minutes later I turn the book I'm reading face down on the table. I stand and stretch. I leave my things and wander out past the security checkpoint and through the crowded entrance hall.

Outside, I pull out my cigarettes and light one, smoking slowly to make it last. I've taken up smoking again for real, though I can barely afford it.

Gideon arrives as I finish my cigarette. I throw the butt down and grind it out with my heel.

"What do you fancy in the way of lunch?" he says.

"McDonald's?"

He groans. Today's Thursday and we've already eaten American fast food twice this week.

We walk to the McDonald's in Tottenham Court Road. He's holding my hand and I'm not really into it.

I order the usual. Big Mac, fries, Diet Coke.

Gideon frowns at the menu. He finally orders a fish sandwich with extra tartar sauce and a chocolate milkshake.

"I don't know what on earth there is to like about this place," he says.

We sit upstairs to eat. Off-putting families surround us on all sides.

"I like it here because even English people can't fuck up McDonald's," I say.

I finish the burger and lick my fingers.

A small child at the table next to us refuses to eat its burger. The mother slaps it and the child throws up all over the table. Its siblings begin to wail.

"For god's sake," Gideon says, "let's get out of here."

He wraps his unfinished sandwich neatly in its wrapper and consolidates the debris on our trays, carrying them to the trash and tipping the rubbish into the bin before replacing the trays on the shelf above.

We go back to my place. He washes his hands. We have sex for twenty minutes. He washes his hands again. Then he returns to work.

"I'll call you in the morning," he says.

Only when he's gone do I remember that my bag's still at the library, manuscript and all. Fuck, I think, I'm an irresponsible fucking loser. I hurry into my clothes and run back to the museum, arriving only minutes before my appointment with the paper conservator. I race past the security guards to retrieve my bag, then waste too much time trying to find the office of Dr. Allan Menzies, which is buried in the bowels of the Museum behind a series of metal doors that warn me to 'Keep Out.'

I'm all too aware that I'm sweaty, disheveled and reeking of sex, but the conservator is courteous as only a British scholar can be. My first impression is all shabby beige corduroy and floppy dark hair, but as we perform our greetings I notice the strength and beauty of his hand in mine, the long supple fingers and the sculptured joint at the base of the thumb, though his cuticles are ragged and the nails bitten down to the skin. He's a soft-spoken Scottish guy in his mid-thirties, and I'm mortified to find myself noticing that he's not wearing a wedding ring.

He's listening to music while he works, and as a new song comes on I exclaim. It's "Hope," by the Descendants, one of the top five masochistic love songs of all time and a regular feature on the running soundtrack to my life.

"I love the Descendants." As soon as the words are out of my mouth I feel ridiculously adolescent, but he lights up and we spend an enjoyable few minutes trading likes and dislikes. We're in extremely good humor with each another when we settle down to look at the manuscript. I haven't brought the sheaf of newspaper clippings at the bottom of the file, just the little stack of homemade books that make up Mary Wild's narrative of her husband's life and death.

"So what have we got here?" he says, drawing the pile towards him with gentle fingers.

I explain how the manuscript came into my possession and give him a brief account of Wild's career returning stolen goods to their owners in eighteenth-century London, the existence of his skeleton and the puzzle of his exhumation.

Preliminaries out of the way, the conservator slips on a pair of latex gloves and begins to examine the manuscript, which I have stored in a large plastic freezer-bag. First he leans down to sniff the first signature, shaking his head.

"Some mildew there," he says, "though the damage doesn't look bad; one should really wear a respirator, but I hate to lose the assistance of my sense of smell. Let's do a quick vacuum, to be on the safe side."

He sucks up spores with a small hand-held vacuum cleaner, brushing each page of the first book with a piece of felt.

"It's a pity this has been bound," he says; "you might want to think about separating the sheets and transferring them to acid-free alkaline folders. Each time you open a book like this you cause a little more damage—it's best to handle it as little as possible, and if you're doing heavy-duty work on the text, I'd advise you to house each sheet in a polyester film folder to protect it from the environment. We can also photograph it for you, of course; it's a bit pricey, but you get an extremely high-quality reproduction."

I'm jotting down notes as he speaks. I like how knowledgeable he seems. The machines covering all the available counter-space remind me of the forensic crime lab where I worked summers in high school, my boss the county pathologist and a golfing partner of my father's.

Dr. Menzies's verdict on the first set of pages is that they're in surprisingly good condition, and that so long as I house the material properly it should remain intact for hundreds of years to come. The remaining material poses more obvious problems. With a pair of tweezers, he tweaks the front page of the next book. It's stuck firmly to the other pages, though, and after what seems to me an unduly finicky set of exploratory maneuvers he puts the tweezers aside.

"Look," he says finally, clearly aware that I'm fidgeting, "this isn't going to be quick. I'll need to explore each signature under a variety of light sources, run a few fiber and pigment analyses and so on before I'll be able to come up with a strategy for making the text accessible. One mustn't rush these things: patience is everything. I suspect it won't be too tricky once we know what we're dealing with. The ink doesn't seem to have run too badly, so it's primarily a matter of washing each page in a solvent that will allow us to separate out the individual pages. Our dry-cleaning techniques are state-of-the-art, but it'll take some time. I realize I'm asking a great deal, but would you be willing to leave the materials with me for a week or two? I promise they'll be in safe hands."

"I don't doubt it," I say. "Are you sure it's not a huge imposition? I can't promise I'll be able to donate the manuscript to the museum; it doesn't really belong to me."

"Not at all," he says, his attention entirely focused on the pages of the book. "This is our bread and butter. No commitment necessary on your part. We'll do tests for authenticity, too, of course (paper, watermarks, chemical analysis), though I must say it looks to me like the real thing."

"I'm impatient to read the next installment," I confide as he strips off the gloves and begins to write out a receipt for the manuscript. "What I've read so far is a bit of a tease. I'm dying to find out what happened next."

"You've got me quite intrigued," he says, grinning at me as he hands over the receipt. "Perhaps I'll stop by the Hunterian Museum to have a look at that skeleton—it's really very exciting."

We shake hands again before I go, with a promise on his part to call me in another week or two to report on his progress. As I give him my phone number I realize I have been treating my mobile like one of those red telephones that sit on the president's desk in cold-war thrillers. It's not actually a hotline to Gideon, so why do I feel like Bluebeard's wife when I think of using it to talk to anyone else? I leave with a feeling of expansive charity towards the British library system for being so generous as to have placed this expert at my disposal. I hit three or four art museums before closing time and write up my copy that night in a fit of diligence.

◉

Gideon calls me the next morning.

"Are you available Friday evening?" he asks.

"Yes," I say.

"Good," he says. "Miranda and I are hoping you'll be able to come to a small dinner party at our place in Hampstead, OK?"

"OK," I say.

I feel sick to my stomach. I light a cigarette.

I write down their address and the time.

"See you, then," I say. I know I'm being ridiculous. My hands are cold as ice.

"Bye, darling," Gideon says.

"Bye."

That afternoon I go shopping. I buy sexy underwear and a bottle of whisky and a big bar of chocolate. At the mini-market round the corner, my eyes linger on a small box of straight-edge razors, attracted to the square retro packaging and the economy of its promise. I have to restrain myself from picking up the box and chucking it onto my heap of groceries (the waxy carton of juice, the green apples, the packets of Hula Hoops—a form of English junk-food to which I have become addicted, whose name reminds me of my childhood in the 1970s and whose reconstituted potato flavor has nothing to do with the vegetable as it exists in nature). They keep razors by the cash register next to the cigarettes: if you thought you could make it out of the store without them, think again. At the last minute I casually pick up a box and add it to my purchases.

At home, I slide one out. I haven't bought razors for a long time. I examine the top fold of stainless steel, the lozenge-shaped hole at the center, the tiny semi-circles nipped out of each side like mechanical analogues to the bubbles in Swiss cheese. I run my finger carefully along the straight sharp edge of the blade. Then I slide it back into the box.

◉

Miranda is gorgeous. She has dark, well-groomed hair, immaculate makeup, amazing legs and long narrow pedicured feet in a high-heeled pair of white Gucci sandals that look like they cost hundreds of dollars. Or pounds, I guess. She wears a white silk shift that exposes various parts of her tanned and aerobicized body.

Miranda is definitely sexier than I am.

And Miranda is also a stunning cook. Mussels steamed in white wine, grilled prawns, mushroom risotto, spinach lasagna, a new wine with each course. The food is so good that I manage to eat more than usual, though by the end of the main course I am nonetheless completely wasted.

My face is flushed. I'm trying hard to look sober, but it's definitely mind over matter.

The unattached man invited for my benefit is horrible. He is an up-and-coming producer at the BBC. He tells me about a documentary he's just finished filming on organized crime and the garbage disposal business. I am interested in organized crime (isn't everyone?), I'm even interested in garbage disposal (I'm interested in everything) but the guy is monumentally dull. He wears a loud tie and a mustard-colored shirt: Michael Caine on a bad day. He spits as he talks. He talks a lot.

I raise my hand to wipe my face.

Miranda catches my eye and almost imperceptibly winks.

I like her more than I expect to.

As we dip homemade almond biscotti into our coffee a tiny old lady appears in the doorway.

"Giddy," she says.

She is a pitiful sight. She clutches a piece of bread in one hand. A drop of blood adorns her pinched upper lip. She's wearing a filthy blue bathrobe and a ratty pair of slippers. The bathrobe falls open to reveal a stained floral nightgown and the flabby wrinkled sacs of her breasts. Her forearms are scratched and bruised.

"Gideon," she says. Her tone is urgent.

He pushes back his chair from the table and moves towards her. He's still holding his wine glass.

"Mother," he says. "What's the matter?"

"Gideon, I've got something stuck in my teeth."

"Shall I help you to get it out?"

"Yes," she says.

She's got a German accent, but there's a hint of something else too. Scotland?

She hands him the piece of bread she's holding. He looks about him and stows it on top of the bookshelf. Then she puts her hand to her mouth and extracts a full set of dentures.

Someone to my left suppresses a hysterical giggle.

Gideon takes the teeth from her, holding them cautiously between his thumb and forefinger. After a moment he pops them into his glass of white wine.

"I'll be back as soon as I can, darling," he tells Miranda.

He leads his mother gently from the room, glass in hand.

Miranda is fuming.

"She does it on purpose," she says. "Whenever we have people over for supper, without fail. You'd think we abuse her or something, I've bought her hundreds of pounds' worth of new clothes at Marks and Sparks but she still insists on wearing those terrible old rags. Did you see the bruise on her arm?"

We all look around at each other, silent and shamefaced.

"She does it herself," Miranda says, "and makes damn sure everybody sees it—she wants you to think the worst! It's probably all for the best that she's not more *compos mentis*, or she'd dream up a lawsuit just to vex me."

An awkward pause follows. We feel sorry for Miranda, but what can you say?

"Haven't seen teeth like that since my old gran died," my boring neighbor remarks finally.

We laugh uneasily.

"Heard a lovely bit of rhyming slang the other day," another guest says, in a valiant attempt to lighten the tone. "Hampsteads. Get it?"

I give him a blank look. Everyone else seems equally annoyed.

"Hampsteads," he repeats. "Bloke asking for Hampsteads at the chemist? Hampstead. Hampstead Heath. False teeth, see?

"Ingenious," Miranda says, in a dry tone. But she's recovered her cool. "Ralph, you've just invented that on the spur of the moment, haven't you?"

Ralph denies it. Nobody believes him.

As a topic, teeth are all too interesting. Everyone has an unsavory anecdote or a painful memory. I myself am completely paranoid about my teeth. I have dreams where they fall out. (What did Freud say this meant?) The last time I went to the dentist, the guy told me I needed a root canal and two fillings. I was seventeen. I made an appointment to go back the next week. I never showed up then and I haven't been back since.

Within fifteen minutes, we're all standing by the door. The party cannot survive the appearance of Gideon's mother and her awful teeth.

Miranda follows me as I retrieve my jacket from the study.

"Oh, god, I'm sorry," she says. "What an utter wash."

I feel sorry for her. "That guy's a real loser," I offer, "the one I was sitting next to."

"The spitting is a bit much, isn't it?" she confides, grinning. "I'd forgotten what a terrible bore he is, I promise I'll find you someone decent next time."

"Do you need a ride?" the boring TV producer asks me.

"I guess so," I say.

Gideon appears as we're leaving and kisses me goodnight.

"Lovely to see you," he says, pressing my hand. "We hardly had a chance to speak."

"Take care," I say.

"I'll call you next week," he says.

◉

Three weeks into the travel guide work, a familiar malaise has hit me. I have a passion for research, but it's bad luck for my editor that I find the past so much more engaging than the present. I have a toxic inability to carry through on projects I don't like. I'm sleeping late, then drifting in to the British Library around eleven for a session with the eighteenth-century pamphlets that recount the life and crimes of Jonathan Wild.

Gideon and I fit in a meal on Tuesday night. We fuck at my place, then go round the corner for a pub supper. The choices are straight out of Monty Python: burger and chips, fish and chips, lasagna and chips.

"Why no birth control?" Gideon asks me as our lasagna is served. His is vegetarian: he won't eat beef because of Creuzfeldt-Jakob disease. "Are you on the pill? If so, you really should stop smoking."

In my experience it's rare for men to inquire so closely into one's birth control—they have a bizarre and often unfounded faith that women reliably take care of these things—but I suppose Gideon's profession gives him a certain investment in knowing.

"I can't get pregnant."

"Why not?"

"It's a long story. I'll tell you some other time."

This is clearly an evasive maneuver, but Gideon doesn't choose to press me. The affair's a busman's holiday, whichever way you look at it. During a normal work week Gideon's hands feel up hundreds of ovaries. One more set can't make that much difference.

"Would you like to have children, though?" he now asks.

I think about it. After a minute, I grudgingly admit that I do.

"Nothing wrong with that," Gideon says. He sounds surprised that I should consider it a guilty secret.

"I don't know," I say. "I guess it depends who you're talking to."

"Miranda's desperate for a baby. As are almost all the women I see at the office," Gideon points out.

For once hearing Miranda's name hasn't sent me into a tailspin of jealousy, shame and self-loathing. Infertility is a great equalizer.

"People reproduce in lots of different ways," I say. "It might be better to think outside the lines. What's your verdict on cloning?"

It's less than six months since Dolly made her debut on the front page of every major newspaper. Cloned from cells drawn from her mother's mammary glands, the sheep is named for Dolly Parton, the other warm-blooded creature whose boobs are her best-known attribute (one of those male scientific jokes about female anatomy).

"We'll be capable of cloning humans within the next five years, I'd put money on it," Gideon says in response, "and I don't see why we should allow professional ethicists to tell us whether to clone or not to clone. Masses of people take a stand against cloning just now, but the same was true for IVF twenty years ago; and how many people any longer think that fertilizing eggs in vitro is immoral?"

"I'm more or less in agreement with you," I say.

Gideon does a double-take. "No!" he says, grinning broadly. "I've said something with which Elizabeth Mann agrees!"

If he'd just ended with the preposition, I think, I might have been able to give him a friendly answer. Instead I ignore him and swallow another mouthful of liquor. "The real test isn't whether you're pro or con," I say. "It's who you'd choose to clone, given the chance."

"How's that?"

"Lots of women are in love with their husbands because they remind them of adorable little boys. Cloning's only one step further—think of how tempting it would be to try again, this time with a chance of getting the guy's upbringing totally right. Erase the bad influence of his mother and all that."

Gideon laughs. "I suppose I can see the appeal."

"You have to be more suspicious of people who want to clone themselves. Especially the men—then they're really just looking for a baby container."

"But surely women who'd like to clone themselves must be equally narcissistic?" Gideon asks.

"Well, it depends whether they're lesbian separatists or compulsive perfectionists," I say. "In reality they're probably both at once: corporate lawyers with long legs and closets full of Prada and Dolce & Gabbana, too proud for facelifts but not really needing them either since they work out twice a day, just too goddamned superior to any potential mate to bother to seek one out."

As soon as I've said this, I have a nasty feeling that I've just described a pathology that characterizes many of Gideon's existing IVF patients. Cloning's not going to make it any worse. And I'm evidently right on the money.

"Can I tell you something, in complete confidence?" Gideon asks.

"Of course," I say. I like the idea that he's confiding in me professionally.

"Post-Dolly, we've all started to ask clients whether they'd be interested in cloning. Can't let the competition beat us to it, you know. Quite a few people express interest, but two of my patients have already made rather more serious overtures, asking me about whether there's any chance they might become pregnant with clones of themselves within the next year or two."

"Are they both astonishingly beautiful but rather stupid?"

Gideon starts to laugh. "Well, yes, now that you mention it," he admits. "One's a former model, the other a rather silly but very good-looking novelist. High cheekbones, long legs, manes of hair: they've both got the goods."

I feel suddenly self-conscious about my pony-tail. Gideon has never used the word 'mane' to describe my hair. Do I have the goods?

"If I were going to clone someone," Gideon says facetiously, "I'd clone you, Elizabeth. You're absolutely perfect."

"I don't think so," I say. "I like the idea of cloning as a real alternative to conventional reproduction, one that gives you the freedom to raise offspring with nothing of yourself in them. I'm squeamish about the normal processes of sexual reproduction."

"Squeamish about sex? You?" Gideon starts to laugh.

We have one last drink. Then we kiss outside the pub like lovers in a French film until a football supporter chucks a can of lager our way and we are spattered with beer. Gideon will have a hard time explaining away the smell when he returns to Hampstead.

◉

The cellphone rings at eight on Monday morning.

I pick it up, expecting Gideon. Nobody else has the number.

To my surprise, I hear Miranda's voice.

"Liz," she says. "Thank god you're there, Gideon and I are at our wits' end. Look, what are you doing over the weekend?"

"Nothing much," I say.

I resist the temptation to tell her I'm hoping to fuck her husband.

"Is there any chance you could do us an enormous favor? I wouldn't usually beg, but we've rounded up all the usual suspects and nobody's free. It's terribly cheeky of me to ask, but do you think you might be able to spend the weekend here in Hampstead with Gideon's mother?"

I think for a minute.

"We'd pay you, of course," she adds.

"What does it entail?" I ask. It seems like a bad idea, but I'm extremely broke and there's also the appeal of combing through Miranda and Gideon's personal possessions under circumstances that are the next best thing to legitimate.

"Oh, she's perfectly continent and so on," Miranda says of her mother-in-law, "just quite confused and forgetful."

"I guess I can do it," I say.

"Bless you, Lizzie, you're an absolute angel and I promise we'll make it up to you. Can you be here at four on Friday? Gideon and I have got to drive to Scotland for my cousin's wedding. We'll be back by ten on Sunday evening."

Gideon hasn't told me he's going to Scotland this weekend.

"Sounds OK," I say. "See you Friday around four."

And I don't hear from Gideon again that week. Finally I turn off my phone. That way I can't even hope that he'll call.

◉

On Thursday afternoon I leave the reading room for a cigarette break. Outside on the steps I realize I don't have any matches, and after rummaging unsuccessfully through my bag I hear the snap of a Zippo. In a haze of butane I lean over to light my cigarette and thank the lighter's owner, who I recognize as the person I've mentally labeled the library guy. I see him almost every day, either smoking outside or sitting with an impressive stack of folios at a seat about twenty degrees further along the same quadrant of the reading room that I prefer. He is small and neatly made, with fair wavy hair and a suede jacket two shades darker. He looks like a three-quarters-scale Robert Redford (dress sense from *All the President's Men*, weatherbeaten colonial skin from *Out of Africa*).

"Thanks," I say.

"Ran out of matches, eh?" he says.

"Let me guess: you're Canadian?"

His name is Robert Forsyth, and he is researching a doctoral thesis on eighteenth-century British literature at University College London. He's excited to hear I'm interested in Jonathan Wild.

"The Al Capone of the 1720s," he says. "The man who put the law enforcement system of his day to shame. Pity he came to such a sordid end. He deserved a medal, not a bad rep."

It's an immense relief to be talking to someone who has nothing invested in being morally upstanding.

"What are you working on?" I ask.

He shrugs. "Did you know," he says, "that the historian Edward Gibbon spent the last years of his life going about with enormously swollen testicle? It hung almost to his knees, but he was startled when a friend commented on it one day—he thought nobody had noticed."

Like all the other Canadians I've met he says 'aboot' for 'about.' Talking about balls to someone you've just met seems a little sleazy, but I find the guy curiously attractive. The feeling of kinship is compounded when I learn that he has a Scottish uncle, a dentist, who keeps Wordsworth's very own false teeth in a display-case in his waiting-room.

We are picking up our fourth—or is it fifth?—round of drinks at the bar in the pub round the corner before I notice that it's been at least two hours since I last thought of Gideon. I also realize that for once I'm hanging out with someone who's an even heavier drinker than I am. At the stage where I'm about to pass out if I don't eat, we transition to a pizzeria for dinner. I'm slightly put off by Rob's connoisseurship—he has a long conversation with the waiter about which bottle of red will best suit our Neapolitan pizza, and there's something fussy and gentleman-amateurish about his interest in the age of Gibbon and Horace Walpole. But he's definitely good company and I make only a token protest when he invites me back to his place for a drink.

His flat is less than a mile away, in the strange dead area behind Euston Station. He pours us each a large snifter of cognac and we sit at opposite ends of the relatively small couch. My skirt keeps riding up my legs and I tug it back down my thighs while Rob dims the light.

"If you testified at an organized crime trial," I say, passing back to Rob the huge spliff he's rolled out of a couple of Rizlas, a wad of tobacco from one of my Marlboros and several large crumbs of hash, "and you had to go underground afterwards in the Witness Protection Program, what kind of a job would you ask them to set you up in?"

Rob takes this question more seriously than it deserves. "I wouldn't mind being a wine salesman," he says. "Drive around with a few cases in the boot of the car, hit a restaurant or two, run through their tasting menu with the choicest bottles, make a sale—nobody to account to but yourself, so long as you're moving the stuff."

Put this way, it sounds fairly idyllic, though my impression of the Witness Protection Program (admittedly drawn entirely from TV) is that you'd be more likely to end up working at McDonald's. Maybe the Outback Steakhouse, if you were lucky.

"What about you?" Rob asks.

"A xerox shop," I say. "I'd like to run a copy shop."

"That wouldn't be very amusing, would it?" Rob says, sliding his hand over my exposed thigh and rubbing his thumb along the soft skin on the inside just above my knee. "You'd make a nice stripper, you know. What about a lap dance?"

"I'm not that kind of girl," I say, well aware of how ridiculous this sounds.

"How do you know if you're that kind of a girl or not? Isn't the whole point of the Witness Protection Program that you leave behind all your bad old habits?" Rob says very reasonably. His hand's encroaching now on my upper thigh and I sigh as his fingers slide into my wet warm pussy.

"Come here," he says, and I scramble towards him across the small stretch of couch that separates us. Now I'm kneeling beside him as he pushes my shirt up with one hand and pulls down my panties with the other. I put my leg over him and nestle down on top of him. I can feel his hard dick through the denim. He grunts as he tugs on the zipper and wriggles out of his jeans. He's wearing a very North American pair of underpants and I slip my hand below the waistband and start rubbing his cock. I unfasten my bra strap to preempt the usual fumbling and pull off shirt and bra over my head, tossing them over the side of the couch and moving further down his body. I'm on the floor at his feet by now, the perfect height for taking his nipples in my mouth, one at a time. As I give his left nipple a gentle tweak with my teeth he pulls me up onto his lap. I rub myself against him till we're both practically foaming at the mouth and then I lower myself onto his cock. Sliding up and down, I keep my eyes open. His are closed. He looks like a baby as he comes inside of me. It's much too soon.

"Whisky dick," he says. "Sorry."

At least he's not defensive.

We lie together on the couch for some uncomfortable minutes. It's not really big enough for two.

"There's a queen-size bed in the other room," Rob says as he gets up and weaves across the room to pour himself another tumbler of brandy. "Why don't we move there and have another go?"

But sharing a bed with this guy suddenly seems like an extremely bad idea. I jump up and reclaim my scattered clothing, taking it into the bathroom to get dressed. When I come back, Rob's still lounging naked on the couch, playing with himself and smiling at me. He looks like the dictionary illustration of the word 'sybarite.'

Against my better judgment I go to him and lean over to give him a long hard kiss. His lips are softer than I could have imagined. He rubs his tongue over my gums in a way that reminds me he's related to a dentist.

"On that note," I say, tearing myself away.

"I knew you wouldn't stay," he says, smiling at me and shaking his head. "I understand you better than you think."

"Good night," I say.

"See you around?"

"Sure thing," I say, though I can see I'll be spending a lot less time at the library in the weeks to come.

As I walk home through empty streets I tell myself to pretend it never happened. This is not my real life. This has absolutely nothing to do with Gideon. This is not my real life.

On the hall table of my building I find a large brown envelope padded with corrugated cardboard. As soon as I open it I really do forget what happened this evening. Allan has sent a sheaf of glossy eleven-by-seventeen photographic reproductions of the next pages of Mary Wild's narrative.

◉

Abraham Mendez was my very great ally in the early days at the Office for the Recovery of Lost and Stolen Property. Mendez was one of Mr. Wild's two most trusted lieutenants; the other was Quilt Arnold, who had been a bailiff before he entered Mr. Wild's service, where he was always called the Clerk of the Northern Roads—an elevated title indeed for a common bully—and Mendez Clerk of the Western Roads. While Arnold had no family beyond a wizened old mother who sold apples at a dirty little stall on Fleet Bridge, Mendez was the black sheep of the Ceixes family, a large clan of Portuguese Jews who lived in Bury Street in the parish of St. Catherine's in the East End. The family house stood in a courtyard off Bevis Marks behind the grand new synagogue, where the Ceixes father and brothers sold wine imported from Portugal in small barrels carried down from the Douro valley on broad boats with rectangular sails and transported across the sea to England. Port's a fashionable drink these days, though I have never had the taste for it: the real wine is fortified with brandy, colored with elderberries and seasoned with pimentos, but more often (and surely as my aunt serves it) you get dirty water and cheap spirits colored with blackberry juice, saturated with orange peel and sugar and steeped with hops or oak chips for astringency.

Now here is Mary Wild, you will be thinking, one who was ever the champion of regularity and order in all things, telling her story all higgledy-piggledy and losing her sense along the way. Well, I come to the point when I say that Mr. Wild had a mind above domestic matters; indeed he seemed to feel that a certain lavishness with regard to the household accounts could only raise his credit. Arnold was a man of simple needs who could not sign his own name, let alone detect irregularities in the housekeeping. Mendez was the only one of the three who had the instincts of a tradesman, and he let me know straight away that I could count on his support for any reforms I might undertake.

"For," as he said to me one morning over a delicious Somerset syllabub (I'd poured sherry into new milk warm from the cow, then stirred in half a pint of heavy cream), "it will not do any longer for such a scandalous parcel of domestics to take advantage of the great man."

I soon discovered that I might leave off at last the pert and insolent manner I had perfected under my aunt's government, for despite my youth I had now the authority to bully the other maids into submission. The servants from all the other houses in the Old Bailey had been used to come in and out at all hours, eating and drinking at my master's expense. I put a stop to that at once, but such practices were legion.

Whenever the cook went to buy anything, for instance, she paid the full demand without bargaining, knowing she'd get a present of cash at the end of the year from the tradesman (or at the very least a beefsteak or two for her own personal consumption). She never washed her hands, combing her head over the cookery and serving up the leavings with the victuals. I had never seen such greasy spits as in the kitchen at the Old Bailey, and when I asked the cook what she was about, she told me—flexing her brawny arms as she stirred the sauce—that the grease served to keep the inside of the meat moist.

"A filthy practice," says I, and made a note to get her dismissed as soon as I could, if I could not reduce her perquisites to a more reasonable quantity and stop the excessive breakages that would otherwise shortly do Mr. Wild out of house and home.

When the cook's back was turned, I threw a lump of soot into her pot, which gave me very great satisfaction; Mr. Wild being away, he would not suffer in his own person, and there was a good chance that Mendez would find it in his soup at dinner and turn her off.

In the kitchen they used the good copper pot for every purpose but its own, recklessly boiling milk, heating porridge, brewing small-beer, etc., to the pot's very great detriment. The day I saw the footman pissing into it I turned him off at once. The butler (who left shortly afterwards, and had no successor) had whetted down all the kitchen knives till he wore out the good part of the iron right down to the bottom of the silver handles; as I learned from the errand-boy, the goldsmith had promised the wretch a present if Mr. Wild could be induced to place an order for new cutlery.

The maids were even worse. They were meant to carry the chamber-pots down each morning to the cesspool in the garden, which would be emptied later on by the night-soil men; but they saved time by tipping them out of the window directly into the street, soiling the passers-by in the process.

One housemaid was always leaving a pail of dirty water with the mop still in it upon the darkest part of the back-stairs, that someone might break his shins on it, while the other girl had a habit of breaking china. When I called her to account in the butler's pantry, the silly girl burst into tears and began to make excuses of the most unlikely sort.

"A dog ran across me in the hall," says she, and I'd have had more time for her if I'd not seen the sly puss eyeing me through her tears all the while to see if I'd swallow her story, "and I could not help dropping the whole tray of plates."

"Oh, and tomorrow you will tell me that the chambermaid accidentally pushed the door against you, or that a mop stood across the entry and tripped you up," says I. "No, girl, you're out."

The one remaining became even more of a slut once all the work fell to her. She'd come in from an errand, skirts muddy to the knees, and flounce about her duties without a thought for the mess.

"Pin up your petticoat," says I to the lass, "or the dirt will be all over the stairs."

"You're nothing but a jumped-up housemaid yourself," says she, "and I'll pay you no mind, no, nor the master neither."

"You have grown so rude and saucy of late," says I, "that I think you are trying to get yourself turned off." And so she did, and I brought in two little girls from the charity-school to take her place. They were too timid to give me cheek, and I enjoyed rolling up to my old school in Mr. Wild's coach and asking them to show me a few of their most biddable girls.

I took to washing the china myself, and showed the new girls how to sand the floors and stairs, using my own two hands to polish the brasses and scour the room with freestone when they flagged.

The laundress who took in the washing did good enough work, at least after the time that Mr. Wild's best linen shirts came back singed with the iron in four or five places; I gave her a proper tongue-lashing and she knew she'd lose our custom if she ruined any more clothes.

I will say that I was not altogether out of sympathy with some of the servants' demands. Good management is a matter of respecting perquisites even as you rule with an iron rod. It was all the fashion in those days to keep the tea and sugar in locked caddies, for one thing, but I went to Mr. Wild and told him that if he kept them locked up, the servants would simply find a way to procure a false key. So the tea and sugar went back into ordinary jars, and Mr. Wild regained the favor of his domestics.

It is not necessary here to enter into the particulars, but at this time Mr. Wild still had the reputation of a mighty honest man. It was surely well enough to carry on the trade of restoring stolen goods, he used to say, so long as he did not actually enter into a confederacy with the thieves. He had of necessity a large acquaintance among that sort of person, however, and whenever he heard that a robbery had been committed, and such-and-such goods taken away, he sent to inquire after the suspected persons, leaving word at the most likely places for them to hear of it, that if they would cause the goods to be carried to his house in the Old Bailey, they should receive the promised reward, and no questions asked. Some charged him with wrongdoing in such matters, of course, yet he neither saw the thief, nor received the goods. He could not carry on his business effectually without an avowed intimacy and acquaintance among the societies of thieves, but this in no wise meant he had become a party to their management. His part was not only serviceable, but very honest, and whatever money he took on each side was no otherwise than as a solicitor takes his fee, on consideration from both parties, for honestly putting an end to a lawsuit and bringing the contenders to a friendly accommodation. (It is a gross calumny to say, as the writer Defoe has alleged, that Mr. Wild encouraged rogues to rob and plunder, then demanded money from the victims for his clients to bring back what they had stolen, out of which he secured always the lion's share for himself.)

Once I had taken things at the Old Bailey rightly in hand, the kitchen became the most comfortable room in the house. Even Mendez and Arnold often found their way to the large open fire, where meats roasted on a jack turned by the kitchen-boy as the new cook (less prone to drink than the last) basted them from the drippings in the pan below the spit.

You must not think that I spent my days sitting about all idle; no, I exacted good service by turning my own hand to whatever task was most pressing. The servants could say behind my back that I was the most odious taskmistress that ever lived, but nobody could have charged me with shirking. My particular province was my lady's chamber, where I made the bed and put things in order, examining the sheets—sometimes more closely than strictly necessary—carrying the jordan downstairs to empty it and generally making everything nice for Mr. Wild's wife.

You may find it strange that I have not yet made mention of her. Her name was Elizabeth Mann; she had been a whore, was then converted by one of her customers (a defrocked priest, or so it is told) to the Roman Catholic religion, confessed, received absolution and became thereafter a penitent for all her former life. Thus she snared Mr. Wild. She was not his first wife; that honor fell to a lady at Wolverhampton, Mr. Wild's childhood sweetheart, who had borne him a son before she expired of an apoplexy—the boy was being raised in Wolverhampton by his mother's relatives, and a considerable time would pass before we ever saw him in London.

For a quiet lady, Elizabeth Mann made very great use of the handbell on the table beside her bed, and I grew to hate its perpetual clanging. She spent her days lying a-bed, pale and languishing, but if you ask me she could have made more of an effort—she showed to great advantage in dishabille, after all, and whenever she held an audience in her bedroom I lost the whole morning dressing her hair specially. I believed that her wax-work complexion owed more to powder and paint than to ill health, though I will say now that she was always very kind to me, and generous to a fault.

I'll confess to you now what you may have already guessed: that I was most extravagantly in love with Mr. Wild, and had been from the time I'd first set eyes on him. The show of violence at our first meeting had only heightened my desire for him. I could think of no other man and thus the pleasures of running his household were distinctly bittersweet. I cannot tell you how many times I accidentally brushed up against Mr. Wild in the hall, or leaned over his desk to dust the curiosities he kept on a shelf behind his chair—pistols, blackjacks, lengths of iron pipe and of rope, a gold watch whose owner had perished at the hands of a notorious highwayman of the last century. He took little notice of me, and was seemingly able to resist my charms with ease, so that I decided one night to force his hand.

He and his wife had not lain together for a fortnight or more, she being ill and in the care of a surgeon who came every morning from Northumberland Court with a jar of leeches to let her blood. No other woman had visited Mr. Wild's bed betimes, as I knew from close inspection of the linen.

That day two housebreakers had been hanged, only a month after being taken in a very public fashion by Mr. Wild, whose testimony sent them to the gallows. I never liked to go to Tyburn on hanging day. When the coiner Barbara Spencer was burned alive at the stake directly opposite the gallows, some years after the time of which I now write, I remember that I kept myself close within doors all day so as not to have to think on it. Afterwards I heard that in the crush to see her, several persons lost the use of their limbs, others had their arms and legs broken, and two men their eyes cut out. (It was Mr. Wild's brother who took Barbara Spencer, and he relished the feat, for he stood very much in the shadow of his older brother. Mr. Andrew Wild kept a poor case at the Black Boy in Lewkenor's Lane, where he received stolen goods which he sold back to their owners only when he couldn't fence them to better advantage. I always hated to see him in our house, as he was like a cheap rude copy of his brother.)

On the day of which I speak now, however, Mr. Wild and his men had all been at the hanging, where Mr. Wild had a very great triumph, toasting the hangman and standing drinks all round for the turnkeys and constables who rode out with those who were about to be hanged. Later half-a-dozen of Mr. Wild's posse had drunk themselves into a stupor in the taproom next door at their master's expense. I knew that after a hanging men often visited whores, to relieve the uneasiness occasioned by the sight of men and women plunging to their death on the gallows. When I thought of it I too felt a curious thrill, despite my distaste for the business; and I resolved that my master should find what he needed at home, without having to resort to some nasty Covent Garden establishment.

That night Mr. Wild had put away even more liquor than the other men, though it did not seem to affect him much. His brown eyes were as hard and bright as ever when he walked in the street door, setting it to with more care than usual so as not to wake the house—did I mention that it was very late, and all the others abed?

I heard him come up the stairs at the front of the house, and scampered down the back stairs from my attic bedroom to turn down his covers for him. I was wearing my very best calico nightgown, having also let down my hair and tousled the curls prettily about my shoulders.

"What are you doing about so late?" asks Mr. Wild, when I came to him with a tray of chocolate, a flask of brandy and a small plate of the biscuits he liked best.

"I have brought you something to drink, and we shall go snacks," says I, setting the tray on the table and leaning over the bed to fold down the coverlet. I plumped up the pillows, making sure that Mr. Wild caught a glimpse of my ankle. I have always been vain of my feet: they are small and slender, and I wore that night a new pair of calf's-leather shoes with pointed toes and diamond buckles (a gift from William Riddlesden, who'd kept them back for me out of a heap of goods whose owner had taken too long negotiating for their return) which showed me off to great advantage.

His eye lingered on the stretch of stocking exposed beneath my skirt. I went to him then and pushed him down onto the bed. "Let me undress you," says I; "you have had a long night of it already."

When my hands reached the last button on his shirt, he laid his own hand on top of mine and said that was enough.

But by that time I lay beside him, and wriggling a little closer, I asked him what he meant. "I will do anything for you," says I, kissing him on the lips—he tasted of juniper berries, sweet indeed—and feeling with my hand for the rudder of his affections. "Let me take your cock in my mouth."

He laughed a little, and buried his head in my hair. "You are my Martha," says he, pushing a lock of hair back behind my ear.

"No," says I, pulling back offended, "I am your Mary."

"I know your name very well," says he, laughing again, "but nonetheless I say you are a Martha, not a Mary, and I like you for it all the more."

I began presently to understand his meaning when all unbidden the text from Luke rolled through my mind. I could thank the charity-school mistress that I knew exactly what Mr. Wild meant, though that did not mean I had to like it:

> Now it came to pass, as they went, that Jesus entered into a certain village: and a certain woman named Martha received him into her house. And she had a sister called Mary, which also sat at Jesus feet, and heard

his word: But Martha was cumbered about much serving, and came to him, and said, Lord, dost thou not care that my sister hath left me to serve alone? Bid her therefore that she help me. And Jesus answered, and said unto her, Martha, Martha, thou art careful, and troubled about many things: But one thing is needful, and Mary hath chosen that good part, which shall not be taken away from her.

I felt this reflection of Mr. Wild's to be a heartless one. As far as I was concerned, I was the one doing needful things, and I resented the thought that Mr. Wild so evidently held his wife to be a kind of saint. My loathsome uncle, when asked which of the two he'd prefer to take to wife, had once made the notorious answer that he'd have a Martha before dinner and a Mary afterwards, and this jest had been a great favorite with the prisoners, for whom it represented the height of wit.

I stood again and pulling Mr. Wild up after me, placed his hand under my skirts. I knew he wanted me by the way he grunted when his fingers found the moist slit beneath my petticoat, but he flipped the flounces back down after a minute and pushed me away from him.

"I am old enough to be your father," says he, "and besides, it will not do for either of us to foul our own nest."

I pestered him a little longer, but in spite of the late hour and the liquor he'd consumed and my very great perseverance, I could not get him to do more than lay one hand on my breast and stroke my hair with the other. Finally I got up and left him there, going up the back stairs to the attic where I slept, half a dozen thoughts jostling about my head. Why was Mr. Wild unwilling to take me up on my offer? Did he think of me, indeed, as nothing more than a household drudge? Surely his affection for his wife would not stop him from dipping his wick elsewhere—unless he feared I'd tell all, and thereby stir up trouble in his establishment?

All I knew for sure when I roused myself out of bed the next morning at six o'clock and knocked up the cook and maids on my way downstairs, was that if Mr. Wild could not take me on my merits, others would. And before the week was out, I'd accepted a proposal of marriage from John Dean—Skull, we all called him, on account of the way his bones showed beneath the skin of his face. Skull Dean lived with his father, a cabinet-maker, in Little Old Bailey next to the sign of the Cooper's Arms where Mr. Wild kept his office. Whenever I saw Skull, he offered no manner of rudeness to me, but only kissed me a while and told me pretty things. I decided that this was enough, though I felt for him none of the fervor Mr. Wild provoked in my breast.

After being married by a parson in the Fleet, with witnesses pulled off the street for the price of a pint of ale, we had six happy months together, living beneath his father's roof while Skull pursued his apprenticeship in the cabinet trade. Imagine, then, my very great sorrow and mortification when my own husband was arrested for burglary. I had not inquired too closely into his nocturnal activities, for it does not do for wife and husband to be living always in one another's pockets, but I suppose I knew very well that his day labor could not have maintained us in our then way of living. It was a beautiful May morning when they came to arrest him; before the sessions came on, Skull escaped from Newgate on the pretext of going to the necessary house, but his ankles were fettered and he came to grief in Giltspur Street, where he was taken and carried back to Newgate in a closed coach. He was sentenced to death at the May sessions and hanged on the 26th of June in the year 1717.

I do not mean to write the story of Skull Dean, nor of my marriage to him, but I will say by way of an epitaph that Skull was as sweet-tempered a cove as ever broke open a house. I spent as much time with him as I could in the ward at Newgate, though it brought back nasty memories of my childhood. What I remember best, I can say now, is the unfortunate prisoner in the bed beside him, who used to press lice to death between the nails of his thumb and first finger, cracking them between his teeth and spitting out the bloody skins onto the floor. Our conversation was punctuated by the crack of each tiny carapace.

I believe I lasted out this period only with the help of liquor, for I loved my first husband in my own way and saw my life falling about me in pieces as his death approached. My aunt made overtures of friendship in those days, as if she liked me better in the role of widow-to-be than wife, and so we achieved an uneasy truce, though not so much that we forgot our former differences. After Skull's death I was for a time beside myself, not with grief but with a kind of panic as to how I should live. I had burned any number of bridges, having already let my aunt know that I did not intend to rely on her charity, and I could hardly skulk back to the Office for the Recovery of Lost and Stolen Property and beg for my place again; indeed, hard words had been exchanged on the occasion of my leaving, Mr. Wild accusing me of being a cold-hearted bitch with an eye to the main chance, and even Mendez staying silent when he could have defended me.

I was still young and comely, but only a brave man would marry a lady so recently widowed by Jack Ketch, and I had fallen into extravagant habits during my months with Skull, who liked nothing more than to see me lolling about without any clothes in a bath of asses' milk or downing a pint of brandy in three minutes flat, a feat he used to time with a very fine repeating watch he'd kept back from one of his marks. Afterwards people would say that it was Mr. Wild who laid the information that led to Skull's capture and conviction, but I am afraid that is simply a desire to tie up the loose ends of the story by putting as sinister a complexion on events as they can bear; for I see now that Skull Dean was bent on death, whether by Mr. Wild's agency or no.

I hardly know how it happened, but I fell after Skull's departure into a highly disreputable line of work. I returned to the intelligence office where I'd first gone to seek a place, but the bitch behind the desk, learning I had no character and was now a widow to boot, said I'd be of little use to them. On my way out I was accosted by a lady in mantua and bonnet, a high color about her face. She took me home with her, and fed me up, and next thing I knew, I'd moved under her roof and joined her company.

I prefer to cast a veil over this part of my history; suffice it to say that I had become a posture-moll, working out of Mother Clap's house in Field Lane. It was a strange place, full of male mollies who gave each other the title of Madam or Your Ladyship and called each other dear and darling till your ears would ring with the sound of their little intimacies. They hugged and kissed and tickled and felt each other up, rigged out in gowns, petticoats, headcloths and fine laced shoes and hoop-petticoats. (As the old rhyme has it, though, and Mother Clap never let the boys forget it, "Who could Women's charms refuse / And such a beastly practice use?") Flogging cullies are always willing to pay a good price for being scourged in their arses by posture-molls, and as for myself, I took to flagellation like a duck to water. "You will be whipped," I used to say, "for not coming to school more often." And whip them I did, at ten guineas a head: the girls did better business than the boys all round, though you would not have known it from the money we kept at the end of the day.

Mother Clap restored maidenheads like no other. She chose children at Smithfield Market as a butcher might choose a mare, dressing them up in paint and patches and letting them out at extravagant prices, calling them young milliners or parsons' daughters. I felt an old lady next to them, though I was not yet twenty years of age, and I scorned the men who couldn't get it up except for a twelve-year-old with a mound of Venus as bare as a baby's bottom.

I did not think I'd go so far as to ruin myself in this line of work, yet over time my virtue was worn down by the persuasions of a gentleman who promised me a very fine diamond ring, and twenty pounds in bankbills, if I would let him attempt what is called the last favor. Many melancholy hours did I spend thinking on this prospect, for I loathed the thought of bedding with him, until at last he prevailed on me to consent. Once he had won his prize, he soon tired of me, and I was now left in a dismal case indeed, my price sinking with each week that passed. One cannot live long in such a line of work without strong drink, and I was in my cups more often than not, so the night that Mendez turned up in Field Lane, I took him at first for a new customer. I gave a crack of the whip and asked this handsome young fellow to stand me a drink while we talked terms.

He gave me a look of such horror that I saw I'd mistaken the fellow, and it was then that I knew him. "Mr. Mendez," says I, dismayed now to think what I was wearing and how the whole business must look to one who'd known me before.

"May we talk outside, or in a quieter room than this?" he asks me, averting his eyes all the while from my near-naked bosom.

"Indeed," says I, and we went next door to the Bull and Bear for a chat over a pint of gin. I had thrown a cloak over my shoulders and gathered its folds about my chest, and the blush on Mendez's cheeks began at last to fade.

He came at once to the point. "I know that you and Mr. Wild did not part on the best of terms, but I can assure you that not a day goes by that we do not sincerely regret your absence."

"Do you speak for yourself here, or for Mr. Wild as well?" asks I, a fierce gulp of gin burning my gullet and running into my belly like fire.

"I speak for Mr. Wild as well as for myself. The house has been all at sixes and sevens since you left, and Mr. Wild has a particular reason just now for wishing all to run smoothly."

"Oh?" says I, resolved not to make the man's task any easier.

"Yes; his wife is with child, and very ill with it. The surgeons do not think she'll live, but Jonathan swears he'll prove them wrong. Thus your presence, as housekeeper and nurse, would be most valuable."

"What price would he set upon it, then, in money?"

"He'd make you a present of fifty pounds as a token of good earnest, and double your old wages thereafter."

"I will think on it," says I, but in my heart, I knew it was too good an offer to turn down. I sold off my whips, Mother Clap taking the lion's share and dunning half Mr. Wild's present off me as well to pay my tally, for no matter how much money you pull down as a whore, the house takes all. And so I returned to the Old Bailey.

◉

I arrive at the house in Hampstead just before four on Friday afternoon and ring the doorbell.

Miranda answers right away.

"Come in," she says. "I'm everlastingly grateful, by the way, you're a real life-saver. We don't like to leave her with someone from an agency for such a long time. I saw a dreadful program on television the other day about home helps abusing pensioners."

We walk through the dining room and sitting room towards the kitchen.

"Her bedroom's directly off the kitchen," Miranda says. "We've put in a shower and a toilet so that she doesn't need to use the stairs at all. She likes to sit in the garden if the weather's decent, that's where she is now."

We walk out to the terrace at the back of the house. The old lady is huddled in her dressing-gown on a wrought-iron bench. She tosses handfuls of crumbs from the Ziploc bag beside her to the sparrows on the flagstones.

"The people next door often telephone to complain about what she's wearing," Miranda whispers to me, "but there's absolutely nothing I can do about it. The last time I persuaded her to put on something nice, she peed in her pants. Just to spite me, too, it never happens unless she's been crossed in one way or another."

We reach the old lady and Miranda raises her voice.

"Mother," she says, enunciating in the awful precise manner English people save for dogs, children and the very old, "this is Elizabeth. She'll be staying with you this weekend."

The old lady looks me up and down.

"She's a pretty girl, isn't she?" she says to Miranda. "What's she doing here?"

She has a strong Viennese accent, but her English is clear and idiomatic.

"She'll keep you company while we're in Scotland," Miranda says.

"I had Gideon in the hospital in Edinburgh," the old lady says to me. "We had driven up to hear a friend of Josef's play a concert. The waters broke all over my evening dress."

She gives me a sly look to see how I will respond to this revelation. I oblige with an exaggerated expression of shock and she cackles with pleasure. Once she begins to speak about the past, Gideon's mother becomes animated, but Miranda has obviously heard the story before.

"You'll have a lovely time telling Elizabeth all your adventures," she says briskly.

The old lady's face becomes vacant again. She throws another handful of crusts at the birds.

I go back into the house with Miranda.

"I've taped detailed instructions to the fridge," she says. "The meals are all in containers, you'll just need to heat them up in the microwave. There's bread and salad as well, it shouldn't be too much for you to manage. Eat anything you like; there's a very nice box of Belgian chocolates in the sitting room, a patient of Gideon's brought them round the other day and they're really lovely. I've locked the drinks cupboard—left to herself Gideon's mother tends to tipple a bit—but I'll leave the key with you, as she does like a glass of sherry before Sunday lunch. Dole it out with a sparing hand, though, and don't get her going on the hard stuff; she can be a real terror."

I do like Miranda.

I also feel extremely sorry for Gideon's mother.

"Any questions?" Miranda says.

The arrangements are clear enough and I tell her so.

"I've put her GP's number by the phone, along with the number of the hotel we're staying at. Don't hesitate to call, even if you just want to check in.

"Mind you," Miranda adds, "it's all right if you leave her for an hour or so, but don't stay away longer than that, or she'll get up to all sorts of mischief."

Miranda's driving up to Scotland by herself. Gideon will take a train later this evening. He has to attend a dinner and award ceremony honoring a hospital colleague.

I wave after the car as she drives off.

At eight I heat up the lamb stew that Miranda has prepared. We eat off trays in the sitting-room. Gideon's mother has perked up since Miranda's departure. She's combed her hair and changed into a reasonably clean dressing-gown.

I pour two glasses of sherry and we sip it together.

Gideon's mother does not eat much of her supper.

"My mouth is very painful," she confides. "It is a nightmare for me to chew anything solid these days, I have horrible sores on my gums."

I am fascinated.

I have never known anyone with false teeth before.

"Take the teeth out if it's more comfortable," I say. "I don't mind, either way."

"You are very kind," she says.

She inserts arthritic fingers into her mouth. The dentures pop out. She rests them on the end-table.

"Much better," she says.

Her cheeks have collapsed into hollows. She looks ancient.

We're listening to Schumann and she begins to tell me about her career as a pianist. I am surprised by the coherence and lucidity of the narrative.

"Clara Stern," she says. "My name was Clara Stern and I began to play the piano when I was four. I played my first concert at twelve.

"When I was fifteen, Hitler came to power in Germany and my father had the remarkable foresight to insist on moving the family from Vienna to London. My English was excellent, of course; I had a Scottish governess—a most respectable lady called Elspeth Pitcairn, of whom I was very fond—and a French bonne and instructors from half a dozen other European nations."

The accent, I think. Her voice is indeed overlaid with the slightest trace of Scotland. I imagine the governess like something out of a Muriel Spark novel: genteel, well-educated and tough to the core.

"I studied music at the Guildhall. I was political—how could one not be in those days?—and at a meeting in Bloomsbury, one of those endless smoky argumentative meetings, I met my future husband. He was called Josef Streetcar, though his name in Poland had been Striedter; the imbecility of those men who helped refugees enter the country, you know.

"Josef had come from Poland. My parents did not approve of him. My parents were highly assimilated Jews with a great deal of money and more pride. My father was a banker; in Vienna, he dined with members of the minor nobility on a regular basis. Josef was Jewish, of course, but shtetl Jewish. He was a disreputable Communist agitator and my parents wanted nothing to do with him. He wasn't really an agitator, of course. He was a musician, like myself. But still they did not take to him.

"We married in 1939, very much without my parents' consent. My father never spoke to me again. I dare say he would have become reconciled to the marriage later on, perhaps when Gideon was born. But he did not have the opportunity. Both he and my mother died in 1941 when a bomb destroyed their Kensington townhouse.

"Two weeks after the wedding, war was declared. Josef enlisted in the Royal Signal Corps. He returned three times on leave. Then his battalion was captured in North Africa."

Gideon's mother falls silent. She has eaten no more than a few mouthfuls of her dinner. The plate of stew sits forgotten on the tray.

"I did not get word from him again for almost a year," she says.

I pour us each another glass of sherry. She thanks me and asks for a biscuit. I unearth a tin of Carr's Table Water and she takes one, nibbling as she speaks.

"I continued to perform throughout this time," she says, "in spite of the danger and the inconvenience of wartime travel. I became quite well known in England. I played music written by the English, the French, the Russians. I played music written by Jews. I did not play Beethoven or Brahms, the audiences would not have it. A pity, really. My agent promised me that after the war, I would play whatever I wished. I worked as hard as I could.

"I remember the morning the letter came, a tattered blue form with penciled characters straggling like spiders across the cover. It was April 1942. A friend had given me a quarter-kilo of cocoa, god knows where she'd gotten it, and I had treated myself that morning to a cup of chocolate: cocoa and a scant spoonful of sugar and a dribble of milk, boiling water poured onto it. Delicious. The small pleasures, my dear, were what we cherished in those days.

"Josef's letter told me that he was safe in a German prisoner-of-war camp. He had written before, he said; I suppose the letter had been lost. The Red Cross got letters out of the camp and gave the men parcels of food. He was hungry all the time. He had chilblains and mouth ulcers and bronchitis and a fungal infection of the feet but he was alive. They did not suspect he was a Jew."

She stops.

"Another glass of sherry, my dear?" she asks.

It's just as well Miranda's liquor cabinet is so well stocked. We've almost finished the bottle. I plan before I leave to dispose of the empties in the builder's skip down the road, so that Miranda won't suspect me of being a secret alcoholic and corrupter of old ladies.

"When he came home after the liberation of the camps," she says, "I hardly recognized him. His hair had gone white. He weighed barely fifty kilos. In the months following the Armistice, I learned that almost all of my Austrian relations had died in the camps. I had feared for their safety, of course, but I had not imagined genocide."

Gideon's mother stopped performing when her husband returned from the war.

"I did not like to travel in those years after the war," she says. "I never felt safe on a train."

Josef taught composition for several years. Then he had the opportunity to take up his old career as a conductor.

"Did you travel with him?"

"No, no," says Gideon's mother, gesturing vaguely towards her stomach. "I suffered very much during these years with what they call female troubles. I was never well."

"What was wrong with you?"

She shrugs. "I had the most lovely doctor, Dr. Foster. I saw him religiously: such a bright man, but even he could do nothing for me for some time. Perhaps it was simply that I wanted a child so badly, yet I could not conceive," she adds with disarming candor.

"But you had Gideon."

"That was after I began to see Dr. Foster. He treated me and helped me to become a little happier. Josef and I had never used any prophylaxis. When I became pregnant in the summer of 1954, it was an occasion for great joy. After Gideon was born, of course, I was allowed to retire from the concert stage altogether."

Josef's career meanwhile prospered.

I clear our trays. In the kitchen, I tip congealing lumps of lamb into the trash and run the plates beneath a stream of hot tap water before sticking them in the dishwasher. Dusk has fallen and the sky is almost dark by the time I finish cleaning up. When I return to the sitting room, I draw the curtains and turn on the lights.

"Is it time for supper?" Clara asks.

The evidence of our meal removed, Clara evidently does not remember that we have eaten.

"We've had supper already," I say. "Would you like a chocolate?"

We spend a considerable time picking the perfect chocolate from the box in the sitting-room. I know better than to suggest that she could have more than one; the pleasure's all in the choosing. After some debate, Clara decides on a marbled chocolate nautilus shell.

"Do you still play the piano?" I ask. I have settled into the armchair opposite Clara's place on the couch.

In response she holds up her hands, gnarled with arthritis.

"There's no piano in the house," she says. "Miranda said there wasn't room. They sold the Bosendorfer when I moved out of our old house."

"You could fit an upright in somewhere," I say.

"An upright?" she says with contempt. "I think not."

I pour us each another drink. Then another. By now we are both a little wasted. Alcohol has the surprising effect of sharpening Clara's memory. She becomes increasingly specific. She tells me the names of the dolls she had as a child, the Vienna concert halls she played, the pastries she liked best at the little café on the other side of the square where she grew up.

"The worst thing," she says suddenly, "the worst of all was the letter I got from Josef just after he went missing. He had written it three weeks before he was captured."

At first I think she's still talking about the letter he sent from the prisoner-of-war camp. Then I see that the timing is wrong: this is a letter she got just after she heard he'd gone missing, many months before getting the news that he was safe.

"What did the letter say?" I ask.

"It was an awful thing," she says. She gives me a tragic look. "A truly terrible thing. He had just returned to the front after his last leave. He was furious with me. I had never seen my husband so angry in my life as the morning he walked out of the front door to go to the train. I was afraid he would never speak to me again."

"Why was he so angry?" I ask.

She shies away from a direct answer.

"My parents were very strict," she says. She looks at me, then looks down at her hands. She begins to pick the crumbs off the lap of her dressing-gown, laying them in a neat row along the small table beside her seat. "I received from them many old-fashioned ideas about the relations between men and women. What happens between them in the bedroom, I mean," she adds. "Between the sheets, as it were.

"In Vienna, my parents slept in separate rooms. My father visited my mother's room once, perhaps twice in a week. She would have been appalled if he came more often. By the time we moved to England, he had stopped visiting altogether.

"The night before I got married my mother told me what to expect. 'Your husband is a Polish peasant,' she said. 'You must not let him turn you into a fat housewife with half-a-dozen squalling brats at your heels.'

"She spoke in German, of course. She refused to speak English. She hated the fact that I was marrying but she gave me money to buy clothes for the honeymoon. I do not need to tell you that I was sworn to secrecy. My father knew nothing. She helped me to dress the morning I went to the registry office. She cried when I left. My father told her afterwards that I would not be allowed again under their roof. I met her for tea once or twice after that. But not often. And then the house was obliterated.

"'He will want to do certain things to you,' my mother told me as she adjusted the gardenia in the buttonhole of my suit. A brown grosgrain suit, I was very proud of it. 'Dirty things,' my mother said for emphasis. 'The duty of a wife is to comply with all her husband's wishes.'

"I let Josef do whatever he wanted," Gideon's mother says now. "And I thought he wanted a great deal. We shared a room for two weeks before he left for the army. His lodgings were very unpleasant, my dear. His landlady did not believe that we were really married. The house smelled of cabbage. You will perhaps remind me that cabbage is an essential part of many delicious national cuisines and that I should not malign this most useful vegetable, but the smell of boiled cabbage is a horrible thing. It was all very painful and uncomfortable.

"When Josef came back to visit, I was happy to see him but I was not so happy about those night-time activities. There was so little hot water during the war, my dear, and I did not like knowing that I would not be able to bathe properly afterwards. But I kept my mouth closed and let Josef do what he wanted."

Clara suddenly loses the thread of her story.

"Where am I?" she says.

She looks about her as though for a physical cue.

I coach her back to her place.

"The last visit," I say. "The last visit before Josef was taken prisoner. The time he was so angry."

As her face crumples, I am smitten with guilt for taking her back to this. Couldn't I have diverted her to something else instead, something happier? But I'm curious to find out what happened that was so awful.

"It was a lovely visit," she says sadly, "just at the very beginning of the summer. They had filled the parks with vegetables and the carrot-tops and Jerusalem artichokes looked so funny in the flowerbeds, it was quite decorative. There was a pig farm, my dear, in Hyde Park!

"We had tea at a Lyons, I think," she continues. "I remember there was nothing nice to eat. I was sad and Josef pressed me to tell him what I was thinking.

"'I want to make you happy,' he says to me. He is upset that I don't like the nasty English patisserie they have served us, scones that taste only of baking soda and horrible stewed tea. I would not have been so foolish as to ask for coffee at an English teashop, even before the war. 'You must tell me what you like.'

"I do not know what to say.

"Josef insists.

"'You do not always enjoy our time in bed together,' he says. 'What can I do to please you?'

"Because of his Communism," Gideon's mother observes as an aside, "Josef feels happier speaking about such things than I do."

His Communism, or simply his gender? It's impossible to say now.

"At last I speak," Clara continues, immersed in the scene as though it's happening here, now, right before her eyes. She has fallen into verbal patterns that suggest she has told this story before, and in exactly the same words.

"'Josef,' I say, 'sometimes I feel that your demands are perhaps too many.'

"I have drawn myself up to my full height. I sit straight up and I try to say what I feel with force, with conviction.

"He does not see at once what I mean.

"'My demands,' he says, shaking his head in puzzlement. 'The war has made many things difficult, but I do not believe that I am a difficult man.'

"I blush. You cannot imagine how hard I find this, my dear. I struggle to say what I mean.

"'I feel I am very generous to you,' I say. 'Perhaps too generous. I wish you would not take advantage so often of my generosity.'

"I put a special weight on the word generosity. When Josef sees at last what I mean, his face goes puffy and pale. He has an allergy to what I am saying, as a man may have an allergy to shellfish. He stands and looks at me with a face I have never seen before.

"'I am so sorry,' I say, raising my hands in a helpless and feminine manner"—and Gideon's mother here shows me what she means—"'but this is what I feel.'

"He stands, turns and leaves the café.

"I have no money to pay for tea. I am forced to degrade myself before the waitress and the manager. I cry as I walk home. Josef is not there. He does not return until very late at night. I am lying in bed in my nightgown. The lights are out.

"He stumbles across the room towards the bed. He knocks over a chair. He stinks of cheap perfume and tobacco and gin, the liquor coming from his very pores.

"He puts his hands on my shoulders.

"'Clara,' he says.

"I turn away from him.

"'Clara,' he says again.

"I say nothing.

"At last he rolls to the far side of the bed.

"In the morning, I cook him the special English breakfast, the one I never cook, the one I have saved many coupons to cook for him today. He eats his eggs and bacon without looking at me and without speaking once. I am not happy. I clear the plates and rinse out the teapot. I say nothing. I do not know what to say. It is the very last morning of his leave and he is due at the station in an hour.

"I follow him down into the street. He carries all his kit with him. He walks too fast for me to catch up.

"'Wait for me,' I say.

"He does not look at me. In the station he will not kiss me goodbye. The train pulls out of the station and he hasn't looked at me even once. I stand crying on the platform, and while I could be crying for the same reason as all of these stupid little English wives, somehow they see the difference and stare at me as though I am an absolute pariah.

"Six weeks later I receive a telegram from the army telling me that Josef has been captured. Six weeks after this visit. It is the next day that I get the letter, the letter he wrote after he last saw me. It had been delayed, you see. War delays so many things.

"'Clara,' the letter says, 'I will only say this once. You must never again suggest that when you are in bed with me you are simply being generous. I do not do this for my own selfish pleasures. I want you to feel pleasure as well.'

"Josef is a Communist, you know," she says again, "and so he writes in this manner."

She looks at me. I hardly know what to say.

"My mother had a dachshund," she says now, as though to introduce the next episode of the story. I pay close attention, willing to believe the connection may be oblique.

"Fritzl was a horrible little dog with short legs and a pointy nose. In Vienna, my governess and I used to walk each day in the park. We took the dog with us. One day the wretched little sausage slipped off his collar and ran under a tram. My mother believed that I had let the dog escape intentionally. I was locked in my room for two days. That was long before the war, of course."

I can't see the link, and indeed there doesn't seem to be one. Not unless both actions fall under a single heading—bad things I have done and been punished for but which I felt were justified by the circumstances. Clara loops back now into the account I have already heard: the war, Josef's return, her mother's advice before the wedding. Her memory is scrambled. She has forgotten what she has just told me.

I once acted in a production of *No Exit.* The play isn't broken into scenes, though it falls naturally into linked sections. At the dress rehearsal, I messed up the transition from one part to the next. Instead of moving forward, we looped back ten minutes and repeated a whole chunk of the play. There was no way out. We simply gave ourselves up to the grimness of repetition.

This is what happens to Gideon's mother. We cover the same ground again and again. I don't mind. After I leave, Clara won't remember me at all.

At midnight, the phone rings. I don't answer. The machine takes the call, and I hear Miranda's clear upper-middle-class English voice asking the caller to leave a message. The caller waits for the beep. He says nothing. I know it's Gideon. I don't pick up. I toss and turn for hours before falling into an uneasy sleep.

I wake up a couple of hours later in a cold sweat from a nightmare that still feels completely real. I'm lying in Jonathan Wild's coffin. Cold flat coins hold down the lids of my eyes and the scent of lilies barely masks the stink of rotting flesh. Then I hear above me the faint sounds of men digging. As they excavate the earth above my head, shovels slam into the surface of the coffin, splitting open the wood. I'm dragged from the lead shell that was meant to keep the worms out, stuffed into a sack and then humped over the rough ground of the church-yard into a coach standing at the end of the lane. As we ride through the streets, we bump about the coach like peas in a colander. It's the middle of the night and there's no other traffic. When we reach our destination, they dump the sack out of the coach and heft me through a pair of doors and up several flights of stairs.

Finally my body is taken from the bag and laid out on a wide table. Fluids seep from my body into the gutters along the side. I see everything but I can't move a muscle. A tall figure in scrubs approaches the table, and at the moment I wake, I recognize my father's eyes above the surgeon's mask.

On Saturday morning I wander down the road to the newsagent for a pack of cigarettes. I walk over to Hampstead Heath and sit outside for an hour. I smoke four or five cigarettes before I can steel myself to return. I have been feeling a little claustrophobic and it is a relief to get out of the house. I pass a small pastry shop on the way back, and guilt prompts me to stop and pick out the most Viennese-looking cakes I can find to bring back for Clara. The woman behind the counter puts the pastries into a box, whipped cream spilling out of them. She ties the box with string which she cuts on a blade set into the marble counter.

When I get back to the house, I know at once that something's wrong. The entrance hall is filled with smoke. The house smells of English breakfast and worse.

I panic. I set the box of pastry down on the hall table and run to the kitchen, where I find Gideon's mother holding a frying pan with both hands and gazing at the flames leaping from a lake of grease.

I spot a fire extinguisher by the back door. It's funny and English-looking but it's definitely a fire extinguisher, and I grab it and douse the flames. Then I dump the pan in the sink and run cold water over it.

I'm overwhelmed with remorse for having left the house, but then I rationalize: they wouldn't keep the fire extinguisher so close to hand if this didn't happen all the time.

The kitchen reveals the signs of Clara's attempt to prepare breakfast. A package of sausages lies open on the counter beside a dish of poached eggs, eight or nine of them, floating in a puddle of brown water. I catch myself thinking that she can't ever have been a good cook.

Smoke still rises from the stove. I open the oven, then bend down to pull out the broiler tray, where six slices of bread have turned to charcoal. I turn off the broiler and throw the 'toast' in the bin. Clara has ignored the high-tech toaster below the microwave. She clearly prefers the old ways.

Clara now begins to cry.

"Who are you?" she says.

"Don't worry," I say. "I'm Elizabeth. I'm staying with you this weekend. I'm a friend of Gideon's."

I lead her to a seat by the window.

"Sit down," I say. "Let's have some breakfast."

I throw away the eggs and put the sausages back in the fridge. I put bread into the toaster and find butter and marmalade in the cupboard. I collect the box of pastries from the hall and set them out on a plate.

Clara looks pleased. She puts a little heap of marmalade on the side of her plate and uses her knife to transfer a dab of it onto each strip of toast. She eats slowly and methodically, chewing each small bite long after I have swallowed my food.

After eating my toast, I tidy up the kitchen, returning odd jars of condiments to cupboards and putting things back in the fridge. I make us a pot of coffee and join Clara again at the kitchen table. She's lingering over a custard-layered pastry whose top is decorated with elaborate swirls of chocolate.

"Where's Gideon?" she says. She looks at me like a small child, cream smeared over her chin.

"He's in Scotland," I say. "He'll be back soon."

"Gideon was born in Scotland," she says. "Will he bring me Edinburgh rock? We liked Edinburgh rock when he was a little boy."

"I think so," I say. I'm not sure exactly what Edinburgh rock is, but Gideon's definitely a mama's boy.

She settles down again to work on her pastry.

Clara does not remember our conversation of the previous evening. She does not remember the fire of half an hour ago. She does not remember anything that has happened since I have been here. The strangest thing about my acquaintance with Clara is that it is not cumulative. She will come away at the end of the weekend knowing as little of me as when she first set eyes on me. She remembers nothing.

We spend the day watching videos together. *Brief Encounter. All About Eve. Adam's Rib.* The films are familiar. She knows the names of the stars and the directors. She has seen each one many times before.

Whenever I leave the room for a few minutes, I return to find her agitated and upset.

"Where's Gideon?" she says.

"He'll be back soon," I tell her. "He won't be gone much longer."

When I hear the car outside on Sunday evening, I hurry to clean up the remains of our supper. I rinse out the tumblers from which Clara and I have been drinking Scotch. I fear that Miranda will smell in them the scent of my depravity.

Clara is happy to see her son. Gideon sits down next to her on the couch. She takes his hand in one of her own and pats it with her other hand.

"Say goodbye to Elizabeth," Gideon says.

"Goodbye," Clara says obediently.

Miranda gives me a plaid-wrapped box of Edinburgh rock—it turns out to be candy, thick pastel-colored logs of edible chalk—and two hundred pounds in shopworn tens. "Gideon doesn't like to handle cash," she says, rolling her eyes. "He says it makes his hands feel dirty."

She has brought a separate box of candy for Gideon's mother, who looks at it as though it's a bomb about to blow. Gideon pulls the cellophane off for her and extracts a pink stick which she puts into her mouth, sucking audibly.

Miranda drives me home.

"We're forever in your debt," she says. "I promise, I won't forget it."

I talk to Gideon later that night. He speaks in a low voice on his mobile: Miranda is already asleep, and he doesn't want to wake her.

"Why didn't you pick up the phone when I called on Friday night?" he asks.

After a brief pause, I tell him the truth: I'm enraged that he didn't tell me he was going to Scotland with his wife. I don't add that I think he avoided calling me all week because he was embarrassed about withholding this information, but privately I'm sure of it.

"Bloody hell," Gideon says, sounding relieved, "why didn't you say something sooner? You seem to have taken it as a personal insult, but I can assure you I didn't mean it as such. In fact, I've got to go to Scotland again for a conference in a couple of weeks. Why don't you come with me this time?"

I pause again. It's not the most gracious invitation I've ever received, and my gut tells me that by saying yes, I'm letting myself in for an oppressive cycle of promises and disappointments.

"Yes, please," I say.

"What did you think of my mother, by the way?" Gideon now asks.

This is a harder question to answer. "It's funny she's always been such an invalid," I say finally. "She's got an unusually strong character."

"Oh, I'm sure the problem was simply that my father hadn't the attention to spare for her. Our family doctor was really a godsend in that regard; he flirted with her a bit, managed to cheer her up, that sort of thing. She got pregnant not long after she began seeing him, and I believe that things were never quite so bad for her again as they'd been directly after the war."

"Why was she infertile? Do you know?"

"Interesting you should ask. I asked Dr. Foster several times before he died, but he simply wouldn't say. Patient confidentiality, I suppose. I imagine it was something fairly minor. As far as I know, she never had a miscarriage and I was born as a result of her first pregnancy—I don't have any ghostly brothers and sisters, not like Pip in *Great Expectations.*"

We fall silent. There's something tense still in the air, though I can't tell exactly what it is. The Scotland commitment I have extorted from him weighs on my mind.

"Gideon, what happens to the embryos you don't implant?" I suddenly ask. "Do they stay in the freezer, like old popsicles?"

Without any explicit arrangement, IVF has become our comfort zone, a safe neutral topic whenever something feels slightly off in the relationship (a word I hate). I've been reading recently about the frozen embryo situation, a problem for which there doesn't seem to be a simple solution. The first major custody battle over "orphaned" embryos took place in Australia. A wealthy American couple went to Melbourne after being turned down by a number of IVF clinics in the US. The wife miscarried the embryos the doctors implanted, but several more were left frozen in liquid nitrogen. Husband and wife died several years later in a plane crash in Chile, and their estate amounted to the relatively large sum of eight million US dollars. You can imagine the media explosion after that: who would bear the future heir to the estate? Massive numbers of Australian women volunteered to serve as surrogates, though the numbers fell off when a California court ruled that the embryos had no right to claim an inheritance. In the end a government-appointed commission concluded that the embryos should be thawed and set aside to die in the laboratory.

"You should have been here last year," Gideon says in answer to my question. His voice warms as he tells the story, and the knot in my stomach begins to loosen. "In the early 1990s the government passed one of our characteristically mad British laws—the British Human Fertilisation and Embryology Act, believe it or not—pushed through by a bunch of nutters who didn't like the idea of frozen embryos surviving past what I can only call their 'sell-by' date. They set a five-year grace period, at which point all IVF clinics would be required by law to destroy embryos placed into storage prior to the passage of the act, except in cases where the parents gave their express consent to continued storage.

"I suppose there are about thirty major IVF clinics in Britain; and just try sometime to get in touch with couples who left embryos with you years before, it's a logistical nightmare. It's virtually impossible—or at any rate incredibly time-consuming—to track people down if they haven't left a forwarding address. By the end of July 1996, there were still over six hundred couples nationwide who hadn't been reached (seven of those on our own list, I'm sorry to say). We all thought about resisting the court order rather than destroying the embryos without parental consent, but the government was hell-bent on enforcing the law."

"Not a very pleasant story," I say.

"The tabloid coverage was absolutely out of this world," Gideon says with fervor. "Of course, the British media are obsessed with reproductive technology."

"It wasn't covered at all in the US," I say. "America's only interested in the home-grown version of right-to-life politics. There's no way the US government could get away with telling private IVF clinics to destroy the embryos they hold. You can't even imagine the evangelical cults that would spring up to carry the 'babies' to term."

"Along those lines, you'd be surprised what we were able to come up with even on this side of the Atlantic," Gideon says. "The Vatican called it prenatal massacre and asked women to volunteer for what the press outrageously dubbed 'prenatal adoptions.' Hundreds of Italian women volunteered, including a number of rather elderly nuns. Several Italian IVF clinics offered to take the embryos, but John Major got on his high horse and declined the appeal. Poor sod, he probably thought that the British public would never stand for the thought of nice little English embryos being brought up as wops."

We are silent for a moment.

"Guess what I'm wearing," I say.

I hear Gideon breathing on the other end of the phone.

"Tell me," he says, wheezing a little.

I proceed to describe a completely fictitious outfit: items of lingerie that I do not possess, that I identified in Miranda's underwear drawer but that I was not brazen enough to steal. We match strokes as we masturbate, getting off at almost the same time.

"Good night," Gideon says afterwards. "I love you."

But later I can't sleep. What is it about doctors? Sometime I'm not sure if I'm having an affair with Gideon or just a tutorial. I'm picking his brains and borrowing books. Did you know that the first baby reconstituted from a frozen embryo wasn't born until 1984? It drives me crazy that Gideon knows so much more than I do about reproductive medicine. Doctors always make me feel like this, but this time it's worse than usual. English doctors are more articulate than their American counterparts (in fact they're impossibly glib), and it's even more galling when you're sleeping with one of them.

◉

"You're not in love with Gideon," Dahlia tells me firmly over sake on Monday night. "You're just using him for sex."

I'm in no condition to evaluate the accuracy of this statement, but I am saved from having to answer by the arrival of the waiter. Dahlia wrangles with him over the particulars of her order—she wants two pieces of smoked eel and a spicy tuna roll that's not on the menu, plus a salad with dressing on the side (de rigueur in New York, in London bizarre to the point of perversity).

"You don't need a boyfriend," she says when the salads arrive, the waiter's expression distinctly sour. "You need a job."

"It's true I always look at help wanted before I turn to the personals," I say.

"Not that the personals aren't a practical way of getting over your obsessive focus on Gideon," Dahlia adds. "Dating, Elizabeth. It's the only solution, especially so long as you refuse to go to medical school."

I don't know why everyone thinks I should be a doctor. Everyone, that is, except the schools themselves: I was waitlisted or rejected outright everywhere I applied.

"And don't tell me about the rejections," Dahlia adds, reading my mind as usual. "You know you only applied to the top six medical schools in the United States."

"Is that according to U.S. News and World Report, or do you rank them yourself?"

Dahlia snorts. "I know you're on the waiting list at Cornell and Columbia," she says. This is true; I told her myself, in a lapse of judgment the previous spring. "One of them will take you in the end."

"If they do take me," I say, "it'll only be because of my father."

"I change my mind," Dahlia says. "You had better turn to the personals. You are clearly showing yourself unfit for the practice of a rational vocation like medicine."

What seemed only minutes ago like the topic from hell is looking better and better. My conjectural future as a medical student is absolutely off limits as far as I'm concerned, and I'm now resigned to talking about dating.

"In this case, the personals are no good," I say. "We've already established that I don't like English men."

"Have we? You could place an ad of your own, you know."

"What would I say? American personal ads are bad enough. English ones are completely useless. Smug, witty, totally offensive."

Dahlia scribbles down a few lines on her napkin and gives them to me with a meaningful look. Her job gives her a lot of practice formulating the verbal drivel preferred by upscale women's magazines. Her description of me is probably more flattering than I deserve: "Looks like Drew Barrymore. Talks like Angelina Jolie. Thinks like Bridget Jones."

"I don't think like Bridget Jones," I protest.

"Close enough," says Dahlia. "Have you anything better to say for yourself?"

Unwillingly I start to laugh. "Avid smoker," I say. "Recently quit reading."

"Start taking this more seriously, girl. We want sexy, not suicidal. Perhaps it's best to be blunt. 'Blond Venusian seeks charismatic Martian with professional expertise.'"

I groan and cover my head.

"Men *are* from Mars," says Dahlia.

Dahlia shares with my father a fondness for the more offensive classics of the self-help movement. I swore off regular boyfriends after my stepmother (with what motives, I don't know) gave me a copy of *Men Are From Mars, Women Are From Venus* for my birthday. On the Metro-North train home from New Haven, I didn't have anything else to read so I started dipping into it. In the end I read it from cover to cover with a kind of demented loathing. The only thing I couldn't figure out afterwards was why the Venusians didn't forget about the Martians and just go out with each other instead.

It's enough—as Dahlia would say—to make you throw your guts up.

"This can't go on," Dahlia says as she pays the check, ignoring my credit card, which looks like a child's toy next to her American Express Platinum. "It's a repetition compulsion. It's no good. The question isn't about the men. It's about you. What do you want?"

This question is impossible to answer.

When I see Gideon on Tuesday, my period's just started and I don't want to sleep with him. He tries to persuade me he doesn't mind the blood, but I'm not convinced.

"Your mother told me how pissed off your father got when she wouldn't put out," I say, hoping to distract him from my own resistance.

"Oh, god," Gideon says, covering his face with his hands. "She must have taken a real fancy to you. Even Miranda's only heard that one at second hand."

"What was he like?" I ask. "Your father, I mean."

Gideon shrugs. We're at the pub round the corner from his office. He's eating a disgusting packet of bacon-flavored crisps and drinking gin-and-tonics. Unlike Gideon, I'm not pedantic enough to call them gins-and-tonic, especially since I'm on my fourth pint of Guinness.

"He was something of a public figure," he says. "A bit too fond of being fawned upon, preferably by good-looking young women, though second-rate music critics also went over rather well. While I was growing up, the house was full of hangers-on. My mother didn't want me to go away to school, I suppose she depended on me for company while father was on the road. I had godawful asthma in those days and she found a series of tutors to work with me at home. I had a piano lesson with her first thing in the morning, then Latin, maths and so on with the tutor. My father was often away for months at a time."

"Difficult," I say.

"Oh, life was far better when he was away," Gideon says. "I wasn't allowed to practice the piano while he was at home, and that drove my mother absolutely round the bend."

"Why couldn't you practice the piano?"

"And disturb the great musician at work? Sorry, it just wasn't on."

"Do you still play the piano?"

"I've got rather a funny story about that, actually, if you'd like to hear it," Gideon says. "I haven't played a note since the age of twelve. My father had just returned from a particularly successful tour of the States, we hadn't seen him for months. He'd invited friends to supper and I was brought down to meet them afterwards.

"I remember he was very taken that night with a striking young cellist in a long amber evening gown. Dark-haired, quite young. I thought her very pretty but she made me feel a bit shy, she was rather too interested in me. At any rate, she'd made a point of being friendly to my mother, unlike many of father's other women. And of course mother's favorite, Dr. Foster, was there in attendance. He never married, though he often brought his American secretary with him to functions."

"Was he having an affair with his secretary?" I ask. It's a cliché, but that doesn't stop it happening from time to time.

"Oh no, I shouldn't think so; she was an old-fashioned Sapphist (as she'd have called herself), she lived with a very mannish lady choir director in Tufnell Park. She wasn't there that night, anyway, as far as I remember. And my mother was always Dr. Foster's first concern. He stood there at her side, small and dapper, a knight-errant poised to intervene in case of need.

"'Will Gideon play something for us this evening, Clara?' the cellist asked my mother.

"My mother put her arm around me and pulled me to her side. I had on a ridiculous velvet suit, in a hideous shade of aubergine—"

"Eggplant," I interject.

"Call the bloody thing what you like, darling, at any rate I hated it with a passion but my mother fancied me in it and begged that I wear it. She's a difficult person to say no to," he adds as an aside; "I don't know if you noticed."

I nod.

"'Would you like to hear him, Josef?' my mother asked my father.

"My father frowned at the lady in amber. He took a seat on the piano bench and beckoned me over. 'What have you been working on?' he asked.

"My mind went completely blank, you can't imagine how horrified I was. 'Beethoven,' I said at last. 'Sonata No. 9, in E major.'

"My father raised his eyebrows. 'No, really?' he said. 'Play it for us, then.'

"Some of the guests must have continued to talk to one another, but it seemed to me at the time as though the room had fallen completely silent. The moment of truth had arrived. I sat down and raised my hands over the keyboard. It was February and the room was absolutely glacial, my fingers were terribly cold and stiff but I didn't dare wait any longer for fear of being completely overcome with nerves. I could feel father hovering over my shoulder. The lady in amber had come to join him, and Dr. Foster remained nearby."

Gideon falls silent.

"So what happened?" I say.

"Oh, I played quite well," he says. "I was certainly old enough to know that I had better play as well as I could. I played the allegro and the visitors clapped and my mother smiled at me. I ran to her once I'd finished, I didn't know what else to do with myself.

"'What do you think, Josef?' she asked my father.

"'Second-rate,' he said, slamming the lid down over the keys. The vase of chrysanthemums on the piano shook with the crash, and Dr. Foster rescued it just before it toppled. 'His playing is quite wooden. God knows what possessed you to unleash the boy on the instrument. Even with your teaching, Clara, he'll never amount to much.'"

"What did your mother say to that?" Somehow I can't imagine the scene. Could Gideon's mother even have heard such words? Wouldn't she have pretended to herself that her husband had said something else?

"Oh, nothing. She turned quite white, though, and the lady in the amber dress put her hand on my father's arm. 'The boy's very good,' she said. 'Really, Josef, you're being rather unfair.'

"My father looked at me.

"'What do you think, Gideon?' he asked. 'Are you either foolish or mad enough to believe that you'll make a concert pianist?'

"I could hardly speak, of course. I was afraid I might cry. My mother clutched at my arm, but I pulled it away from her.

"'I know perfectly well that I will never be a first-rate pianist,' I said loudly.

"'You see, the boy's no idiot,' my father said. 'At least he knows he doesn't have what it takes, as they say in America.'

"The amber lady laughed and took his hand. 'Josef, you're quite ruthless, aren't you?' she said. 'Shall we put on a record and have some dancing instead?'

"My mother said nothing as the lady led my father away. Only a few people had overheard his comments, so it wasn't a full-fledged catastrophe. Dr. Foster lingered, gin-and-tonic in hand. I don't think he knew which one of us to console first.

"'Don't listen to your father,' my mother whispered to me.

"I stared at her.

"'I will never play like you do,' I said.

"Her eyes fell. 'Perhaps I should have found you a different teacher,' she said under her breath. 'I thought it could do no harm; how should I have known?'

"Now Dr. Foster intervened. 'There's no reason you should be a professional musician,' he said. 'We're not all bound to enter our fathers' professions. My own parent was a clergyman; and if I had a son I'd be very careful not to press him to enter the medical line, not unless he wanted it for himself. I'm sorry, Gideon, but you mustn't make a meal of it.'

"I turned and left the room. At breakfast I told my mother that I wanted to go away to school.

"'I suppose it must be time,' she said. And she dismissed the tutor that day. A month later I was at Shrewsbury."

"And you never played the piano again?"

I believe his story, but I also find it uncharacteristically melodramatic. I know I haven't kept the incredulity out of my voice, and Gideon looks annoyed.

"I have no patience with people who insist on doing things badly," he snaps. "I play squash very well. I play a rather poor game of golf. Why should I play golf instead of squash? I'm not a musician, I'm a doctor, a first-rate doctor in fact. My father was absolutely right to steer me away from music."

I have nothing to say to this. I'm superficially uncomfortable with his first-rate/second-rate distinction, but secretly I believe it's valid.

"When I was eighteen, by the way," Gideon adds, "I lost my virginity to the cellist in the amber dress. She'd become quite well-known as a soloist by that point, but my father had gotten tired of her and taken up with an older woman, a platinum-blond German mezzo-soprano with absolutely enormous tits. I was at home that summer, about to go up to Oxford. My father sent me to deliver a score to the cellist's suite at Claridge's. She gave me an American cocktail and seduced me. She was quite straightforward about it, she wouldn't take no for an answer."

He gives me a suggestive leer.

"What kind of cocktail did she give you?" I ask deliberately. "Do we have time for another drink?"

"You're trying to rile me, aren't you, sweet thing?" Gideon says. "Don't you mean to ask what we did in bed?"

"What did you do in bed?" I'm not really in a bad mood, I'm just pretending. I know that Gideon finds me endearing when I'm sullen.

Gideon smiles. "If you'll wait till we're alone together, I'll show you. A real-life re-enactment, as they promise on American television."

"Sounds appealing," I say. I'm suddenly dying to get into bed with him. I'm not sure what's come over me, unless it's the drink. In other words, Gideon's story has had exactly the effect he meant it to.

"You're very lucky, you know," he adds, as I pay for our last round of drinks. "Your father's so appreciative of your abilities. My father died the year before I went to America. He approved of medicine as a profession, in fact he suspected that my lack of imagination rather suited me to it. But he never thought I'd do so well as I've done."

At Gideon's allusion to my father, my jaw figuratively drops. Has there ever been a less perceptive observer than Gideon Streetcar? I'm about to get pissed off, but I skip it. I say instead what Gideon wants to hear.

"My father thought very highly of you," I say. "That year, you were the favored son. You could do no wrong. He still speaks about you sometimes, he hasn't had anyone nearly so good since."

"Do you mean that?" Gideon says, with pitiful eagerness.

"Of course," I say.

To my own ears, I sound absolutely sincere.

◉

History cannot furnish an instance of such complicated villainy as was shewn in the character of Jonathan Wild, who possessed abilities, which had they been properly cultivated, and directed into a right course, would have rendered him a respectable and an useful member of society; but it is to be lamented that the profligate turn of mind that distinguished him in the early part of life, disposed him to adopt the maxims of the abandoned people with whom he became acquainted.

—*A Particular Account of the Life and Trial of Jonathan Wild* (1773)

What I want, I've decided, is to know absolutely everything about Jonathan Wild, down to the smallest detail. My pockets are full of canceled library slips for the pamphlets and broadsides in which Wild's contemporaries chronicled his exploits. All that I've learned so far from Mary Wild's story has little to do with her husband's dealings, though I tell Rob—as we smoke a cigarette outside the library on Saturday afternoon—that it might qualify me to write the first chapter of a thesis titled "Sexual Predilections of the British Male, 1700-1998."

"Make that British and North American," Rob says.

I've had coffee with him a few times but have resisted his invitation to do another pub crawl. Even an ounce of alcohol inside me and I know I'll be overcome with lust.

"What are you doing tomorrow?" he says. "We could take a picnic and a few bottles of champagne to Kew Gardens and look at all those sexually suggestive flesh-eating plants collected by good old Queen Victoria."

"Sorry," I say. "I've already got plans."

In the event I spend the whole day Sunday tracking down the old coach roads out of the city—I locate sites for some of the more notorious hold-ups whose perpetrators were later apprehended by Jonathan Wild—and I'm tired and dusty when I meet Gideon toward the end of the afternoon.

Gideon has just attended the christening of one of his clinic babies, and children are high on the conversational agenda.

"I'd like a son," Gideon says, "a baby boy. I'd take him to football games and teach him how to bowl a cricket ball."

We're lying on the grass in Holland Park. Gideon's hoping nobody he knows will see us together. I'm wearing bright red lipstick and a little blue polka-dotted dress that I picked up for two pounds in the Portabello Road. I look like a slutty 1940s munitions-factory worker. Gideon's wearing jeans and a polo shirt, but he still looks like a doctor.

"I guess I'd like a baby too," I say, "but only under certain circumstances. I want Jonathan Wild's baby. To bring him back to life."

As soon as the words are out of my mouth, I feel that they're true.

"That sounds impractical," Gideon says lazily. "You'd be hard put to collect child support from a man who's been dead for almost three hundred years."

"I don't care about child support," I say. I sit up and run my hands through my hair. "I want to have Jonathan Wild's baby. Well, not exactly his baby: his clone."

Gideon thinks I'm joking, but I'm not. Not really.

"No, I'm totally serious," I say. "It's Dolly meets *Jurassic Park*."

Gideon has neither read *Jurassic Park* nor seen the movie—what planet is he living on?—so I explain the concept. Scientists extract dinosaur DNA from blood in the abdominal cavities of mosquitoes preserved in amber, the resin having protected the integrity of the DNA for millions of years. They then use the DNA to grow authentic dinosaurs in an egg hatchery on an island off the coast of Costa Rica.

"Utter rubbish," says Gideon. "Even supposing that you could extract the genetic material in the first place, why shouldn't the mosquito have bitten something else, something quite ordinary? A small rodent, say, or a worm?"

"I don't think mosquitoes bite worms," I say. "Anyway, in this case we wouldn't have such a hard time."

"No?"

I lay out the procedure.

First you get a bone sample from Jonathan Wild's skeleton. You extract the DNA and multiply it with a PCR machine, an amazing invention that's now in practically every chemistry lab in America. The polymerase chain reaction lets you turn a few cells into a whole test-tube full of DNA: disgusting, in a way, but highly useful for genetic profiling in court cases and so on. As well as for cloning.

Gideon tickles the back of my knee with a piece of grass. I roll over onto my back and swat his hand away.

"You're telling me that you want to clone Jonathan Wild?" Gideon asks. "To give birth to a perfect replica of a notorious eighteenth-century criminal?"

"Yes."

Gideon puts his hand to my face and I pout and toss my hair. He sees he's going to have to enter into the spirit of the thing.

"It's an amusing idea," he admits. "You could deactivate the DNA in a fertilized egg, and then you could inject the nucleus of Jonathan Wild's DNA through a hollow glass needle into the center of the egg."

His hand's creeping up my thigh and I roll towards him. Gideon is an expert in intra-cytoplasmic sperm injection, a technique he thinks could be readily adapted to cloning. He often picks up a single sperm and injects it directly into the egg cytoplasm.

"Actually," Gideon adds, "I have a friend who does DNA work at a laboratory in Scotland. I expect he could give you a few pointers on how best to deal with Wild's genetic material."

"I need more than just a few tips," I say.

"Oh?"

"I want to try an experimental procedure," I say. "A really radical one."

"What's that?"

"I'll make you a bet. I bet you anything you can't clone Jonathan Wild."

Gideon starts to laugh.

"You've got a wild imagination," he says. "Shall I start calling you my Dollybird, then?" He makes a series of baas, sounding surprisingly like a real sheep. He's so convulsed with his own wit that he doesn't notice my expression.

"Stop teasing me," I say. "I'm dead serious."

Looking at Gideon snorting with laughter, I do not know whether I can trust him to help me or not. But it seems that my best chance at enlisting Gideon's help depends on a cunning combination of skepticism and flattery.

"There are only a handful of people in the world who are talented enough to take on a project like this," I say, though I'd afraid I'm overdoing it. "It would take remarkable skill. I bet you can't do it. But I hope you can."

Gideon slides his hand further up my thigh. I drape a sheet of the *Independent* (Gideon's paper of choice) over my midsection.

"How do you suggest that I go about doing such a thing?" he says. He can never resist a challenge; he doesn't know it yet, but he's hooked.

"You're the guy with the magic hands, right? You tell me."

"I suppose I might well be able to put Jonathan Wild's DNA into your enucleated fertilized eggs in vitro," he says thoughtfully, "and then implant the cloned embryos into your uterus."

He slips his hand inside my panties and begins to stroke my pussy.

"Come up with a plan," I say, "and you can tell me all about it. At your leisure."

I'm breathing faster. I reach over and ease my hand down the front of his pants. I grab his cock and start jerking him off.

His eyes roll back in his head.

I hope nobody can see what we're doing.
Gideon comes right away.
So do I.

◉

I buy a dress the next day in a ridiculously expensive Chelsea boutique, the kind of place I think Miranda might shop (but only if she were slumming). I spot the thing in the window, a black rayon frock patterned with tiny swirls of red, yellow, white. I lurk outside for a few minutes, then I go in and ask to try it on. I'm not well enough dressed for the saleswoman to treat me with respect, but she grudgingly lets me take the dress on its hanger into an enormous high-ceilinged changing-room at the back of the shop.

The dress suits me. I turn around and check myself out in the dressing-room mirror. I pose. I show a little leg. I think I look OK.

As I wait at the counter for my credit card to clear, abjectly and unrealistically hoping that I haven't yet reached the limit, I run the fabric between my fingers. Only then do I notice that the tiny pattern, abstract at a distance, actually represents the two linked strands of a double helix, the image that Watson and Crick created to describe the structure of human DNA. It's perfect.

The most basic insight into genetics occurred in the nineteenth-century Moravian monastery where Gregor Mendel crossed different varieties of the garden pea, varieties that maintained clear alternative traits, some dominant and some recessive. Distinctive characteristics in the parents were redistributed in all possible combinations in the progeny, an entire range of hybrids, each trait (tall/short, smooth/wrinkled, yellow/green) passed down independently of the others according to simple mathematical rules.

One of the students in my ninth-grade biology class was shattered to learn that he could not possibly be the brown-eyed child of two blue-eyed parents. Blue eyes are recessive, so his father must have been somebody else, somebody with brown eyes. I don't know. I think a discovery like that could be liberating. And not uncommon, either. The results are ambiguous, but one hospital study has shown "extra-pair paternity" (where it's genetically impossible that the father named on the birth certificate contributed the sperm in question) running as high as thirty percent.

Gideon's out of town till Thursday at a conference, and I have too much time to think about these things. He calls me every night from Leeds and we have phone sex. Afterwards I find it hard to sleep, sitting by the window and smoking cigarettes, sometimes until dawn.

◉

Allan Menzies calls me Thursday morning at nine. I'm only half awake as I struggle to identify his voice.

"Did you get the photographs I sent?" he says.

"Who is this?"

"Sorry," he says belatedly, "did I wake you?"

"No, no," I babble. I'm mortified to realize I never called to thank him. "I've been up for hours. The pictures were unbelievably clear, too. I could read every word. Thank you so much for taking care of it so quickly."

"I've got another set of pages for you, and they've come out really beautifully. It's slow work, but not especially difficult. Would you like to pick them up sometime later in the day?"

We arrange to meet in the museum café at half-past two. This time I'm early and I buy a pot of tea and sit and reread the first couple parts of the narrative while I wait for Allan to arrive.

He joins me and we look together through the new sheaf of papers, each image protected by a plastic cover. These are the originals.

"I suppose we tend to forget how salacious eighteenth-century writing could be," he says, a deep flood of crimson staining his face.

"That dirty, huh?" I ask. I can feel my own cheeks turning hot with sympathy.

"I hope you don't mind, but I couldn't help reading the narrative as I cleaned the pages," he confesses.

"That would be desperately ungrateful of me," I say politely, though what I'm really experiencing is a flood of competitive rage. How could he have read it first, before I got to? "I really appreciate the time you've put into this."

He brushes off my thanks. "As I mentioned, it hasn't been a particular challenge, technically speaking," he says, "but you've certainly got me fired up about the story. I'm away on holiday for the rest of the week, and the soonest I'll have the next bits ready for you is a fortnight from now. I'll send the photos of this lot as soon as they're processed—you should have them before the weekend."

"Well," I say, "I'll just have to wait it out. Half the pleasure is in the anticipation."

"I know just what you mean," he says. He checks his watch. "Look, I must get back to work. I've got loads of things to finish off this afternoon before I leave."

"Where are you going?" I ask.

"To Inverness," he says, grimacing.

It seems to be my fate to hear of nothing but other people's trips to Scotland. He notices that something has put me off. "Visiting the aged parents," he explains. "Duty calls."

He stacks his cake plate underneath the saucer and teacup, then lays the teaspoon neatly beside it. He's stalling for some reason. I'm an expert, I can always tell.

"My girlfriend ditched me a few weeks ago," he says then, giving me a shy look, "so I'm all by myself. Have you ever been to Scotland? I don't suppose you'd fancy a quick trip?"

Before I can say anything, he backs off. He's completely flustered, needless to say. "I'm sure you're attached, I don't mean to be forward but I just thought you might enjoy the countryside."

"It's a sweet invitation," I say, "but I've got commitments in London that can't be rescheduled."

"Of course, of course, such short notice," he says, blushing again and restacking the crockery on his tray.

"But maybe when you're back in London, we could get together for a meal?" Even this suggestion makes me feel disloyal to Gideon—I'm setting up a date with another man!—though I know my scruples are absurd.

"Yes, that would be lovely," he says. He's standing now, looking hopelessly down at his tea-tray and not knowing what to do next.

I stand and kiss him on the cheek. "Have a nice time in Scotland," I say. "I'll call you in a week and a half, right? We'll do dinner."

"Right," he says.

◉

"I missed you," Gideon says when he gets back to town that night.

"Any more word about the Scotland trip?"

Gideon shakes his head.

There's a Woody Allen revival at a small movie theater near my flat, and we're walking at top speed (his arm round my shoulders) to make the 7:30 show of *Hannah and Her Sisters.* Though I have seen the movie before, I am struck this time round by the force of the infertility sub-plot. Mia Farrow divorces Woody Allen because of his low sperm count, among other things. As soon as she marries again, she's pregnant with twins. Woody takes this as conclusive evidence of his own inadequacy. Somehow Woody ends up blissfully married to Mia Farrow's hapless sister, Dianne Wiest. In the final scene of the movie, Dianne tells Woody that she's pregnant. It's a redemptive little moment; Woody's ecstatic smile fills the screen.

Gideon likes to stay and watch the credits, but I'm dying for a cigarette. I go outside and wait for him.

All the way home, we argue about the ending.

I push for the cynical interpretation. Dianne has slept with someone else and it's not Woody's child.

"Preposterous," Gideon says. "That can't possibly be what he meant to get across. You're being wayward, darling."

I light another cigarette. We've stopped for a drink at a pub along the way.

"Persuade me," I say.

We go back to my room and have sex.

"I still think it's not Woody's child," I say afterwards.

"You're very like your father," Gideon says.

"I'm nothing like my father."

Gideon starts to tick off points of resemblance.

"Obstinate as hell," he says. "Remarkably intelligent. Exceptionally charming."

Each phrase sounds more like a reproach than a compliment. I am made to feel that I am not living up to Gideon's estimate of my character.

"Naturally blond," he adds as an afterthought, running his hands through my hair.

I say nothing.

"You can't do much about heredity," he says.

"Fuck you," I say.

I have noticed that English people prefer to say fuck off. This I find annoying. When Gideon says blond, he probably says "blonde" with an "e."

"Besides," I say, "my father dyes his hair."

I take malicious pleasure in confirming what I suspected: that there is nothing I could say that would shock Gideon more.

"He does not!" Gideon now exclaims. He's genuinely outraged. Men of science do not dye their hair.

"He does too," I say, "and when I was in high school he used L'Oreal Preference, champagne blond."

Gideon starts tickling me and we begin to fight in bed, wrestling and punching each other until Gideon has effectively subdued me.

"Take it back," he says, once he has pinned my arms and maneuvered me into a position of immobility. "Tell me your father doesn't dye his hair."

I remain obstinately silent.

◉

Towards the end of the week I make a few phone calls to track down some information for the travel guide. I'm currently writing on Sport.

Football: Arsenal, Barnet, Brentford, Charlton Athletic, Chelsea, Crystal Palace, Fulham, Leyton Orient, Millwall, Queen's Park Rangers, Tottenham Hotspur, West Ham United, Wimbledon.

Football's not my scene.

I swim at the Britannia Leisure Centre, the Serpentine Lido, the Chelsea Sports Centre, the Oasis Baths. Only men are allowed to swim in Highgate Pond.

I do not care for sport.

In an attempt to liven up an extremely dull batch of copy, I visit a small lab near Notting Hill Gate and pay a huge fee to spend half an hour in a sensory deprivation tank.

The envelope from Allan arrives at my building on Saturday morning. It contains only a few pages, but I read them over and over until I know the words practically by heart.

I think more about the past than the present.

I do not think about the future.

◉

I hated to feel myself a pensioner on Mr. Wild's charity, and I strove to make myself even more useful than I had been before. I did not know what to think of Elizabeth Mann's situation, the child being the first she'd conceived, and she at least five-and-thirty years of age. Mr. Wild did not seem over-pleased, expressing great concern about his wife's health and hardly letting her leave her bed for fear of accidents. I thought he coddled the lady to no purpose, though indeed she tired rapidly whenever she left her bed, and found it easier to lie still and follow Mr. Wild's orders.

The physician came every week, dressed like a gentleman right down to his sword and gold-topped cane, in which he kept a vial of vinegar. He charged a fee of a guinea a visit, which I resented on Mr. Wild's behalf: ten shillings would have been more than enough, I thought, and even that an extravagance, as the visits seemed to do no good whatsoever. He'd told Mr. Wild that likely neither the lady nor her child would survive the lying-in.

In the lady's seventh month, after one long visit in which the physician warned Mr. Wild once again to expect the worst, Mr. Wild finally sent the doctor packing, dismissing at the same time the nurse he'd recommended, who stank of brandy and tobacco, with breath rank enough to make you vomit. He asked me to nurse his wife myself, saying that he knew he could rely on my good sense to do what was best for her.

I gained a grudging respect for Elizabeth Mann during that time. She never griped, sitting up instead in her bed doing plain-work and making light of her condition. Meanwhile, Mr. Wild brought her one present after another. Her first-floor chamber seemed a magpie's trove of bright and glittering things, the walls hung with rich tapestries and the tables littered with the trinkets he brought her: bright enameled pill-boxes, curious fans, letter-openers, a pretty little writing-desk of ivory and sandalwood, sugarplums, oranges and comfits.

As if cashmere shawls and diamond bracelets were not the limit, Mr. Wild came home one day with a grotesque little monkey he'd bought from an East-India sailor by the docks.

Mrs. Wild exclaimed when she saw it; whether with delight or horror, I was never to know, for I put my foot down when it came to livestock. "Never have I seen such a thing," I told Mr. Wild, "that a man should see fit to import into his wife's bedchamber a filthy disease-ridden creature from the tropics, bringing all manner of vermin into the place."

Mr. Wild's face fell. The monkey was duly returned to its original owner, and a better day's work I dare say I never did. The idea!

I sat with her during the daytime, and Mr. Wild nights, though he was there as often during my watch as his own. He would sit by the bed holding her hands, which had become cold and stiff and swollen, the nails tinged with blue.

Meanwhile I would heap more coals on the fire, keeping the room as hot as she liked it.

A month before she was to be brought to bed, Mrs. Wild called me to her. "Say nothing to my husband," she warned me, "but I believe that it is time for me to shed my worldly possessions. I will not go to heaven with so many rich things about me. Will you see for me that they are given away to the poor, leaving nothing but what is necessary?"

A fine commission, thought I, and one that might put a penny or two in my pocket. I would worry later about Mr. Wild's wrath; besides, his wife would bear the largest share of the blame. I sold the things piecemeal, giving ten shillings or so to charity (as I had promised) and keeping the rest for myself, to feather (as I called it) my nest. I had my eye on the writing-desk, in particular, and indeed I pen these very words on it still, and it is one of the few things I will take with me to the Americas.

"Service is no inheritance," says I to Mendez, when he took the liberty of observing that I might have followed Elizabeth Mann's instructions to the letter; "my work is great, and my wages small, and besides, she does not mind what I do with the goods, she simply wants to be rid of them."

"What have you done with your things?" Mr. Wild cried out that night, when he came to see her.

I loitered about the doorway, in case she meant to say anything to get me into trouble.

"I have no more use for them," said Elizabeth Mann. "I have made my confession to the priest, and am prepared for what will come hereafter."

Perhaps I forgot to say before that she was a devout Catholic, whose observance in matters of religion might be attributed to her having been a very great sinner in her former life.

Mr. Wild sank to the floor beside the bed and buried his face in the covers. He hardly seemed to remember that I was there.

"I have found a wet-nurse," I heard him whisper. "She will be ready."

I saw her hand move to caress his head. In a sharp motion, he stood and cast her hand away from him. He pushed past me out of the room, not making a word of apology for knocking against me. I thought I heard him say something: "I cannot bear it," it might have been, or "No man could bear it."

I bustled into the room now on the pretext of scolding the chambermaid; indeed, the nasty girl was using the tongs to stir up the fire, though the poker was directly to hand. Elizabeth Mann said nothing that night, looking thinner than ever in the face—though her belly was monstrous huge—and hardly able to lift a finger to help herself.

And after all the money Mr. Wild threw away on physicians and surgeons and nurses, she died. The baby was born dead as well, and the watchers came from the parish to inspect the corpses for signs of plague.

I washed the lady's body myself, under Mr. Wild's watchful eye, and wrapped it in a fine woolen shift. I would have preferred linen, but Parliament in those days forbade the use of linen or cotton inside a coffin. To encourage the domestic manufacture of wool, even the grave-clothes had to be sewn in woolen thread. To think of these things at such-and-such a time is commonly supposed to be disrespectful, and nobody will like you for being the one to do so, yet somebody has to be the one to think about wool. If this kind of forethought has not made me well-liked, it has been at any rate indispensable about the house.

The cabinet-maker came from the Naked Boy and Coffin in a coach filled with the tools of his trade. He placed the body on a bed of bran inside a one-inch elm inner coffin with a recessed lid. I put the baby there in her arms, so that they could be buried together. The coffin was lined and covered with cambric, a length of beading tacked inside the upper rim to support the lid. Screws anchored the lid to the sides.

Next he caulked the inner joints with Swedish pitch and gimped the cotton with cambric. He covered the coffin with a plumber's shell of lead, five pounds per square foot, folding up the edges and tacking them onto the side. Strips of lead covered the lid and the head- and foot-ends. The plumber then smoothed and soldered the joints to make the coffin airtight and resistant to damp.

Mr. Wild watched everything. "I want to be sure the worms won't get at her," he told me, when I asked him to leave the men alone at their work.

The undertaker card-wired a diaper design onto the lead sheet with his template and straight-edge, then soldered the lead depositum plate into place and affixed four pairs of gilt grip-plates.

The coffin sat in state for three days in Mr. Wild's house. Two rows of gilt upholstery nails fixed the drapes of scarlet and white Genoese velvet to the coffin.

When the time came for the funeral, I handed round sprigs of rosemary for everyone to carry in their hands. We spread a white pall over the coffin, and six undertakers' men in white gloves, silk scarves and black hat-bands carried the body to the churchyard, the beadles marching at the head of the procession with their long silver-knobbed staffs.

When we arrived at St. Pancras Church-yard, a gust of wind almost knocked the men aside. They struggled with their burden until they could lay it down beside the open grave.

"Man that is born of woman hath but a short time to live," intoned the priest, "and is full of misery. He cometh up, and is cut down, like a flower; he fleeth as it were a shadow, and never continueth in one stay. In the midst of life we are in death: of whom may we seek for succour, but of thee, O Lord, who for our sins art justly displeased?"

The coffin was let down into the ground. We threw our sprigs of rosemary in after it.

Earth to earth, ashes to ashes, dust to dust.

I need hardly say that I thought it the most natural thing in the world that after the death of his wife, Mr. Wild should look to me for a replacement.

◉

It's funny what lengths people will go to in order to hold on to their loved ones.

Bones aren't the only things that survive, though I'm amazed that Wild's skeleton remains on public view. Embalming's the most popular way of retaining the dear departed. I'm padding out my travel guide copy with all kinds of curious information ("Did you know . . . ?"), and while I'm saving my best attention for Jonathan Wild and his wives, I've dug up lots of shocking little-known facts. Did you know that Jeremy Bentham put his money where his mouth was when it came to dissection? After years of arguing strenuously that dead paupers' bodies should be made available to doctors, he saved his admirers the trouble of commissioning a portrait bust after his death by asking his friend Dr. Southwood Smith—author of *The Uses of the Dead to the Living*, a polemical intervention into the contemporary debate about the ethics of dissection—to dissect him in public and then articulate his skeleton. Smith desiccated Bentham's head and put the skeleton in a seated position; he gave the body a wax portrait head and dressed it in a suit of Bentham's clothes, padded and stuffed to the philosopher's proportions in life. The auto-icon is housed in a glass-fronted showcase at University College, London, Bentham's shriveled head resting beneath its feet.

In the eighteenth century, Sir John Price embalmed his first wife and placed her body by his bed. His second wife apparently had no objection to keeping the remains in their bedroom, and when she herself died, Sir John embalmed her as well and placed her beside the first. When Sir John's third wife said she wouldn't marry him unless he removed the embalmed bodies from his bedchamber, everyone thought her very unreasonable.

The technology of embalming has taken a long time to perfect. Reading the books, you'd think innovation in this field was driven solely by men's need to keep their hands a little longer on their dead wives.

In the middle ages, bodies were preserved by the *mos teutonicus*. When Henry V died in Normandy in 1422, butchers cut up his body into pieces and boiled them in wine until the fat and flesh fell away from the bones. They preserved the soft remains in spices and sealed them up in a lead case with his bones, then shipped him home to England for burial.

Through the centuries that followed, every high-street wax-chandler, undertaker and apothecary tried his hand at embalming. During the reign of Charles II,

Robert Boyle wanted to preserve corpses to use in anatomy tutorials during the summer season. He drained all the blood from the arteries and veins and replaced it with a fluid that hardened in place. Unfortunately the procedure worked better on bird embryos than on human bodies.

The eighteenth-century surgeon William Hunter knew that many people wished to have the bodies of their friends preserved, so he took the problem in hand. First he examined an Egyptian mummy and saw that the embalmer had taken out the viscera of the head, thorax and abdomen and cut all the flesh off the bones. The body cavities were filled up with tar, the limbs were nothing but linen rags dipped in pitch and wrapped around the bone, and the flesh had been buried or burned. Hunter felt that this hardly counted as embalming.

Then a man came to Hunter and asked him to embalm the body of his dead wife. It was midsummer. Hunter said he'd try. Hoping to prevent putrefaction by getting rid of all the body's moisture, he put the woman in a wooden coffin filled with plaster-of-Paris and replaced the body's natural juices with embalming fluids.

The body rotted anyway.

Some time passed before another subject came to hand. Martin Van Butchell had been one of Hunter's brother's original pupils, practicing dentistry before becoming an eminent truss-maker and scientific eccentric. He rode around Hyde Park on a gray pony that he'd dyed purple, carrying a large white bone that had been used in battle on the island of Otaheite (a.k.a. Tahiti) and which he claimed to need to defend himself against robbers.

After Van Butchell's wife Maria died in 1775, he approached Hunter and asked him to embalm her. Hunter agreed to take the job.

A statuary took an impression in plaster of Maria Van Butchell's face for a death-mask. An apothecary injected her veins with five pints of oil-of-turpentine, Venice turpentine and vermilion. The next day Hunter opened up the body and began to embalm it. He removed the thorax and abdomen and placed them in water. Then he emptied the trunk of blood. He washed the cavities and the exterior in spirits of wine, then injected the trunk again with a preservative solution. He left the brain in place and returned the viscera to the cavity with a dose of camphor, nitre and resin.

Three days after her death, Hunter placed Maria Van Butchell in a box with a hundred and thirty pounds of plaster-of-paris. He then returned the body to the woman's husband. Van Butchell placed between his wife's thighs a bottle of camphorated spirits rich with gum. He secreted vials of oil of rosemary and lavender about the rest of her limbs. He washed and dried the body, then rubbed it with fragrant oils.

Finally he put her on display. Members of the public who wished to see his wife had to obtain a personal introduction from a friend and visit between the hours of nine and one, Monday through Saturday. When his wife's green parrot died some time afterwards, Van Butchell had it stuffed and put into a glass case beside her.

Van Butchell died in 1814. Their son donated his mother's embalmed body (as well as that of the parrot) to the Royal College of Surgeons, and she remained there in the Curio Room well into the twentieth century.

Is it appropriate to put your dead mother's body on public display in the name of science? My own mother died in a drunk-driving accident when I was twelve. She was the one who was drunk. She lay in a coma on life support for a few days. The organ team from my father's hospital harvested her heart and kidneys. Then they unplugged the machine.

We cremated her and put her ashes into a small silver box. My father meant to have the ashes scattered over the Long Island Sound but he never got around to delivering them to the helicopter pilot.

The box sat in the hall closet for several years.

Then my father married my step-mother. She had the whole house redecorated. In the course of the renovations, the contractors misplaced my mother's ashes.

My father threatened to sue but his lawyer told him he might come out looking worse than the builders and he changed his mind. This is not a joke or an exaggeration. It is a true story.

◉

The summer has been unusually hot.

I struggle around historic houses and out-of-the-way museums. The tube trains do not have air-conditioning. As I push my hair back behind my sweaty ears, I think about getting that famous Mia Farrow summer haircut, the one from *Rosemary's Baby.*

Gideon thinks short hair is sexy.

I book an appointment.

I cancel it.

I do not know what to do.

Though Gideon never guaranteed the trip to Edinburgh, I have somehow forgotten my native caution. Without even knowing it I've been banking on going to Scotland with him and it comes as a major blow when Gideon tells me on the phone later that week that he may not be able to get away after all. I'm a person who feels emotion like a punch in the stomach. This time I'm so disappointed that I'm afraid I'm going to throw up.

"Hold on a second," I say, and grab the bucket from underneath the sink.

The worst thing, I realize, is that I have absolutely no clue what Gideon's thinking. The small voice of reason tells me that this is for him nothing more than a routine extramarital affair, one of perhaps three or four he's had since he got married, with the additional spice of me being my father's daughter.

"Elizabeth?" Gideon says. "Are you there?"

I mutter assent. Why did I expect him to take me to Edinburgh in the first place? I should never have brought it up, and to remind myself of this I bite my tongue. Literally: I taste the blood.

"Elizabeth? Are we still on for lunch tomorrow?"

"I guess so," I say.

Gideon believes himself to be a good husband, a family man, a benefactor to humanity in his work. And in some sense it's true, just as the same things are true of my father. But Gideon's not necessarily a good person. He's good at his job. It's a crucial difference.

◉

The next afternoon, we sit upstairs at McDonald's. Milkshakes, burgers, fries: Gideon struggles to overcome his aversion to the food, to which he objects not on caloric grounds but as a matter of taste. We're not talking about Scotland. Gideon won't know until the very last minute whether he'll be able to get away. We're being deliberately chipper, which means we're talking about cloning instead.

"Imagine if you could order a vial of sperm from Amazon.com, along with your books on cloning and fertility," I say.

"Well, the Human Embryology and Fertilisation Authority has issued a national warning against buying sperm over the Internet," Gideon tells me, "mostly on the grounds that there's no certainty that donors have been properly screened for HIV. But I see no reason why it shouldn't be allowed, given a reputable provider."

The latest fuel to the flames of my cloning obsession is a bizarrely brilliant book called *In His Image*, billed by a well-known science writer as a non-fiction account of one business tycoon's quest to clone himself an heir. Author David Rorvik is approached by a multimillionaire, a self-made man who has an elaborate scheme for cloning himself. Part of the deal is that the journalist is sworn to secrecy; this allows Rorvik to fudge crucial details that might give away the self-made man's real identity (and that certainly would have shown his story to be a fraud). The book came out in 1978, the year I turned six: I remember sneaking it from my mother's bedside table and skimming through the science to get to the racy parts, which involved Asian settings and what seemed to me at the time to be extremely decadent and exotic sex. When my copy arrives from Amazon UK, I am shattered to realize that there's hardly any sex in it at all: I've become immune to vague raciness, I need my sex harder-core.

Nineteen seventy-eight: the same year that an English woman gave birth to Louise Brown, the world's first test-tube baby. You can see how hard it must have been to separate science fact from science fiction.

And the best cloning novel of all time, for the record? That's easy: *The Boys From Brazil.* (Runner-up is *Brave New World*, a little highbrow for my taste but still prescient in its view of a world in which sex has been entirely decoupled from reproduction.)

One of Gideon's more human traits is that he reads science-fiction novels at night before he goes to sleep. He claims to be increasingly taken with the technical demands of the cloning project.

"It's an interesting scheme," he says, pulling a piece of imaginary gristle out of his McNugget and laying it fastidiously on his tray. "Of course you can't be sure the bones actually belonged to your chap. Your sorry skeleton's likely to have been a common-or-garden highwayman or housebreaker, dug up to defraud the surgeons."

I shrug.

"I'm willing to take the chance," I say. Privately I think that Gideon's being unnecessarily scrupulous. We both know the bones are Jonathan Wild's.

"Whenever you mess about with this rubbish," Gideon says, "the chance of genetic defects goes up. Are you prepared to risk an error in the reconstructed genome? Down's syndrome, fragile X chromosome?"

I stare him down.

"I suppose you're absolutely sure that you want to have a baby," he says then.

This question makes me nervous. I'm not at all sure I want to have a baby. But this is not something Gideon is capable of understanding. Every woman he meets is absolutely sure she wants a baby.

I lean across the table and put my hand behind his head. I kiss him hard on the mouth.

"What do you think?" I say.

"I'll do it," he says, holding up a hand to forestall premature celebration, "but only on one condition."

"What's that?" I say, my heart in my mouth.

"That we pursue ordinary IVF concurrently. Your eggs, my sperm."

I sit there and look at him.

"It won't cost you anything," he adds.

"It won't cost me any money," I correct him.

"Well?"

I know I'm not getting pregnant the regular way. I can't help it. I start grinning and he grabs my hands and squeezes tight.

"What the hell," he says, taking a puff from his inhaler. "Let's go for it."

◉

We have only a week before the conjectural Scotland trip to get started on the baby project. I tell myself I won't care if we don't go to Scotland—that I only want to go so that I can meet Gideon's friend the DNA expert—and I book an appointment to see Gideon as a patient.

It's the grown-up version of playing doctor. Mrs. Beardsley greets me when I arrive. I ask after her daughter and the baby.

"Both in fine fettle," she says, "and thanks very much for asking. Have a seat and Dr. Streetcar will be with you as soon as he's able."

I've been on antibiotics for three days in preparation for the hysterosalpingogram Gideon is about to administer. Basically he's going to X-ray my uterus and fallopian tubes. The antibiotics are meant to prevent infection. I've told him my tubes are blocked, and that the problem wasn't endometriosis or pelvic inflammatory disease but a minor surgical procedure gone wrong. He's going to check for adhesions and generally scope things out.

Gideon appears and ushers me into the examining room. He steps out of the office while I undress. I put on the cotton robe and climb onto the examining table. I place my heels in the stirrups at the bottom of the table.

Gideon comes back in.

He locks the door behind him. In America this would be against the law. In England it's just bad judgment.

"God, you're sexy," he says.

He comes over to me and begins to caress my breasts.

"Doctor," I say, "I want you to examine me."

I pull up the robe and start stroking my cunt.

Gideon groans.

"I'm a little nervous," I say. I smile at him and stretch out on the table.

"Just relax," he says.

Gideon puts on latex gloves.

He brushes his hand up along my calf and back down the thigh towards my vagina.

I moan a little. Actually I'm disgusted by the latex, but the turn-off is its own kind of turn-on. I feel very distant from my body.

He holds up the speculum for my inspection. He lubricates my vagina with K-

Y, then inserts the speculum, clicking it into place. He rotates the X-ray so that it's directed at my uterus. The video monitor now displays a flashlight-sized view of my reproductive organs.

I squirm. This hurts a little.

Gideon kisses me.

"Don't fret, little girl," he says.

"I don't think my tubes are in great shape," I mumble.

"You're in good hands," he says.

I take his wrist and kiss the palm of his hand.

"I know," I say.

“Married?” says my aunt, when I came round at last to pay her the courtesy of a visit. She had received me civilly at first, until she learned my errand, whereupon she gave me a look as though I was ten years old again and caught out in some dire mischief. “Why would you wish to marry such an outright rogue? That man has more maggots in his noddle than there are nits in a mumper’s doublet! Besides, there’s no honor in common-law coupling, and I promise you Mr. Jonathan Wild will never stand up with you before the parson.”

“Of course we will be married in church,” says I, though I’d not thought of it before; “a common-law marriage is not the same thing at all.”

“I have it on the very best authority, you know,” says she then, shaking her head in a very affected manner, “that he cannot have offspring, on account of the salivation the surgeons applied after his last bout of pox.”

I would rather have died than let her know it, but her assertion gave me pause. I had seen men who’d tried to cure their syphilis with mercury. My uncle, indeed, had spewed out a pint of spittle every hour the last time he took a salivation. I did not believe, however, that Mr. Wild had come to such a pass.

“Jonathan’s venereal performances with lewd women have made his body rotten,” persisted she, “and to keep his body in repair, he has been a constant customer to Dr. Askew at Northumberland Court in the Strand—I have it from my friend Mrs. Smith, nurse to Lady B———, who is a frequent visitor to Askew’s house.”

I scoffed at her. “I have been living in his house these two years, more or less, and never heard a whisper of it,” says I, and hearing my voice rise, I cursed myself for giving the old bitch the satisfaction of knowing her words troubled me. “Moreover, his last wife died in childbed, which would put the lie to your tale.”

“Of course if you have been living in his house you’ll not have heard of it,” answers she. “No, Mary, I wish for once you’d listen to your old aunt. We’ve had our differences over the years, but I have knowledge of the man you mean to marry that would make your skin crawl. He was an old associate of your uncle’s, you know.”

As she looked at me, I kept my expression stony, though I was surprised as could be.

“Everyone knew your uncle for a hard, brutal man. But Mr. Wild, for all that bluff forthright northern manner, is ten times worse than Mr. Spurling ever was.

I would not wish such a husband on my worst enemy, my dear, and I urge you to think again, while you still can. If you don't marry so soon, you'll make yourself amends by marrying safer. Anyone who gets a bad husband is married too soon."

She took a deep draught of brandy-and-water and swilled the liquid around in her mouth as if to rinse out the taste of her words. The contrast between her present gravity and the usual frivolity of her manner could not have been more marked.

I smirked. I couldn't help myself—the idea that Mr. Wild had anything in common with my wicked uncle struck me as absolutely ludicrous. No, worse: it was a mortal affront.

She saw my expression and slapped me hard across the face.

"If you marry that man," says she, "you may depend upon it he'll come to a bad end, and you with him; I warrant you I may even have a hand in it myself."

My aunt's settled enmity notwithstanding, Mr. Wild and I were married at St. Pancras-in-the-Fields on the 13th of February in the year 1719. It was hanging day at Tyburn, and Mr. Wild had taken two of the men who were due to be executed, Sam Linn and a man called Sinnamond. Some said it was a strange day to choose for a wedding, and I dared not ask Mr. Wild why he had fixed upon it—he was still beside himself with grief on account of his dead wife, and I feared that any questions might put it into his head that he didn't want to be married at all.

We rode there in a coach and four. The ceremony being performed, we traveled next to the foot of the gallows, where the Ordinary of Newgate and the hangman—Mr. Richard Arnet—appeared with gloves and favors, handing them out to all the officers who attended at the melancholy scene.

"What goes?" one man cried out. "Is one of the malefactors to be married to some tender-hearted virgin under the gallows?"

For as you must know, it had become a fashion to be married in such a way—girls gave themselves airs thinking on the fine prospect of being joined in holy matrimony to the soon-to-be-martyred.

"No, not at all," said Mr. Arnet, "but Mr. Wild has been married today, and wishes the world to celebrate with him."

Afterwards we gave out favors to the turnkeys at Newgate, and even the prisoners were issued anchors of brandy for making a punch. We kept court at our new house in the Old Bailey for three days, brewing up bowl after bowl of punch at the sign of King Charles's Head, right up until the liquor ran out. This establishment was grander by far than the last, though I sometimes thought we'd moved simply because Mr. Wild felt the ghost of his dead wife in every room of the old house. Moreover, Mr. Wild had taken a coach-and-six for his own use, stabling his horses in Red Cross Street, Southwark, which was most convenient, and very fashionable as well.

Not until the third night after the wedding were we finally alone together. As my new husband shut the massive door to the best bedchamber, I lay on the bed, my hair loose over my shoulders, my bodice unlaced. I knew that I looked very well—the festivities had gone on far too long, but I'd made sure to have a good sleep that afternoon so that my husband would find me as lively as a new bride should be, at least when she's a widow with none of bashfulness that makes a virgin dread her wedding-night.

I have always been blessed with a naturally good complexion. Other women might resort to rouge and paint, but not I: of course, a little red-pomatum to plump out my lips, burnt cork to blacken my eyebrows, lotion for my hands, all these I use when necessary. I sweetened my breath that evening with cloves, cinnamon and orange peel, and felt ready for anything in the world.

I suppose, looking back, that it was a little perplexing that Mr. Wild had waited till the third night to savor the sweets of the marriage-bed. But at the time, it seemed sensible enough that the obligations of a host should outweigh the need to discharge the marital debt.

Mr. Wild made a good beginning at the business, and before half-an-hour had passed, I lay quite naked on the bed. Mr. Wild had taken off his shirt—like Esau, he was a hairy man—and I ran my fingers through the thick dark mat of hair on his chest (though his back was smooth, a fortunate thing as I never could abide a pelt of fur over a man's shoulders). When I moved to his breeches, though, he laid a hand on mine and effectively halted my progress.

"I will have your cock inside me now," I said at last, having seen that modesty would only get me so far. He had suckled my nipples and rubbed his fingers up and down my slit and I was more than ready to receive him.

"Not yet," says Mr. Wild, renewing the assault with his fingers and using his other hand to hold me down on the bed.

I sat up, and gave him my best glare. "I grow tired of waiting," says I, and refused to listen to any more of his equivocations.

"Well, then, if you are set upon it, I suppose we must proceed," says Mr. Wild, a strange kind of sorrow in his voice. I wondered for an instant whether he had sworn to his last wife a vow of celibacy or some other idiocy. Then I dismissed the thought.

Mr. Wild threw off the rest of his clothes now in a kind of frenzy. Snatching up the candle, he held it before his groin. He seized my head with his other hand and forced my face towards his member, and my stomach churned as I contemplated what he meant me to see. The genital area was covered with small hard chancres; some of the pustules were enlarged, while others had broken open into shallow ulcers, pus crusting about the edges.

You must know that I felt quite faint.

"It was my fault Elizabeth died," says he. "My fault."

"Your wife died for the sins of Eve," says I, having had a moment to collect myself and decide I had no patience for this line of argument, for it would profit us none. "Childbirth is always dangerous."

But I knew in my heart what he meant to say, and say it he did.

"It was the pox," says he. "The French disease. Syphilis."

I was silenced at once.

"Now you see why I hold myself responsible for the death of Elizabeth Mann, and why I will on no account lay you open to the same risk," says Mr. Wild, letting me go and pulling his breeches back on, then sitting beside me at the end of the bed. "I will not hold it against you if you take other lovers, though I urge caution; I have no desire to raise another man's by-blow in the place of my own child, and as you see, disease threatens at every turn."

"There are no lesions," says I, grasping at straws; "and your joints are hardly swollen at all; it need not be the French disease, and if it's just a clap, you can be cured at once. I am willing to take the risk, at any rate, that I may bear you a child."

"I can have no issue," Mr. Wild said then. "Those physicians who are acquainted with the fatigues my constitution has undergone, give me but little encouragement to hope for any."

I suppose I had not known until that moment how much I wanted a child by Mr. Wild. I burst then into tears, and Mr. Wild comforted me as best he could. A sad night we made of it, and when I fell asleep at last, shortly before the dawn, my dreams were uneasy indeed.

I woke refreshed, though at a later hour than usual. Mr. Wild was gone, and I dressed with particular care, it not being my way to resign myself to affliction without first putting up a good fight. I wandered about the room in my stays and stomacher before pulling a linen chemise over my head. I drew up about my ankles my favorite pair of black silk stockings with the lace clocks, and tied the garters about my thighs. I will never wear worsted again, I thought to myself, and felt a flicker of delight at the uncontested advantages of my situation. I had no small trouble with my petticoat, a new model whose hoops of whalebone were strung together with tapes, but I did not fancy the maids assisting me with it so soon after my first night in my old master's bed. At last I covered my bosom with a handkerchief and let myself out of the room.

At my friend Mrs. Betty's shop in Covent Garden that afternoon I purchased a packet of eight condoms, manufactured out of sheep's intestines and guaranteed to be of the best quality. I hesitated between the different sizes, but settled at last on the largest, not wishing to offend. Each one was bound in a pretty sachet with silk ribbons; Mrs. Betty gave me a choice of pink or blue, and I chose the pink, on the grounds of it being better suited to my complexion, though (as she said) it was not as though I meant to wear the things on my head.

That night the men asked for a good supper, and I gave it to them: cod, mutton, soup, chicken pie, pudding, pigeons, veal, asparagus and sweetbreads, with jelly, fruit and madeira to follow, and as nice a piece of Dutch cheese as I'd ever laid eyes on. I always loved a good piece of fish—trout, shad, lampreys, barbels, roach, dace, eels, flounder, salmon, sturgeon—and the fishmonger two streets away knew better than to fob me off with any but the freshest. We were well situated for food by now, despite the dirty stuff that was sold in so many shops. A man came round each morning leading his donkey, and we had fresh asses' milk in our silver can for three shillings a quart. The bread the baker sold was no good, being heavily adulterated with alum and white lead, but it was no trouble to do our own baking. I was never one to take out my frustrations on other people's stomachs, in other words, and I knew already that the satisfactions of marriage to Mr. Wild would be little different in kind from what I'd already known as his housekeeper, the only difference being that now nothing was too good for me: I had fine milled French soap scented with roses or lavender, the most expensive dresses and baubles, etc.

Yet I'd not given up altogether on the idea that my husband might be coaxed into bedding me properly. In bed that night, I loosened the ribbon at the end of the condom, then put it to my nose to sniff the scent of almond oil.

Mr. Wild smiled at me, though I thought it took some effort, and began to recite the Earl of Rochester's "Panegyrick upon Condoms, useful against unwanted Brats."

I gave him a hopeful look, and he laughed a little.

"After all," says he, "I suppose we may chance it."

And so we did, my own satisfaction somewhat hampered by the intrusive membrane, but knowing well enough that discretion is the better part of valor.

The one thing I could not understand was why Mr. Wild continued to go back to St. Pancras Church-yard every morning to visit the grave of Elizabeth Mann.

"Must you wear that dowdy mourning-ring?" asked I one night the week after, disturbed despite my best intentions by the lock of his dead wife's hair lying so close to my own on the pillow.

He took his hands off my breasts and turned me over. Rolling a condom onto his cock, he began to thrust into me.

"She only came to me because she had nowhere else to go," he grunted, addressing the words mostly to himself. "She foreswore her former trade, became a penitent for her former life and feared to fall back into the old ways. She came to me and we were married at once."

I knew better than to say it, but I thought she had been a cast-off whore who'd spotted Mr. Wild as a mark, and sought him out to better herself—odds were she'd been the one to give him the pox, making his scruples about her death singularly unnecessary. But I kept my mouth shut. As soon as he came into the condom, he rolled off and lay on his back beside me, covering his eyes with his hands. I saw a tear slide out from under his fingers, and said no more about the ring.

◉

> One of the most common mistakes in asking for support is the use of *could* and *can* in place of *would* and *will.* "*Could* you empty the trash?" is merely a question gathering information. "*Would* you empty the trash?" is a request. . . . On Mars it would be an insult to ask a man "*Can* you empty the trash?" Of course he can empty the trash! The question is not *can* he empty the trash but *will* he empty the trash. After he has been insulted, he may say no just because you have irritated him.
>
> —John Gray, Ph.D., *Men Are From Mars, Women Are From Venus* (1992)

"Do you think you can bring me to Scotland with you?" I ask Gideon the next time we talk.

"I certainly *can,*" Gideon says. "It's a question of whether it's really a good idea. Won't it be rather dull for you, darling? Miranda always has a bloody awful time at these affairs."

I don't know what to say. I can't tell him how much I want to go to Scotland.

"What about Jonathan Wild?" I ask after a long pause. I would much rather argue about Jonathan Wild than squabble about whether we're going away next weekend. This displacement doesn't solve any problems, but at least it clears the air.

"Don't set your heart on cloning this character," Gideon warns me. "I've been looking into it, and I think we're likely to run into all sorts of difficulties. Why didn't you tell me sooner that Wild had syphilis?"

I'm silent. Syphilis is one of those words you never want to hear. Do they still use the Wassermann reaction to detect syphilis cases? It sounds like a Robert Ludlum title to me, but for the 80-and-over set the name Wasserman still conjures up what was just about the worst diagnosis you could possibly get.

I was born in 1972, the year the national press finally exposed the horror of the Tuskegee Study of Untreated Syphilis in the Negro Male. Beginning in 1932, government health officers told four hundred syphilitic black men in Macon County, Alabama that they had "bad blood," but that they'd be eligible for a few perks if they came for regular checkups. The district nurse and the doctors involved all knew that "bad blood" was a euphemism for syphilis, but they kept the men in ignorance. Even when penicillin was found to be an effective cure, they chose to continue the study rather than provide the drug and cure the disease. All in the name of science.

Did you ever see a single spirochete under an electron microscope? Corkscrew-shaped, its tightly wound coils reproduce in the body's tissues unless they are destroyed by penicillin. Tertiary-stage syphilis can incapacitate or kill; neurosyphilis produces intense back pain, lack of muscular coordination and wasting, while cardiovascular syphilis destroys the tissue of the aorta. Even benign tertiary syphilis patients present with ulcerated lesions of the skin, bone and organs (liver, testicles, brain).

"None of the doctors who've examined Wild's skeleton over the years have spotted any sign of syphilis," I object now. "It must have been gonorrhea or some other venereal disease."

I have asked Gideon to write me a letter on his office stationery that I can present at the Hunterian Museum.

"What shall I write?" Gideon says.

He doesn't want to do it, and in the end I compose the text myself. It is an understated masterpiece of English formality. My credentials are laid out in four-syllable words on expensive letterhead, Gideon's illegible doctor's signature at the foot of the page.

I make another appointment at the College of Surgeons. The curator is happy to see me again.

"What can I do for you this time?" she says.

She has already shown me several recent acquisitions and the draft of an article about Hunter's tissue-grafting experiments.

"I'd like to take a small sample of bone from Jonathan Wild's skeleton," I say.

"Whatever for?" she asks.

"It's on behalf of a forensic historian in Massachusetts," I say. "He's collecting samples from well-known criminals. He wants to model the criminal genome."

She looks skeptical.

"He's a little crazy," I say, "but the project's basically legitimate."

Now she's worried about the damage my sample-taking may cause. "We can't just allow people to come in and hack away at the things we've got here," she says. "They may be curiosities, but they're still worthy of preservation."

"I've done this before," I say. "The damage will be minimal."

She hesitates.

"The potential gain to science," I say, "is worth the risk."

In the movie version, I'd save myself some trouble by planning a bone heist, but I have no talent for breaking and entering. It takes some time more to obtain her permission, and the expression on her face is almost comically worried as she accompanies me upstairs.

She unlocks the case with a small key on a ring retrieved from her desk drawer. The glass door swings open and I face Jonathan Wild directly. I put out my hand to touch the bones of his thighs and pelvis. Then I kneel on the floor by the case and place my kit in front of me. I take out several test-tubes and put on a pair of latex gloves. With a straight-edge from my personal stash, I carefully scrape Wild's femur. I transfer the sample to a test-tube. I take additional samples from the ribs and the collar-bone. The bones don't look syphilitic to me, and I'm sure one of the nineteenth-century doctors who looked at the skeleton would have commented on it, if only to drive the final nail into the coffin of Wild's reputation.

I seal the other samples and strip off the gloves. I scribble the date and time on a couple of labels and slap them on the tubes.

"Do let me know what you find out," says the curator, calmer now she has seen how respectable my equipment looks.

I promise to keep in touch.

Gideon's friend in Edinburgh will extract the DNA from the bone specimen. Gideon has promised to take him out for an expensive meal in return for his trouble. I still don't know if I'll be there myself, but even if I'm not, Gideon's friend will still reconstitute Wild's DNA for the cloning project.

I call Gideon as I walk to the tube. Mrs. Beardsley puts me on hold for five minutes.

"What is it?" he says when he finally gets on the line.

"I got it!" I say.

"Good show, darling. We'll talk tomorrow, all right? My hands are a bit full at the moment."

The fact that I have Wild's genetic material in my possession sustains me for the rest of the afternoon. So, too, does the fact that I run into Robert as I'm coming back from lunch.

"Let me cook you dinner," he says. "You're free, aren't you? I'm an excellent cook, you know."

I promise to bring dessert. I leave the library early as I am overcome by an entirely uncharacteristic compulsion to show off my domestic side. I can believe, based on my previous visit to his apartment (the bottles of rice wine and sherry by the stove, the mason jars of fresh fish and chicken stock in the fridge), that Robert is an intimidatingly good cook. I don't have an oven, so regular baking is out, but I can do an acceptable tarte tatin in the cast-iron skillet that sits on the single gas-ring in my efficiency.

I have almost forgotten that I like to cook. Even in adverse conditions (the

Swiss Army knife I use to peel and slice the apples, sacks of flour and sugar spilling out onto the surface of the desk) the tart turns out well. English butter is strangely better than the rock-solid refrigerated bricks you get in America: it's soft and fresh and I shave off a deep-yellow sliver and put it in my mouth as I wait for the apples to caramelize.

I call Rob at 6:30 to see if there's anything else I can bring.

"Well," he says, "I'm in a bit of a fix at this end."

His words are slurred, and I already have an inkling as to the nature of the problem. It emerges that he ran into an old friend from Canada and they spent a decadent afternoon getting incredibly stoned and drinking pints down the pub.

"Don't worry," he says now. "I've thrown money at the problem. It's all going to be fine. It's a simpler menu than I planned, but everything will be all right. You do eat British beef, don't you?"

"Of course," I say. "Anyway, what should I pick up on the way over?"

"Well, I'm sorry to say that I accidentally left the second bag of shopping in my friend's car. Could you pick up a few salad things? Greens, a cucumber, tomatoes?"

"Are you sure you still want me to come over?"

He says he's sure, but I arrive at his place forty minutes later and he's massively drunk. His kiss barely hits my cheek and I follow him into the kitchen with a feeling of despair.

As I unpack the salad stuff, a bottle of wine and the apple tart (which I want somebody to praise and appreciate), Robert picks up a knife and starts chopping potatoes into small cubes, which he says he'll deep-dry in the oil and butter that's already bubbling in a wok on the top of the stove. A minute later he cries out. I turn towards him and he's practically cut off the top joint of the index finger on his left hand. Blood's spurting out all over the potatoes and I hustle him into the bathroom, holding a wad of paper towels to his hand while I root around in the cabinet for the band-aids (or sticking plasters, as they are called here). After applying pressure for what seems like a very long time, the bleeding stops enough for me to plaster up his finger with lint and tape. As I bend over him, my hair falls forward and he brushes it back with his uninjured hand, then runs his finger down the side of my face.

I hear the oil bubbling in the other room and realize I'm the one who's going to have to cook dinner. Once I've persuaded Rob to sit down in the living room with a glass of wine—the last thing he needs, but it's the only way to keep him quiet—I take over. The menu will have to be even more drastically simplified. I throw away the bloody potatoes, turn off the burner under the wok and pour the oil down the drain. Part of me hopes that the sink will be clogged for weeks to come as punishment for his bad behavior.

I unwrap the two fat pieces of filet mignon on the counter and chop shallots and mushrooms. My glass of wine sits untouched on the counter. I am full of rage. Rob ambles in periodically to refill his glass without picking up the evil vibes I'm sending his way. He criticizes my slicing technique and sloshes into the frying pan a slug of red wine that promptly shoots up in flames. I glare at him and tell him to go and set the table.

By the time we sit down in front of the food my legs are aching and I'm sick with rage. The last straw is when he saws off a huge chunk of meat and spears it on his knife, then shoves it into his mouth, grinning at me as he chews.

"My roommate's away," he says conversationally. "We can get naked whenever we want!" He takes off one of his shoes and chucks it theatrically across the room, where it crashes into a stack of videos and knocks over an empty cocktail glass.

At this point I push back my chair and get up from the table. "I have to go now," I say.

He looks so disappointed that I almost relent.

"What about dessert?" he says.

"You should go to bed," I say.

"That's more like it," he says, taking this for an invitation. He stands and sways towards me.

It takes a good twenty minutes for him to understand I don't want to join him there, but finally he passes out on the bed and I make a run for it.

◉

Two Martians go to lunch to discuss a project or business goal; they have a problem to solve. In addition, Martians view going to a restaurant as an efficient way to approach food: no shopping, no cooking, and no washing dishes. For Venusians, going to lunch is an opportunity to nurture a relationship, for both giving support to and receiving support from a friend. Women's restaurant talk can be very open and intimate, almost like the dialogue that occurs between therapist and patient.

—John Gray, Ph.D., *Men Are From Mars, Women Are From Venus* (1992)

At eight the next morning my phone rings.

"Sorry about last night," says Rob, sounding cheerful as ever. "I'm hoping I might lure you over for breakfast. Your tarte tatin looks good enough to eat!"

"I'm working now," I say, though I'm obviously still completely asleep. "Hope you enjoy it."

"Well, if you're sure I can't persuade you. . . ."

I'm still so angry that I don't fall asleep again for hours, and I barely wake up in time to meet Miranda for lunch. She wants to thank me for taking care of Gideon's mother.

We meet at a Greek restaurant off Kensington High Street. She's in the middle of redesigning the interior of a nearby townhouse.

"How do you like life in London?" Miranda asks over our first cocktail.

"It's all right," I say. "I like New York better."

"I'm not surprised," Miranda says. "But I suppose it must be nice to have a change of scene. Not that Hampstead offered you much relief from the rigors of family life. You know, I really must thank you again for spending the weekend with Gideon's mother."

"Not at all," I say.

"By the way, what was your impression of her health?"

"I thought she was tough as hell," I say.

Miranda groans. "I was afraid you'd say that. I do worry about her, though. For a lifelong hypochondriac, she's certainly extraordinarily averse to seeing a doctor! Of course, she was very attached to the family doctor, who died four or five years ago—a sweet little man, rather good-looking, very soft-spoken. A strong connection between those two, you might say."

"You're not implying that Clara had an affair with him, are you?" Miranda's carefully chosen words have put a new spin on Gideon's account of his mother's relationship with Dr. Foster.

"Oh, surely not," Miranda says, in a tone that means precisely the opposite. I like her in gossip mode. "Of course I'd never mention it to Gideon, there's no doubt he'd fly completely off the handle. Dr. Foster's old secretary still sends us a Christmas card every year—she's a lovely American lady, a Bryn Mawr graduate circa 1948 with a very pleasant light accent and impeccable manners. She's called Fanny Ravish, Gideon always makes rude jokes about her last name. Which reminds me that I must invite her for tea one day, I know Clara would love to see her. You look rather as she must have done in the old days, actually, what with those wide-set eyes and that clear open expression of yours; I always think of it as such an American look."

I am mortified (not for the first time) by the fact of my own duplicity.

"You know," Miranda continues, "Clara said something about you the other day, I was completely bowled over that she'd even remembered your name. She really took a fancy to you."

"I liked her, too," I say. I am surprised to realize as I say it that this is the truth.

"I wish I could say the same," Miranda says.

"It's easier," I say, "when you're not related."

"Don't I know it," says Miranda, shaking her head. "While I love my parents dearly, I also live in sheer terror of landing up a dead ringer for my mother. I suppose they have a happy enough marriage, but I certainly wouldn't want one like it myself. My father treats my mother as a precious object of some sort, he's really a pathological collector."

I'm not supposed to know anything about Miranda's father, so I pull myself together and ask her what he collects.

"Absolutely everything," Miranda says. "Wedgwood. Tin soldiers. Nineteenth-century medical equipment. Americana. You name it. He and Gideon actually first met one another on the auction circuit, though of course I didn't know Gideon until later on."

"How did you meet?"

"Oh, the usual, I suppose," Miranda says, rather vaguely. "My marriage was falling apart, Gideon swept in and rescued me from the ruins."

"I didn't know you were married before," I say.

"My first husband was a real control freak," Miranda says. "Isn't that what you say in America? A heart surgeon, of all things. God knows what possessed me to marry another doctor, though of course Gideon's nowhere near as bad."

Miranda's face is animated but her eyes are sad. It's begun to be the great sorrow of her life that she can't have children, though she's hardly admitted it to herself. She'll adopt if she can, but Gideon won't like that.

"Doctors are pretty awful," I say. "Sometimes I think about writing a book: *Awful Doctors I've Known*. I used to work for one guy who was really the worst of all. . . ."

"Do tell," Miranda says, leaning towards me.

I finish my drink and Miranda orders another round. It's taking a long time for the food to come. What I'm really tempted to tell her is a comic version of the previous night's disaster, but I can't risk it getting back to Gideon. Instead I start talking about the distant past.

"I was a temp," I say, "a Kelly Girl in fact, and I worked one day a week at a hospital that treated Connecticut prison inmates. I took a bus out to the end of the line, then I got on the hospital shuttle with a motley collection of other employees. It was one of the grimmer parts of Connecticut, I won't tell you exactly where since I don't want the guy to sue me for slander. My employer was a weird Central European psychiatrist who specialized in sleep disorders. He must have been Jewish, but he had this awful accent that made him sound like a Nazi dentist, kind of like the Nick Nolte character in the Hollywood remake of *The Vanishing*."

"How creepy," Miranda says. "Tell me more."

"Of course I learned a lot about sleep apneas and narcolepsy and tryptophan and all that stuff," I continue. "I'm addicted to expert knowledge, so the job had its consolations. But there were major drawbacks. I spent most days sitting in front of the computer with my dictation earphones on. When you type from dictation you use the foot pedals to adjust the playback speed, you know? You feel like some kind of retro cyborg, it's all straight out of a fifties sci-fi space-porn sitcom. I typed letters. I typed notes on patient visits. I typed revisions of articles and lecture notes and thank-you letters for gifts from patients.

"Unfortunately Dr. Herzog also liked to dictate narratives of his dreams. 'And then my wife appears,' I'd type. 'She is completely naked, except for a basket of fruit on her head.' His dreams were always totally graphic, though with the veneer of respectability: more Dali than *Hustler*."

"How shocking," Miranda says. Her elbows are on the table, her chin rests in her hands; she's hanging on my every word and I find the quality of her attention extremely flattering.

"The thought of Dr. Herzog sitting in the room next door and speaking these words into his tape recorder was quite terrifying," I say.

"I can imagine," she says. "Would he say more?"

"Oh, of course," I say. "His wife would have lost her purse, and he wouldn't be able to find it anywhere; then they're making love on a feather mattress in an enormous curtained bedstead, a bed that reminds him of his great-grandmother's bedroom in Cologne before the war. Then he penetrates his wife's anus, just as the maid enters carrying a roast suckling pig on a silver platter with an apple stuffed into its mouth. His wife wants him to give her the apple, and he tells her that the basket on her head is already full of apples and he wants it for himself."

I'm performing for Miranda's benefit, but I'm not exaggerating much. It's basically a true story.

"Oh, the old apple business," Miranda says. "For heaven's sake. I once had a boyfriend who swore that sooner or later, every woman he had a relationship with offered him an apple, without fail. I told him he was being ridiculous and I made a special mental note never, ever to give Roderick an apple. But lo and behold, the next day, without even thinking, I offered him a Cox's Orange Pippin. He was appalled, he called me a temptress and ran off to the Orkneys to paint pictures."

Our food arrives and we sort out utensils, napkins, condiments.

"Tell me more about Dr. Herzog," Miranda says, once we've begun to eat our salads.

I put down my knife and fork and take up my glass of wine.

"Dr. Herzog asked me out to lunch the first day I worked for him," I say. "I turned him down; needless to say, I found the doctor completely off-putting. His office was on the fourth floor of an old brick building that stood apart from the main hospital. The building had been condemned and scheduled for demolition and all the other offices were already vacant. The place was completely empty.

"Once I spent the entire morning hooking up Herzog's modem."

Miranda raises an eyebrow. I ignore the innuendo.

"To test it out, we went into Medline and did a literature search for all Herzog's own articles. He stood behind me, leaning over my shoulder and clucking with satisfaction as the text scrolled down the screen. He smelled of whisky and baby powder.

"Herzog didn't like the bills he got from the temp agency. They charged him twenty dollars an hour, and I only got ten. He tried to persuade me to work directly for him. 'I could pay you eleven dollars an hour,' he'd say in his creepy but courtly way. 'Let us cut out the middleman.'

"The thing was that in a moment of insanity I'd given him my home phone number. I spent the next two months screening my calls. I'd wake up to the sound of the phone and the answering machine's click. I'd hear him leave yet another crazy message on the machine. I'd pull the covers up over my head to drown out the sound.

"Even worse, the temp agency became extremely suspicious. My supervisor called several times a week to check up on me. 'Are you sure you're not taking work on the side?' she'd ask. 'Believe me,' I'd say, 'I wouldn't dream of it.'"

"What a terrible story," Miranda says.

"I guess it wasn't that bad," I say. "Nothing really awful happened in the end. But I'm still suspicious of people who have dreams about sex and dictate them into tape recorders for their secretaries to type. There's something inherently erotic about typing from dictation. Bosses should know better than to take advantage."

"It's a funny thing about doctors," Miranda says. "You'd think they'd be really saintly, but they never are. And they keep such terrible hours, too. I'm constantly quarreling with Gideon about how late he stays at work. It's completely mad to work so hard."

"I don't know," I say. "I always go for guys who exhibit compulsive professional behavior. Not when they're actually my employers, though. But under other circumstances, it's pretty appealing."

"You seem to have quite a lot of experience," Miranda says. "Perhaps it's time for you to get a proper profession of your own."

She gives me a sharp look. Suddenly the combination of the previous night's rage and Miranda's current watchfulness makes me sick to my stomach. I take a big gulp of wine.

"I know, I know," I say. As this is remarkably close to what Dahlia tells me, I figure I'd better agree. I raise my hands defensively. "Tell me about it."

"What will you do when you finish your travel guide?" Miranda asks now.

"Actually," I say, "I'm thinking about writing a novel."

"Brilliant! What's it about? Or is that a terribly tactless question?"

"Not at all," I say. "It's a historical novel."

"Oh, I love historical novels," Miranda exclaims. "I used to devour Georgette Heyer when I was at school. I hope it's full of nice clothes and steamy sex. Bodice-ripping and so on."

"Not exactly," I say. "It's about organized crime, really. Gangs of thieves fencing stolen goods. Charismatic gang-leaders. Random acts of violence."

Miranda's taken aback. "A kind of mystery novel?" she suggests.

"Well, detective fiction," I say. "You know. Noir. Raymond Chandler. Chester Himes. Derek Raymond. Robbe-Grillet and the French new novel. No psychology. Lots of brutal sex and violence. Man reduced to sheer environment."

"How intriguing," Miranda says, clearly put off by my description and meaning exactly the opposite. But I don't take it personally. Hard-boiled's an acquired taste. "You'll have to promise me a signed copy when it's published!"

Now she looks at her watch. "God," she says, sighing, "I'd really better get back to work, I'm meeting the contractor at three. Will you be all right getting home from here?"

"Sure," I say. "Thanks for lunch."

We stand, we kiss each other on both cheeks. We're more than just polite, we're actively friendly. I wave to her as she rushes back to the house she's renovating.

After she's gone I totally crash: that is, I am seized with feelings of despair, self-loathing and general worthlessness. I trudge home calling myself a stupid bitch under my breath, until a middle-aged lady overhears me and takes it personally. As I cross to the other side of the street, it occurs to me that the problem with living in a place where you don't have many friends is that you end up becoming friends with exactly the people you should avoid at all costs. I stop at a pub on the way home for another drink. I'm pissed off with myself for talking so much to Miranda. Why the fuck did I tell her so much? I resolve that the next time I see her I will keep my mouth shut.

When I get home I can't settle down to work. That night I toss and turn like the cartoon of a person who can't sleep. I wrestle with the duvet. I kick my legs in the air. I punch the wall with my fist. Finally, at three in the morning, I throw myself out of bed. I'm standing in the moonlight in the middle of the room and I can hardly tell if I'm awake or asleep. There's nothing in my head but the clear clean image of the sharp metal blades in my desk.

Now I'm over by the desk and picking up the box of razor blades and weighing it in my hand. I slide a blade out of the box. I hold it for a long time before I put it back. I have no idea what I'm thinking but it's hard to let go.

In a daze, I rummage now through the desk drawer until I find the scissors I use to cut and paste my travel-book copy. I switch on the light and cross the room to the mirror over the sink. Pulling my hair out of its ponytail, I run my fingers through it. It comes down as far as my breasts, covering the faint scars above my collarbone. Resolute, naked to the waist, I take the scissors and start hacking.

Twenty minutes later I am surrounded by heaps of hair. I've evened up the sides a couple of times and I now have a neat short bob, angled upwards from my jaw towards the back of my head. Not till I have cropped the hair at the nape of my neck to stubble do I breathe freely. The hard cold steel of the scissors feels outrageously sexy against my skin. I stuff the handfuls of hair into a brown paper bag. Then I get back into bed and fall into a deep dreamless sleep.

I'm secretly appalled the next day by how short my hair is, but I decide to brazen it out. Fortunately Gideon seems to like it, though he gives me a hundred quid to get it finished off at what he calls a proper hairdresser's.

"I'm going to do a laparoscopy to check out the condition of your fallopian tubes," he says. We're in his office. It's after hours and nobody else is in the building. "The ovaries look perfect," he continues, "but I'm not so sure about the tubes. The results of the HSG weren't promising."

"What exactly are you going to do?" I say.

I slide a little further forward on the table, bending my knees and easing my feet into a more comfortable position in the stirrups. He's given me an intravenous sedative and the whole middle part of my body feels like it's not there.

"I'm going to make a small incision in your navel," he says.

He takes a scalpel and cuts open my belly button.

"And now one more, just above the pubic bone, so that I can insert the probe," he says. His movements are quick and sure.

"You have to tell me everything you're doing," I say.

"Of course," he says. "I'm inserting the laparoscope now into the abdominal cavity. You shouldn't feel any pain, let me know if you do."

"I'm fine," I say.

"Now I'm inflating the cavity with carbon dioxide to force the walls away from the organs."

He picks up a large syringe.

"I'm going to pass dye though the tubes," he says.

He pokes around inside me, muttering to himself.

"What do you see?" I say.

"Hold on a sec," he says. "I'll need a bit longer before I'm able to tell."

We wait twenty or thirty minutes.

Carbon dioxide escapes slowly through the incision.

"OK," he finally says. "I'm ready to stitch you back up."

The consultation doesn't take long.

"Well," he says, "your tubes don't look good. They're completely sealed, almost as though you'd had a tubal ligation."

"What can I do about it?"

"We could do a reanastomosis to re-open them."

"And what would that entail?"

He's not listening to me.

"I think I can re-open the tubes through a laparoscopy," he says thoughtfully. "The fimbria seem to be intact. I'll cut the tubes open, then stitch them together again. I'll suture the inner canal and reattach the outer layer of the tube."

I'm freaking out at the thought of all this surgery.

"Do you have to do all that?" I say. "Isn't there a simpler way?"

He stops to think.

"Yes," he says. "That is, if you really want to try IVF. It might actually be easier to plant the embryos directly in the uterus. Then we won't have to worry about the tubes at all."

"That's what I want," I say.

I want to try IVF. I am determined to bear Jonathan Wild's clone.

Gideon kisses me now and promises to call by my place later that evening. He has taken to bringing me gifts, not presents in the normal sense of the word (flowers, jewelry, books, chocolates) but household appliances: all the apparatus of the home.

Tonight he shows up with a brand-new microwave.

"What am I supposed to do with this?" I ask.

It's a serious question. All the available counter space is already taken up with things he's brought: toaster oven, coffee-maker, electric mixer. What the hell am I going to do with an electric mixer? When people get married, they're given so many pieces of equipment that they can no longer imagine living without an electric juice-squeezer, an automated garlic press, a bread machine. "Jonathan Wild would have had no use for a microwave," I add.

"On the contrary," Gideon says, "Jonathan Wild would have been down the East End flogging it off the back of a lorry. Don't you like it?"

"Of course I like it," I lie. "But I'm not comfortable with the idea of you spending all this money on me."

"What I don't like is the thought of you camping out in a cramped little bedsit without any of life's necessities."

As far as I'm concerned, a microwave is not a necessity or even a convenience but a useless piece of junk.

"Well, I guess I'd better stock up on microwave popcorn," I say, making the best of it.

Now Gideon's face lights up. He pulls out of his briefcase a box of Orville Redenbacher popcorn. The last time I was in England, nobody would have known what this was. I don't like it that times have changed.

"See, I knew you'd like it!" he shouts.

"Well, at any rate I like *you*," I say sourly.

Gideon finds this very funny. "Of course you do, darling," he says. "Of course you do."

◉

Here they will meet with a system of politics unknown to Machiavel; they will see deeper stratagems and plots formed by a fellow without learning or education than are to be met with in the conduct of the greatest statesmen who have been at the heads of governments.

—*The Life of Jonathan Wild, by H.D., Clerk to Justice R—-* (1725)

"Here's what we're going to do," Gideon says.

It's several nights later and we're drinking in a pub near his office. He's got half an hour before he has to meet Miranda for dinner. I've visited maybe a dozen museums today and I'm sick of looking at things. I have a date on Thursday with Allan Menzies, who's back from vacation and has been working hard on the manuscript.

"It's a two-pronged plan," Gideon explains now. "First, I'll harvest your eggs, fertilize them with my own sperm, and culture the embryos in the lab. That's the real-world option. Meanwhile we'll attempt to clone Jonathan Wild by inserting his DNA into cow eggs whose DNA has been deactivated. We'll hope to get a couple of embryos that way too. Say we implant three embryos. Two real embryos, one science-fiction. Usually I'd say four, but you're young and healthy and we don't want to end up with triplets or quads."

They used to think that you could transplant the nucleus of a cell directly into an enucleated unfertilized egg. It turns out to be easier to fertilize the egg first and then put it into hibernation before putting in the DNA of the organism you want to clone. Cow's eggs are the easiest to work with (one embryologist in Wisconsin has used cow eggs as a universal incubator for mammal clones), and this is what we'll try first. Nuclear transfer had already been performed in many species before Dolly and Gideon tells me that the word on the street is that they've accomplished nuclear transfer in rhesus monkeys at a facility in Oregon. The technique's similar to intra-cytoplasmic sperm injection—Gideon's experience injecting sperm into egg cells will serve him well.

Science fiction makes us surprised that cloning hasn't been done more often, but Dolly is in fact the only animal to have been born after nuclear transfer from an *adult* donor cell. Far more amazing is the fact that scientists are so close to developing ectogenesis—an artificial womb. The latest version comes from Japan, a clear plastic box of warm amniotic fluid in which the fetus swims, its blood cleansed by dialysis. It's possible that mothers might soon become as extraneous as fathers have been for some time.

"Why two normal embryos and only one clone?" I say now. "You're stacking the deck against Jonathan Wild."

"We're certainly not implanting more than one cloned embryo, in any case," Gideon says, outraged. "What the hell would you do with not one but *two* replicas of Jonathan Wild?"

"I don't know," I say, "but identical twins are pretty cool."

"Well, I'm backing the ordinary embryos."

"And I'm backing the clone," I chip in. "Jonathan Wild to win!"

It's a deal. We shake on it, very serious.

"Then I'll transfer a total of three embryos back to the uterine cavity," Gideon says, more to himself than to me. "We'll bypass the fallopian tubes altogether."

We clink glasses and drink.

"What's the obsession with Jonathan Wild all about?" Gideon asks me suddenly. I can tell he wants a serious answer, and I try to give him one.

"I like Wild," I say slowly, "because he invented his own job when he found there wasn't one to suit him. His work was made for him, and he made himself out of his work."

I don't say it, but Jonathan Wild reminds me of all the men I've ever been drawn to. They're schmoozers, wheeler-dealers, rain-makers; they talk a big game, even if they turn out in the end to be no larger than life. My father's a fine scientist, but it's not the science that got him where he is today, it's the force of his personality.

"Also," I say, knowing that my answer hasn't satisfied Gideon, "he wasn't a doctor."

Gideon laughs. "I give up," he says. "I'll just have to reconcile myself to the fact that your affections are divided."

"As are your own," I say. "You'd better leave now, or you'll be late for Miranda."

Gideon shoots out his wrist and curses when he sees the time. He throws down some notes on the table and kisses me.

"Sorry, darling," he says. "We'll talk later."

◉

"So," says Dahlia over drinks at a ridiculously expensive bar in Notting Hill Gate. "There's a nice Scottish guy who wants to go out with you. You're not attracted to him. There's an alcoholic but single Canadian who wants to go out with you. You're sexually attracted to him but you don't trust him enough to fuck him again. And then there's the married man."

"If the library guy was married," I say, "I'd take him as an acceptable replacement for the married man."

"Which library guy? The Canadian or the Scot?"

"Don't be stupid. The Canadian, of course."

"Why refer to these men by their nationalities? Names, please."

But I find myself completely unable to utter the name Gideon in Dahlia's presence. I try and try, and when she sees that I'm experiencing a real physiological impediment—a kind of stammer—she lets me off the hook.

"Practice, though," she warns me. "You will do better next time I see you. By then you will know enough to write a book about it."

"It's true," I say. "Come to think of it, I can't believe nobody's ever written the obvious sequel to Helen Gurley Brown's *Sex and the Single Girl*: *Sex and the Married Man*."

"Now you're talking like a magazine writer," Dahlia says with approval. "More suggestions?"

"*Self-Hurt*," I say.

"*How to Lose Friends and Alienate People*," Dahlia answers, frowning. She is serious by nature. Losing friends is her specialty: the number of ex-friends with whom she's not on speaking terms is large enough that every time I call her, I'm afraid I'll have joined the list.

"*The Seven Habits of Highly Self-Destructive People*," I say.

"And what are those?"

I think for a minute, then list them on a cocktail napkin with a felt-tip.

The seven habits of highly self-destructive people:

Letting your recycling pile up
Procrastination

Shopping on credit
Drinking on an empty stomach
Screening phone calls
Calling yourself a loser a hundred times a day
Having a secret affair with a married man

When I get home that night I tape it to the wall. Then I think twice. Gideon had better not see this. I fold it carefully and put it in the desk drawer.

> We hear that Jonathan W—d, Gentleman, has projected a Scheme for raising a great Sum of Money by an Insurance on Robberies: this Policy is calculated for the Advantage of Insurers as well as the Projector: and seems to carry with it more Fairness and Demonstration than any modern Scheme either of our own or our Neighbours' Countries: it differs from other Policies in this remarkable Instance, that whereas in those the Adventurers were robb'd, and none escaped but such as had no Dealings with them: in this the Projector can demonstrate that no Persons shall be robb'd, except such as do not insure: which must raise the Value of this Stock above any Other, because it will put all People under a Necessity of insuring in their own Defence.
>
> —*Weekly Journal or Saturday's Post* (6 Jan. 1722)

Gideon arrives at the Indian restaurant in a state of greater excitement than I've ever seen him. He orders a bottle of Veuve Cliquot and won't tell me a thing until it arrives. The waiter pops open the bottle and pours the champagne into two flutes.

"What are we toasting?" I ask.

Gideon smirks. "Guess."

"We're going to Scotland after all?"

"Yes, yes," Gideon says, waving his hand dismissively. "I told you it wouldn't be a problem."

In fact, he's told me nothing of the kind, but I'm in no mood to quibble.

"What, then?"

"Www.reproduction.co.uk!"

We clink glasses and drink. "And what the fuck is that?" I ask.

"Don't swear, darling. We've finally raised the money to launch a web-based clinic that will offer the full range of reproductive services. The venture capital chaps think we might be able to swing an IPO as early as next year, assuming the thing takes off."

I can almost see the dollar signs in his pupils. He's off now in his own venture-capital universe, and I tug his arm like a child trying to get her parent's attention. “Gideon,” I beg, “tell me what the hell you’re talking about?”

“We’re going to provide a central clearing-house for egg and sperm donors and surrogates; our own clinic will serve as the chief provider for IVF information and services. We’ll start on a small scale, steering British clients to our operation here, though of course the real money will come when we move into the US market.

“Don’t say anything to Miranda,” Gideon adds. “I want it to be a surprise.”

It’s a surprise to me, and I hate surprises. I’m one of those people who turns to the end of a detective novel before I’ve even finished the first chapter. I just don’t enjoy it unless I know what’s happening ahead of time. Foreknowledge never stopped anyone from racing towards the end.

Web-based reproduction certainly seems to be the cutting edge. Post-Dolly, the members of the Canadian cult Raël, who believe that cloning will save the world, have started a company called Clonaid® (incorporated in the Bahamas) that will clone individuals with fertility problems and members of gay couples. I’ve already lobbied my editor to include the Raëlians’ headquarters in the Canada guide: Centre UFOland, in rural Quebec, includes a life-size mockup of the flying saucer in which the cult’s founder paid his first visit to aliens in 1973. The Clonaid® home page tells me that the company also offers a service called Insuraclone® that guarantees a new clone if your cloned “child” should be subsequently diagnosed with a terminal disease. (The second clone will either provide replacement organs or itself serve as the child’s permanent replacement.)

Though people have undoubtedly already conceived children by IVF for similar purposes, cloning’s not going to lose the tabloid taint any time soon. In the news most recently is Dr. Richard Seed, who appeared on *Nightline* and threatened to steal Ted Koppel’s blood and clone him without his permission. (Does the world need more Ted Koppels?) Dr. Seed is affiliated with the Human Cloning Foundation, which puts up a respectable front. Their website invites you to order a DNA storage kit and get started as soon as possible. Seed, whose Harvard credentials are blazoned all over the page, recommends liquid nitrogen for DNA storage; he also suggests that the blood thinner heparin might be used to stop blood from clotting and preserve it for cloning. The real progress isn’t happening in mad cults, of course, but behind closed doors in American biotech companies and wealthy IVF chains. You can already order eggs off the Web; it’s no more complicated than buying real estate.

While I am more than ever hell-bent on bearing Jonathan Wild’s clone, I’m secretly horrified (though I won’t admit it) by the mouse chimeras that have been created in laboratories by fusing embryos from mice of different colors: they’re easily identified by their bizarre patchwork of black and white fur. Gideon says that there are lots of natural human chimeras as well, but that you usually spot abnormalities only when one embryo is male and the other female, since the XX-XY mosaic gives you a baby with visible genital anomalies.

Gideon's vision, in his own words (he's clearly been talking to American venture capitalists), is "to meet IVF and cloning needs throughout the archipelago," a fancy word for the British Isles.

Meanwhile Gideon's offended that I haven't congratulated him more effusively. Exerting all my willpower, I smile at him across the table. In Jonathan Wild's day, IPOs were a fascinating financial innovation. Now they're fodder for cheesy movies and self-help books.

"You're cool," I say.

"No, darling," Gideon says triumphantly. "I'm hot!"

And he proceeds to tell me all about the financing, the stock options and the advertising campaign the publicist's already sketched out. My attention wanders. Scotland, I tell myself. Everything will be better once we get to Scotland.

◉

I meet Allan at a Chinese restaurant in Islington. After soggy deep-fried wontons and inadequately sweet-and-sour shrimp, he puts out a hand and takes my own in his.

"May I?" he asks.

He turns over my wrist and runs his fingers along the ridged scars on the inside of my forearm. "What's this?" he asks, his voice soft.

I sit back. I swallow a large gulp of wine. Then I tell him a story.

It's 1991 and I'm home for the summer after my first year of college. My father and I are sitting in the living room drinking brandy and listening to Bach. My stepmother's in New York spending inordinate amounts of money on clothes and my father's just gotten home from a secret adulterous date with a sexy pharmacologist who works down the hall from him at the hospital. I'm filled with rage but I don't say a word. Once I start, I'll spew venom.

He stops the CD to listen to the track again. And again. And again. The fourth time round I snap. I stand up. I walk slowly up to my room. I know what I'm going to do. I lock the bedroom door. I sit down at the desk. Slowly, deliberately, I open the pack of razors and pull one out. I peel off the cardboard protector and lay the blade before me in the center of the blotter. In the circle of light cast by the gooseneck lamp, the blade looks like an artifact from an earlier age, as though it has been transported perfectly preserved from a lost culture of steam-engines and power-looms.

I roll my left shirt-sleeve to my shoulder. I'm calm as I pick the razor up with my right hand. I touch it gently to my lips, kissing the blade. Then in one sharp motion I slice through the flesh of my upper arm, a long deep cut from which the blood pours. I feel no pain, only the tranquilizing flood of endogenous opioids.

And then the knock at the door, my name called out. I say nothing. All I want to do is sit and watch the blood flow out of the gash on my shoulder, crimson tributaries streaking my arm and collarbone. He's kicking the door now. A minute later and he breaks through. The sight of the blood stops him for only a moment. Then he continues towards me and pulls me up out of the chair. He doesn't do anything to stanch the blood. Instead he rolls up his own sleeve. He grips my right wrist—I'm still holding the blade in my fingers—and with his left hand he drags my own hand along his right arm, pressing down so that the blade cuts through layers of skin and muscle.

His blood spurts out in red jets.

I grab a towel from the back of the chair and wrap his arm in it. I know enough to see that we're headed for the emergency room.

We stagger downstairs in a perverse embrace, me holding the bloody towel to his right arm, his left arm clasped round my bloody shoulder. I drive him to the emergency room. We both bleed all over the car seats. Fortunately they are leather, easy to clean.

"If you ever do that again," he says to me inside as the nurse runs towards us, "I'll fucking kill you."

I've never heard my father say "fuck" before. He sounds like a stand-up comedian doing Robert DeNiro. Involuntarily I smirk. My father looks at me, and after a minute his eyes begin to crinkle at the corners. As the nurse reaches us, we turn to each other and burst out laughing. It's a major breach of emergency-room etiquette. We're laughing hysterically and the nurse looks at both of us like we're totally crazy. Fortunately my father's reputation is such that he can live this down without losing face. I can't remember the last time I felt so close to him.

"He's right," I tell Allan now. "Doing it to someone else was the thing that finally made me realize I'd better stop doing it to myself. I haven't done it for seven years."

He gazes at me, still holding my hand.

"Not that you need me to tell you this," I add, "but don't ever start. It's like smoking. Even after you quit, you still smoke in your dreams."

There's an awkward pause. "Are you seeing anybody?" Allan asks then.

"Not right now," I say, defensively bristling. "In the United States, therapy is a luxury, not an entitlement. I saw a psychiatrist for a few years in college, but I haven't had health insurance since then."

Allan blushes. "I suppose I'd better rephrase. Are you involved with anybody just now, romantically speaking? I know I'm not particularly eligible—a girl like you can go out with anybody she wants. But I do find you awfully attractive. And you seem sad somehow, lonely. . . ."

His voice trails off. He can tell from my face that I'm not interested.

"It's nothing personal," I tell him. "I'm having a secret affair with a married man."

"Are you in love with him?"

It takes me some time to answer. "I guess so," I say finally. "Yes."

"Is he going to leave his wife?"

"No chance."

"Well, then," Allan says hopefully.

There is something so claustrophobia-inducing in his kindness that I drop my napkin on the floor and make a run for the bathroom. I sit in the stall with my head in my hands, then wash my face in the sink and take a few deep breaths. When I get back to the table, Allan has called for the check. As he fumbles with his wallet, I put all my remaining cash on the table. It's just about enough to cover the bill.

"This one's on me," I say.

"Are you sure?

"Of course. I owe you, remember?"

I'm desperate to get out of the place now, and I stay standing up till the waiter hurries over with a little tray.

"Mint?" says Allan.

"No thanks," I say.

Outside I light up as though another nicotine-free moment's going to kill me. It's raining as I walk Allan to the bus stop and I have to knock away his arm with its intrusive umbrella. He protests.

"I hate umbrellas," I tell him truthfully. "They make me want to punch somebody."

He switches the umbrella to his other side and makes no protest when I move a good three feet away from him.

"Don't you want the pages?" he asks me reproachfully when we reach the glass bus shelter and I show no sign of stopping.

I take them from him and slip them into my bag. I kiss him quickly on the cheek. Then I keep on walking.

In the year 1720, Mr. Wild seemingly made a packet out of the South Sea Bubble, though it was a gross libel to suggest (as the writer Defoe has insinuated) that the company he meant to float would protect subscribers against theft by Mr. Wild telling his criminal associates to avoid breaking into houses that bore his plaque. It is true he thought of starting a company for insurance, but it was to have been founded on the most modern principles; and besides, he never got it off the ground for lack of capital. To the best of my knowledge he had no money invested in the stocks, but as the country went mad for South Sea stock, the general increase in trade led to a commensurate growth in thieving, as any fool could have told. At the height of the Bubble, receipts were stolen in Exchange Alley at an astonishing rate, and I believe that in the space of a few weeks, Mr. Wild helped the owners to retrieve two thousand pounds in Salter's Hall stocks, eight hundred in Sword-Blade bank-notes, a thousand in Arthur Moore's Royal Fishery, another thousand in Wyersdale's Turnpike, two thousand each in the Company for Insuring Seamen's Wages and Shale's Insurance, and thousands more in funds I could not name for the life of me.

I soon became as fine a lady as any in the City: barring, that is, the stout aldermen's wives in their silks, satins and furs. Usually I wore my hair in a net at the back of my head, the curls waved about my face, but for special occasions a Frenchman came to the house and dressed my head in the latest mode. Each morning I greased my hair and powdered it with rice meal, repowdering later in the day as needed.

We held lavish dinners for aldermen, councilors, magistrates, all the great men of the City, though most of them were nothing much to look at—crude overfed fellows who seemed laughable in their finery, like pigs tricked out in ruffs and ermine.

Mr. Wild started to hold a levee each morning in his bedroom, where he was waited upon by a court of lawyers, bailiffs and other supplicants. He heard petitions for bail and for the use of his favor, all the attorneys begging him to handle their cases. Mr. Wild invariably wore on these occasions his callimanco dressing-gown and slippers, a cloth over his head to cover the scars and silver plates that were the marks of his success as a thief-taker. He breakfasted on a pint of sherry and a bowl of thick chocolate, which he liked to eat with a spoon. I made it for him myself with my own hands, boiling the cocoa nibs with white sugar, cinnamon, Mexican peppers, cloves, almonds, vanilla and orange-flower water, then beating in eggs and milk to give it body and froth.

At about this time, however, and likely as a consequence of his great prosperity, the public began to take notice of Mr. Wild's practices and started the alarm. Mr. Wild's prominence was attended with no few ill consequences, among them the government passing a bill designed to close down the Office for the Recovery of Lost and Stolen Property for good, by making it illegal to return goods to their owners without also taking the thieves. While the bill purported to punish all those persons who had secret acquaintance with felons and who made it their business to help people to their goods again, it was actually put through by a group of men who envied Mr. Wild his success, a parcel of magistrates who thought that by taking their greatest competitor straight out of the business, they could reserve all the profits for themselves.

This new law, then, though my husband's name was never mentioned therein, so obviously targeted his practice that it soon came to be known as the Jonathan Wild Act:

> And whereas, there are divers Persons, who have secret Acquaintance with Felons, and who make it their Business to help Persons to their stolen Goods, and by that Means gain Money from them, which is divided between them and the Felons, whereby they greatly encourage such Offenders.
>
> Be it enacted, by the Authority aforesaid, that wherever any Person taketh Money or Reward, directly or indirectly, under Pretence, or upon Account, of helping any Person or Persons to any stolen Goods or Chattels, every such Person so taking Money or Reward as aforesaid (unless such Person do apprehend, or cause to be apprehended, such Felon, who stole the same, and give Evidence against him), shall be guilty of Felony, according to the Nature of the Felony committed in stealing such Goods, and in such and the same Manner, as if such Offender had stolen such Goods and Chattels, in the Manner, and with such Circumstances as the same were stolen.

One night shortly after the act had passed into law—I believe it was April of the year 1721, though I cannot swear to it—Mr. Wild tossed and turned in bed until I smacked him on the back and asked him to tell me what troubled him.

"I was at Newgate today," says he at last, once I'd persuaded him he'd not sleep till he got the matter off his chest. "I visited a man called John Thomson in the condemned hold."

"Thomson?" says I. I'd not heard the name before.

Mr. Wild let out a sigh, and opened all the matter up to me. It seemed that Thomson was a veteran of the War of the Spanish Succession who had been at the taking of Gibraltar but had the bad luck when he returned to England to marry the first whore he took up with. They kept an alehouse together, but business being poor, he began to make a better living by returning to their owners small matters they'd lost: watches, handkerchiefs and the like. When he was arrested and brought before the magistrates, they resolved to prosecute him under the Jonathan Wild Act, to teach my husband a lesson; the man swore he'd never heard of an act prohibiting the taking of a reward, Mr. Wild told me, but was condemned to death regardless.

"Before I could speak with him, the keepers had to drag away his wife," says Mr. Wild; "she hung about his neck, railing at him like a fishwife and saying he'd ruined their children and herself."

I snorted, finding it a ridiculous picture, but all the same drew the blanket closer about me.

"I spoke with him some time," says Mr. Wild next.

"And what did he say?" I could see I was to get no rest until Mr. Wild had finished this sorry tale.

"He said that when he found himself included in the Dead Warrant, he knew he had no reason to desire life, and that he believed that no man had ever passed his time in such a turbulent hurry as he, without having leisure to consider whether he was running to happiness or destruction."

Hoping he'd not take it amiss, I put my hand to Mr. Wild's member and began to stroke it. He let me be for a minute, then pushed my hand away. We had come to an accommodation as regarded marital relations, but in making our truce, as so often happens, we had arrived at a state of affairs that suited nobody: I pestered Mr. Wild frequently with my attentions, and he showed in return a combination of uneasiness and indifference that was hardly calculated to set my mind—no, nor my body neither—at rest.

"The vicious women he'd conversed with, the riotous houses he had kept, the intrigues he'd pursued," says Mr. Wild in continuation, though my thoughts had strayed now to more pressing affairs than Thomson's, "all were so far from affording him that happiness which he expected from them, that he found they gave him great uneasiness. They were frequently alarmed, he said, many times suddenly surprised, always in terror and under apprehensions of danger. One of their company was always in trouble."

Mr. Wild fell silent.

"All his friends had forsaken him in his distress," adds he slowly, after a minute or two. "Though he lately had such numerous acquaintance, he said he knew not that he had one left who would procure a coffin for him, or take care that he should be buried."

I thought to myself that the man must have preyed most unscrupulously on Mr. Wild's darkest fears, to wit, his doubt whether a corpse might ever be kept safe from the surgeons. I always set out to protect Mr. Wild from beggars and supplicants, but I had a nasty feeling that in this case, I would be unable to prevent him laying out his money to bury the miserable Thomson.

And I was right. "I promised him I would pay for his burial," said Mr. Wild, who ever had death in view. "He was very grateful, too, you know, and swore he'd pray for me tonight."

As I was about to remonstrate, Mr. Wild put his finger on my lips. "Say nothing," says he. "Every man has a right to know that his body will lie below ground, undisturbed. These damned surgeons have no respect for the dead."

The next day it was as though we had never spoken. Mr. Wild made exceptionally merry, and ribbed Mendez on his new lady-friend (an ample-bosomed mercer's widow who kept a very good shop on Fleet Bridge). When Mendez asked him about Thomson, Mr. Wild said in a short and impatient manner that there was nothing to fear.

This was also what Mendez wanted to believe, and so he launched into a speech.

"When you help honest people recover their goods, you do a service that none but yourself can manage," was how Mendez began, though I thought he spoke more to persuade himself than to comfort Mr. Wild. "I question whether it be in any man's power to hurt you for carrying on this trade. Of course, it must be that those of our clients who obey your orders, who let us into the secrets of their robberies and commit the goods to our disposal may depend on your protection."

"Yes," said Mr. Wild, more at ease than when Mendez had first raised the subject, "it is certainly true that when I send for a man with the guarantee of a safe conduct, he may come to me directly, though he knows it be in my power to hang him. If he agree with my proposals, we will part good friends and I will protect him to the utmost of my power, and so it must be, or people who lose their things would give up any hope of getting them back again."

I noticed that Mr. Wild afterwards became very careful, however, when a client asked him what he would have for his trouble, to appear indifferent.

"You may do as you please," he would say, affecting a kind of carelessness that did not suit him. "I am glad it has been in my power to serve you. If you see fit to make me a present, it is of your own volition, a gratuity the result of your own generosity. What I have done is from a principle of doing good, without any views of self-interest."

It seemed by now that half London went in fear of my husband. "Those who follow my instructions may be sure I will not disturb them," said Mr. Wild in private. "But if one of my people should presume to leave my government and dispose of what he steals without consulting me and submitting to my terms, or if he should forfeit my favor by any other act of rebellion, he is sure to feel the effects of it. I am vigilant to bring such offenders to justice."

And so he did. I do not mean to bore you with tedious scenes of riding out upon the road, etc. etc. There is a certain sameness to the business of thief-taking and after a while all particulars become redundant. The long and short of the matter was that I was not getting what I needed from Mr. Wild while he was so occupied, and I resolved to seek it elsewhere, if it could be made safe. Yet Mr. Wild's words on our marriage-night rang still in my head. What I wanted was a child, and though I dared not get one with any other man than my husband, he himself refused to comply with my wishes.

In the end, though Mr. Wild was a jealous husband, suspicious of trifles and enraged by the attentions of other gentlemen, I became smitten with a tall, big-boned swarthy fellow called John Malhoney, an Irishman, and had the bad luck to lose my head. I suppose I had grown sick of being suspected when I had committed no offense, and resolved I might as well enjoy in reality the imaginary pleasures for which I had often taken a beating. Malhoney had an uncommon fierceness in his looks, and swore with a voice like thunder. He had a wife living, a rich old lady who he had married only to find that she'd given all her money and furniture to her daughter the day before the wedding, and I suppose this made him a safer object for my affections than an unmarried man could ever have been.

Malhoney was soon enough domesticated. I reserved the third-best bedchamber for our meetings, and he became (at least for the length of the affair) almost a member of the household. He often brought presents for the house, always of the kind I liked best—a pair of fowls, a snare of rabbits, a barrel of oysters—and I cooked him meals with my own hands that were calculated to heighten desire. I always say there's nothing like a nice salad for quickening the blood—I like to mix the lettuce with cucumber, watercress and a few sprigs of mint, dressing it with oil and vinegar, pepper and salt to taste—and I served him privately so that we could sate our desires as we would. I lay with Malhoney a number of times, until the day came when Mr. Wild took him aside and told him if he ever was with me again, he'd find himself in Newgate before he knew it.

I had thought that Mr. Wild was too busy to notice what I was up to, and I now sincerely regretted my actions, or at least having been caught out; though had not my husband told me with his own tongue that I might do as I liked? I was quite outraged at my husband's intervention, although not over-sorry by then to be rid of Malhoney, who turned out after all to be a boorish fellow, a heavy drinker and a blockhead with little idea of how to satisfy a woman. These men are a useless parcel of creatures, I said to myself afterwards, and yet I found it hard to be done with them altogether; by this time I could only call the state in which I coexisted with my husband a marriage of convenience, with all the real inconveniences the phrase implies.

If my response to having no children was to take a lover, Mr. Wild's was very different. He served already as patriarch to a family of sorts, keeping as many of them as he could on the straight and narrow. I liked the boys who used to come by the place; they were about my own age, and we often had a laugh together in the taproom next door. My favorite was Blueskin Blake, a large young fellow who'd known Mr. Wild since their days together long ago in the Wood Street Compter. Blueskin had spent his life in and out of institutions, from the workhouse and the houses of correction to Newgate itself, and Mr. Wild went to continual trouble to save him from reaping what he had sowed. He brought excellent stuff to the Lost Property Office, making us a mint of money before he became so much trouble that Mr. Wild had to cast him loose. There was a good humor about Blueskin that made him hard to dislike, at least until the last year of his life, when he came to express such very great bitterness and resentment against Mr. Wild.

Thinking now on how matters came to their present pass, and trying to determine when exactly Mr. Wild's fortunes turned for the worse, Blueskin comes to mind, for you could say in a way that Blueskin's actions have led indirectly to all Mr. Wild's late troubles. To give a complete account of Mr. Wild's dealings with Blueskin is out of my line, but I will mention the time three years since, about when our marriage came to be in such a bad way, when Blueskin and his friends robbed and murdered a Chelsea pensioner on his way home from visiting a friend in one of the Hyde Park regiments. They set upon the old man in the meadows by Chelsea Hospital, hard by Buckingham Wall—they did not take much from the pensioner, but they robbed others that night as well, and the hue and cry soon went up, the people calling for the murderers' blood.

Mr. Wild was very vexed that Blueskin did not come to him at once with the goods they took. Blueskin had visited us several times a week ever since Mr. Wild had set up him and his friends in a house together some eight years before. His absence now gave rise to great suspicion, said Mr. Wild, willing to make allowances and leave him out of an information or two but greatly impatient for Blueskin's own account of the fact. When Blueskin finally paid his visit, with a meager present for Mr. Wild, my husband made it known that the courtesy was long overdue. But Blueskin refused to impeach the gang he worked with, and the next we heard, Blueskin had sworn publicly at an ale-house in Cock Lane that he'd rather die than be taken by Mr. Wild again.

How could he denounce his benefactor to all his friends, you may ask? I suppose a certain resentment may come from being always at the receiving end of another's kindness. Whatever provoked it, Blueskin had now turned against Mr. Wild. He stole rings, watches, etc., and none of them did he bring to the office to be returned to their proper owners. It hurt Mr. Wild greatly, and not just in his pocket, he having always viewed Blueskin in light of a son, he said, and continuing to entertain the hope that Blueskin would return to the fold.

But he could only be patient for so long. Finally, one of Blueskin's friends laying an information against him, Mr. Wild went with Arnold and Mendez to take Blueskin at his lodgings. It grieved Mr. Wild very much to do so, I can assure you, yet he had no other choice.

Mr. Wild waited in the yard behind the house while Mendez went to Blueskin's third-story room and kicked open the door. Entering with pistols cocked, he found the room empty, Blueskin having broken through the boarded-up window and climbed out down the outside wall, which provided ample hand- and toe-holds for a climber. Mendez saw Blueskin's shadow in the fog, then heard a curse and the sound of a rough landing.

"Hold your position," Mendez called out, and I believe that none of what happened afterwards can be blamed on my husband or his men—Blueskin had been warned, and he chose to ignore the caution and take the consequences.

Mr. Wild waiting downstairs, Blueskin appeared suddenly out of the fog. The boy stopped dead in his tracks when he saw Mr. Wild, then circling round one another, Mr. Wild drew his sword and Blueskin his also. They skirmished for a minute until Mr. Wild slashed Blueskin's head with his saber, Blueskin never having been known for his swordsmanship.

Blueskin cried out when the blood ran into his eyes. Mendez came up behind him then and knocking him to the ground, shackled the boy's hands together behind his back.

Even then all had not been lost, had Blueskin taken it right. Mr. Wild told him that he was a very great fool, who deserved to hang for his ingratitude, but that if he proved grateful, Mr. Wild would be again his friend.

At first all was well. Blueskin lodged an information at Mr. Wild's direction, and three of his friends were condemned on his evidence. But afterwards, they told all and sundry that Mr. Wild had turned them over on account of a grudge, because they would not give him the things they took, and that he meant to teach their fellows a lesson by punishing them for leaving his government. Most men knew better than to credit such nonsense, but some listened, and the gossip corroded Mr. Wild's reputation like acid.

Blueskin himself then began to show the most rank ingratitude towards his benefactor. He claimed to deserve part of the reward Mr. Wild had procured for the conviction of his friends, although the court told him that he was entitled to neither reward nor release, and that as he had put up a violent resistance at his arrest, he should be very grateful to Mr. Wild for his good fortune in being accepted for an evidence at all.

Blueskin was remanded in custody at the Wood Street Compter, and Mr. Wild paid for the cure of his wound and three shillings a week maintenance besides. But once he was let out, he took up with a very bad sort, Jack Sheppard, the housebreaker who had the city all a-stir last year. The city made a hero of Sheppard, who broke out of every gaol in the city, including the condemned hold at Newgate, and the part Mr. Wild would play in the boy's execution let the mob make my husband out to be as great a villain as ever lived.

At this time Sheppard was in prison but not yet hanged, though he'd made his last escape, while Blueskin remained at liberty; this was October last, a mere seven months since, though it seems a lifetime. Mr. Wild went with Mendez and Arnold to arrest Blueskin at his mother's house in Rosemary Lane. Arnold went to the door first, and told Blueskin to open up. "Damn you, I will not," says Blueskin (as Mendez told it me over the punch-bowl later the same night).

Mr. Wild told Arnold to break open the door, and Blueskin inside drew his penknife, swearing he would kill the first man that came in.

"Then I am the first man," says Arnold, "and Mr. Wild is not far behind. If you don't deliver up that knife at once, I'll chop your cursed arm off."

Blueskin threw down the knife and they took him easily, carrying the boy in a coach to Justice Street's house at Westminster.

"There's the house," says Mr. Wild as the coach draws up to the place.

"Make no more of that, Mr. Wild," says Blueskin; "I am as sensible as you, that I am a dead man."

Mr. Wild had nothing to say to this, as the boy was in the right of it. In great agony, though, did Mr. Wild recount to me the next part of the conversation, some little time thereafter.

"What I fear most," says Blueskin to Mr. Wild in the coach that day, "is that I shall afterwards be carried off by the surgeons and anatomized."

You will remember that Mr. Wild had known the boy from when he was eight years old. "I'll take care to prevent that," says he, "by making you a present of a coffin to be buried in." And a very generous offer it was too, for he'd otherwise have been laid to rest in a pauper's grave, unmarked and with no coffin at all.

I will unfold to you now in brief the last chapter of Blueskin's story. On the fourteenth of October last, the sessions began at the Old Bailey, and Blueskin was put into the bail-dock in the sessions-house. Mr. Wild went into the yard to drink a glass of wine with him, and they had a brief conversation.

"You may put in a word for me as well as the next man," it is said that Blueskin told Mr. Wild.

"I cannot do that," said Mr. Wild. "You should have turned in Sheppard."

And these words spurring Blueskin to violence, he drew a clasp-knife, seized Mr. Wild by the neck and cut his throat. The knife was dull and Blueskin had to saw through the muslin stock at my husband's neck, but it was sharp enough to sever a vein and blood spurted from the artery until at last the turn-key Ballard laid hold of Blueskin and threw him against the wall.

I was not there, thank god, but heard all of it afterwards from Mendez, who was hard by but could not reach his master through the crowd in time to fend off his attacker. It was Mendez who stopped the bleeding in time to save Mr. Wild's life, and who came back to the house in the Old Bailey drenched from head to toe in my husband's blood, bringing heavy news indeed. Nothing like this had happened since my own uncle's murder, and the town was all agog for the particulars.

The court sentenced Blueskin to death. The prison ordinary suggested to Blueskin that some third party must have prompted him to commit violence against Mr. Wild, Mr. Wild having paid for the healing of his wounds, allowed him money and even promised him a coffin.

"No man prompted me to the assault," says Blueskin, and this time I was there to hear him, having left my maid in charge of Mr. Wild's sickbed. I was frighted out of my wits that Mr. Wild might die leaving his affairs all in disarray, and I hoped to put my mind at rest by hearing the sentence pronounced against (as I then thought him) my husband's murderer. "If I had thought of it sooner, I might have got a better knife."

We all gasped, of course, at the lack of remorse he showed. Yet I understood what might make a man hate my husband. I will tell more of that in my own good time—I'll not be rushed, though even as I write the bailiffs are banging at the house doors waiting to carry off all our worldly goods to satisfy Mr. Wild's creditors.

"I wish I had cut off his head directly and thrown it among the rabble in the yard," adds Blueskin, that day in court.

"What have you against Mr. Wild?" asks the ordinary.

"He could have obtained transportation for me. Instead he got me death. If I had only murdered him, I should have died with satisfaction."

Satisfaction or no, die he did, riding in the cart to Tyburn so drunk he reeled and faltered in his speech. He cried right up till the moment he hanged, and the crowd cried with him.

We were too wrapped up with Mr. Wild's illness to attend to Jack Sheppard's final capture. He was taken shortly thereafter, sentenced to death and so on, still thought he could elude justice by making a great escape, but was foiled when the knife he concealed about his person was taken off him in the press-yard at Newgate before the procession began to Tyburn.

Never did a more popular man go to his death on the gallows. The crowd begged for his reprieve, and though they were silent while he was hanged, there was a riot afterwards when someone set about a rumor that his body had fallen into the hands of the surgeons. Sheppard had asked his friends to cut him down as soon as he was hanged, to put his body into a warm bed and to call for a barber to bleed him back to life, believing that if they let enough blood, they would be able to resuscitate him.

It was a messy hanging. After about a quarter of an hour, a soldier cut him down and delivered the body to his friends, who carried him to the Barley-Mow in Long Acre, where they tried to bring him back to life. But Sheppard was well beyond hot blankets and brandy. The crowd rioting outside the house, the army sent a detachment of infantry from the Savoy Barracks to disperse the mob with bayonets. Mr. Wild's name was on everyone's lips, as the man who had brought this youthful hero to the gallows, and people began to hate him as they had not before, when he still had the reputation of bringing vicious criminals to justice for the good of the nation.

Meanwhile Mr. Wild lay in this house in a high fever, clinging to life by a thread. The gash across his throat would not heal, and if you had told me six months ago that those troubles would pale in comparison to our present ones, I'd have laughed in your face. Now all the broadsides say what a pity it is that Mr. Wild did not die when Blueskin stabbed him, for at that time he still retained some part of his former reputation, while when he is sent off now, it will be with infamy and hate.

My mind returns now to Mr. Wild's magnanimity in promising to pay for Blueskin's coffin and making sure that it would stay underground. Mr. Wild had a strange look when he talked of the surgeons, as though he feared most of all—more than public disgrace, poverty, death itself—that his corpse might fall into their hands. If you wished to punish the man, I'll just say, above and beyond the penalty the government was determined to exact, it could not have been clearer how you would go about doing so.

◉

Friday evening finds me sitting next to Gideon on a train halfway to Edinburgh. It's a major tactical victory. We'll get there too late for Gideon to go to the inaugural dinner, but he'll give his paper at the conference the next morning while I do a little semi-professional sightseeing (my main target's the Roslin Institute, where Dolly was cloned). Gideon's reading the *Financial Times* and jotting down biotech share prices, while I'm occupied with a pile of books about Edinburgh—not run-of-the-mill guidebooks, but chronicles of the city's seamier side.

In its long history of medical preeminence, Edinburgh has been better-known for grave-robbing than for cloning. Edinburgh is Burke and Hare's hometown, and I figure on taking advantage of the train ride to read up on this notorious episode in the history of medicine.

In 1828, a parliamentary committee was appointed to investigate how the schools of anatomy obtained subjects for dissection. One famous surgeon testified to the committee that he could get any anatomical specimen he wanted, assuming that money was no object: "There is no person, let his situation in life be what it may, whom if I were disposed to dissect I could not obtain. The law only enhances the price. It cannot prevent the exhumation."

The committee submitted a bill to prevent the unlawful disinterment of human bodies and to regulate schools of anatomy, but during Parliament's summer recess, two men called Burke and Hare were caught in Edinburgh luring vagrants with promises of food and drink, then killing them and selling them to a medical professor called Knox. Hare turned King's Evidence and testified against Burke, who was sentenced to be hanged and publicly dissected. Ticket-holders watched Burke's dissection the day after his execution. Forty thousand members of the public subsequently paraded through the building where his partially dissected body lay on display. As a consequence, the verb 'to burke' entered the language, meaning "to murder with the purpose of selling the victim's body to surgeons." Body-snatchers were now called burkers; the fear of grave-robbing, Burkophobia.

We get into Waverley Station after midnight and take a taxi to the hotel. We fall into bed and have cursory sex. Afterwards I look at Gideon with surprise. I have never seen him asleep. I can hardly keep my eyes open but I struggle to stay awake. I don't want to miss a second.

Gideon leaves first thing in the morning. I'm supposed to meet him back at the hotel room before dinner. Meanwhile, I'm free to do whatever I want. I go straight back to sleep.

I get up at eleven, finally responding to the knocks of the cleaners who beg me to let them in so that they can do their job. After a leisurely breakfast (ruinously expensive, but it's on Gideon's tab), I hop on a tourist bus and ride a couple of circuits round the city, phasing out the obnoxious kilt-clad tour guide (the inevitable professional Scot). The New Town is beautiful. It corresponds exactly to my architectural aesthetic. Back at the station, I check the bus timetables for a more important destination: Roslin, the small town outside of Edinburgh where Dolly was cloned.

The bus leaves less than half an hour later. I sit on the top of the double-decker and watch the countryside go by. Everything is on a small scale. From up here, the sheep look like toys. I like the flat-fronted yellow stone houses and the multicolored roses in the front gardens, pink and red and orange splotches of color on a soft green-gray landscape.

I get off in the village of Roslin and follow the asphalt pavement to the Institute. The bus-driver has explained how to get here; they get quite a few tourists on the "Dolly" route, he tells me.

As I approach the place, I realize I don't know what to do now that I'm finally here. I haven't made an appointment, since my press credentials are flimsy at best. Wilmut's original goal was to genetically engineer animals that would produce human insulin in their milk. Cows, ultimately, since the volume of milk is so great; but sheep are far less expensive to work with. Who would have thought that animal embryology would turn out to be such an exciting field? I jot down a few notes in case my editor can be persuaded to add the Roslin Institute to the list of Scotland's most popular tourist attractions. Then I find a low stone wall and sit and smoke a few cigarettes.

By now it's mid-afternoon. At the end of an hour of sitting and smoking, I still haven't been rewarded by a sighting of Ian Wilmut himself. I pick up my stuff and wander downhill to the pub, where I order a pint of bitter at the bar and take my drink to a table by the window.

It gradually dawns on me that Ian Wilmut's not going to show up in this dingy pub either. I'm going to have to use my imagination. I close my eyes. I can see Wilmut wandering in and chatting with the publican. Journalists always describe him as mousy-looking, but the Ian Wilmut in my head (based on the pictures posted on the Web) looks pretty normal: fair complexion, receding hairline, neatly trimmed beard.

Wilmut asks for a single malt. I join him at the bar. "You must be sick to death of this," I say as I lean over to catch the bartender's eye, "but if I buy you a drink, can I ask you questions about cloning?"

He laughs, and nods. He's in a good mood. "What do you want to know?" he says.

"What do you think about the press's reaction to the work you guys are doing here?"

"Completely over the top," he says. "Ta," he adds as the barman brings us a glass of whisky and another pint of beer for me. "We never said anything about cloning humans—speaking for myself, I'd say it's ethically unacceptable, though of course if you really wanted, it could be done—but that's all these maniacs can think of."

"Oh, well, then you'll think I'm being completely ridiculous if I ask you what you think about cloning dead people?"

"Yep." He starts laughing when he sees the look on my face. "Cheer up, love," he says, "it'll never happen. I've been a bit disappointed by the public's rather limited concentration on science-fiction applications. Cloning's all about medical uses: compatible clotting factors for hemophiliacs; pig organs that can be transplanted into human beings. I reckon that in my lifetime we'll see some amazing developments—none of the apocalyptic nonsense you read about in the papers, but perhaps a really effective therapy for cystic fibrosis, which when you think about would be quite incredible enough."

"Don't you ever get scared when you think about what you've done here?" I take a sip of Wilmut's Laphroaig. It's delicious.

"I won't say I haven't had occasional qualms. No sleepless nights, though. We're a moral species, when it comes down to it."

We have an agreeable discussion about Robert Wilson's book *The Moral Animal.* I say it's an offensive rationalization of many unattractive human behaviors in the name of morality, and that you might as well call it reactionary polemic and be done with it. He thinks it's a useful and moderately responsible popularization of some interesting new ideas in evolutionary biology, but agrees that it's a pity to justify—for instance—male promiscuity as "moral" and downplay the element of choice.

"What I think people fail to remember," he says as we return to our original theme, "is that we mustn't throw the baby out with the bath water. The potential here is simply unbelievable. You can't stop science; it's a mistake even to waste time thinking about it. I don't think it's a good idea to clone people, I won't pretend otherwise. Each child who is born should be treated as an individual. You make a copy of a person and you're saying that you don't want a child, but a replica. You're choosing his path for him, and it's not right."

We shake hands and part.

"Something wrong, love?" says a voice at my ear. I open my eyes and see the barmaid wiping down the table next to me and looking at me with concern. I feel a deep blush spread across my face. There are several empty glasses in front of me and I have been having a serious conversation with someone who's not even here. I wonder if my lips have actually been moving as I speak.

"I'm fine," I say, getting my things together to go. It occurs to me that even the imaginary Wilmut looked like a man whose mind was on his job, unlike Gideon, who's essentially a man on the make. If Gideon's such a great doctor, what's he doing fucking around with me when he should be at work?

I barely make it back to the hotel in time to meet Gideon. He's showering when I walk in the door, and I shed my clothes and join him in the bathroom. We have never showered together before. I share a bathroom in London with the three other people down the hall. Besides the privacy issue, the anonymous hairs in the drain gross out the fastidious Gideon. To the best of my knowledge, Gideon showers at the office or at the squash club, whose old-fashioned Imperial Leather soap won't leave a suspicious scent.

In the shower we fuck, me pressed up against the wall under the shower head. The sex is good, but mostly I'm annoyed my hair's getting wet—I don't want to have to blow it dry again before dinner. Afterwards I leave it wet and slick it back instead with the last of Gideon's mousse.

As we dress, Gideon tells me about his friend Steve, who is coming to meet us for a drink at the conference hotel. Gideon says we'll then slip away so that we can eat somewhere decent, since the banquet fare will be what you always get in Scotland at this time of year: overcooked salmon. The real reason, I know, is that he's afraid of being spotted with me.

Our taxi driver is a Scottish nationalist. He takes against Gideon from the first (it's the public-school accent, I don't blame him) and recites Burns to us all the way to the conference center, confirming my suspicion that Scotland's main problem is self-parody. I'm all dolled up in what I think of as a "doctor's wife" outfit—a long dark-green beaded dress that put me back twenty quid at the Oxfam shop in Tooting Broadway, a pair of four-inch heels that make me feel elegant if somewhat unsteady on my feet. I've also got on my grandmother's clip-on diamond earrings, earrings I never wear. Gideon looks immaculate as usual in a tuxedo; he says the occasion's not fancy enough to merit white tie.

We get out of the cab and we're completely surrounded by gynecologists. Steve isn't here yet. Gideon parks me in the lobby and goes off to get some whisky from the bar. He brings me a drink and vanishes into the hive of activity that is the main ballroom. Once he's done schmoozing, he rejoins me in the lobby, where he stands nervously in front of me, shielding me from passersby. I know he's hoping nobody will take note of my presence.

But the doctors haven't all confined themselves to the ballroom, and even in our obscure corner he's foiled. I've already gotten a couple of curious looks (who's Gideon Streetcar's new girlfriend?) and also some puzzled glances from friends of my father's who see in my face the ghost of the fourteen-year-old they remember, then fail to place me and finally move on.

Now someone bumps into me, spilling white wine down my naked back. I turn around and it's one of my father's oldest friends, a hearty Argentine Jew whose four kids went to school with me in New Haven.

"Elizabeth!" shouts Dr. Mendoza, drunkenly embracing me. "What can you possibly be doing in this neck of the woods? Richard isn't here, is he?"

"No," I say.

Gideon knows Mendoza from his own days in Connecticut. He reintroduces himself to the doctor, who looks back at me with sudden suspicion.

"You naughty, naughty girl," he says, clucking and shaking his finger at me. "Aren't you even going to ask after your father's health?"

"No," I say, which causes Mendoza to burst out laughing. He doesn't take me seriously, in part because he sees me still as his second son's prom date (combat boots, blue hair, tattered Japanese paper minidress).

"You should call him sometime, you know," Mendoza now says. "He worries."

I shrug.

I'm saved from further advice by the arrival of Steve. Gideon performs more introductions. Steve is short and stocky, with dark curly hair and bright blue eyes. He's smoking a cigarette and the hotel guests nearby have turned around to glare at him, edging away from us as the smoke drifts their way.

"We've got dinner reservations at eight," I tell Mendoza. "Don't tell my father you saw me."

He looks hurt. "Oh, Elizabeth," he says, "whatever are we to do with you?"

I kiss him on the cheek. "Say hi to your kids for me," I say.

Outside, Gideon gives me a funny look. "Don't you ever talk to your father?"

"Don't give me a hard time about it right now," I say. "What about dinner?"

Shortly we're ensconced in a booth at an extremely fancy downtown restaurant. Gideon's apologizing—unnecessarily, we assure him—for failing to secure a reservation at La Potinière, the famous husband-and-wife prix-fixe place in nearby Gullane. Even Gideon couldn't get us in on such short notice; dinners during the summer are booked a year in advance.

"Don't be a wally," Steve finally says. "I've eaten McDonald's every day for the past two months; even if the food here is crap, it represents a significant step up."

Gideon laughs. "Don't insult McDonald's to the company's most loyal customer: Elizabeth's a die-hard fan."

"Oh?" Steve asks. Steve is nice. He's on the brash side, but he's got a lovely north-of-England accent, on which I now compliment him.

"I'm from Wolverhampton, love," he explains.

I beam at him. "That's where Jonathan Wild was born!" I say. I'm drunk enough to forget that this statement might need clarification.

Steve looks puzzled.

"Elizabeth has a quasi-erotic attachment to one of Wolverhampton's best-known native sons," Gideon explains coldly, "a notorious criminal who hanged all his friends before coming to a sticky end himself."

Steve laughs. "Don't get your knickers in a bloody twist, Gid," he says comfortably.

This evening I'm getting on Gideon's nerves, though this is an expression he'd never use himself. If pressed, he might admit he's a bit cross. One symptom of Gideon's irritation is that he refers to me only in the third person: he's not speaking to me, he's speaking about me. When Steve comments on his bad mood, Gideon is brought to confess that someone challenged the results he presented during the afternoon session, accusing him of statistical misrepresentation. Over our smoked salmon and caviar we go through all the numbers, agreeing that Gideon's critic must have been (in Steve's phrase) off his tree.

I have responded to Gideon's touchiness by drinking more whisky and unfolding to Steve the full scope of the cloning project.

"Is she from America or outer space?" Steve asks at the end of my account, laughing uproariously at his own joke.

"Your guess is as good as mine," Gideon says. He's also drinking more than usual. We have a bottle of white wine with the first course and several more of red when they serve the entrees. Unfortunately the restaurant specializes in game, never my idea of a good meal, and when my quail arrive (ordered mostly because I like the name), I am more than ordinarily disgusted by the miniature gray carcasses, blood oozing pinkly from their breasts.

"Do you think it's technically feasible, then?" I ask Steve. I've put the vials from the Hunterian Museum on the table between us.

Steve spears a huge chunk of venison with his knife.

"I've been reconstituting DNA since I was in the cradle, sweetheart," he says, chewing aggressively. "I see no reason why we shouldn't try it."

He pockets the genetic material.

"I'll work on it this weekend in the lab and post you whatever I come up with early next week," he adds. "Gideon's the one who'll need to manipulate the cow eggs; but I've had some success recently getting them into the right state of receptiveness. I'm not directly involved with the animal trials, of course. You're not anti-vivisection, are you, love?" he asks, turning to me and looking pointedly at the untouched bodies on my plate.

"Of course not," I say. I push the food around on the plate and wish I'd ordered something that came with a side of mashed potatoes. I hate wild rice. "And I'm totally pro-genetic engineering," I add, just to be on the safe side. "I can't wait to taste a genetically engineered potato."

"Chances are you already have, doll," says Steve, "though Europe's likely to ban genetically altered foods sometime this year. Not everyone's in love with genetic engineering, more's the pity."

"Fifty percent of Americans say they would refuse to eat meat from cloned animals," I say, "but I think that's ridiculous."

"Don't know about that myself," Steve admits. "It's the accelerated aging, really; my mate at the Roslin Institute thinks that Dolly's going to age at double the rate of an ordinary sheep. Talk about mutton dressed as lamb! Gives me the heebie-jeebies."

Over dessert I start flirting more heavily with Steve. I get him to start talking about their university days. He and Gideon shared a flat during their last two years at Oxford and first years of postgraduate work.

"Gideon was the most fastidious bloke I'd ever met," Steve says. "He'd put on a poncey-looking pair of pink rubber gloves and scrub out the bath whenever one of his dolly-birds was coming over."

"Steve was absolutely filthy," Gideon counters.

It's better now they're talking about each other in the third person as well: I'm sick of the sound of my own name. Suddenly everything's become more comfortable, possibly because we're all extremely drunk.

"He managed to render the kitchen absolutely unusable in the first week we moved in," Gideon continues; "the cooker was literally encrusted with grease."

"At least I cooked," Steve argues amiably. He's flushed with wine and his voice has become even louder, though not unpleasantly so.

"If you can call that cooking," Gideon says. He turns to me and begins to describe the heights of Steve's culinary achievement: cut-rate vegetables boiled to a muddy green sludge, mince and tatties with an inch of congealed fat, bricks of lard in the fridge.

Steve looks apologetic. "My mum's a bloody awful cook, you see," he explains, "and everything I cook I learned at my mum's knee."

I leave the restaurant briefly to pick up another pack of cigarettes at the bar round the corner. When I get back, I see that Gideon and Steve are the sole customers left in the restaurant. The waiters are hovering, hoping we'll clear out. I sit back down and nudge Gideon, but he ignores me; he finds my attention to the needs of the wait-staff painfully American and middle-class.

They're talking now about girls, the ones Gideon fucked and the ones Steve fucked and the ones they both fucked, including a mad debutante called Cordelia who liked to have them both at once.

"But she doesn't hold a candle to the one you've got here," Steve says in the end to Gideon, reaching his hand over and squeezing my knee.

Finally Steve sees that we're the only people left in the whole place and leaps to his feet. "Right, Streetcar," he says, "we'd best be off." Gideon and I rise to follow.

"Back to my flat for a nightcap?" he says outside.

Gideon looks at me.

"Sure," I say. I'm so drunk now that I have to reserve all my attention for tottering along in my heels as we go to the corner to hail a cab. It's only five minutes to Steve's place, a fifth-floor walk-up in one of Edinburgh's old tenements, now swanky crash pads for bachelors who don't have to worry about lugging groceries, children and other loads up a million stairs.

Steve's place is flash but messy. Empty cans of lager sit by the couch in the living room, and the most conspicuous piece of furniture is an enormous satellite TV for watching the football.

"Gideon, I really fancy your bird," Steve says, once he's handed round more drinks. I'm sitting next to Steve on a monstrous leather-and-chrome couch. "What would you say if I made a pass at her?"

"She's all yours, mate," Gideon says.

I can't read his tone. Am I supposed to get up off the couch and go over to him? Instead Steve leans over and kisses me. I'm already in a state of acute sexual arousal and this tips me over the edge. I can feel the rough lace of my bra against my nipples. I bite my lip.

"At Oxford Steve always used to fuck my girlfriends," Gideon says. He's sitting in a chair on the other side of the room, swigging from a tumbler of vodka.

"Can I fuck this one?" Steve asks.

"Since you've been so considerate as to ask my permission," Gideon says, "I suppose I'd better grant it. Not to mention the fact that Elizabeth should sleep with at least one Staffordshire terrier before she goes back to America."

I'm not about to stand up and insist that I don't want to get fucked by Steve. I wish I were back in the hotel room with Gideon. I would rather have Gideon sitting next to me than Steve. But I'm turned on and I'll take what I can get.

Steve roughly undresses me as he kisses my neck and breasts. Gideon watches from across the room. In a haze I notice that he has pulled out his asthma inhaler and taken several urgent puffs.

Steve has unzipped my dress, tearing a seam in the process, and I stand up and step out of it. I'm now in bra, panties, heels and stockings. Steve is kissing me roughly, his stubble abrading the skin on my cheeks. I press harder against him, banging my head into his. Now Steve drops to the floor in front of me and begins to run his hands up my thighs.

He hams it up a bit. "Your girlfriend has a beautiful body," he tells Gideon. The etiquette again involves talking about me as though I am not here.

As Steve pulls down my panties, I see out of the corner of my eye that Gideon has taken his cock out of his pants and started to jerk off. I'm rubbing my left hand up and down my pussy, and Steve's moaning on the floor in front of me. Now he stands, spins me round and pushes me forward onto the couch. I'm lying on my stomach and he digs through the clutter on the coffee table until he finds a small foil packet. He tears it open and fumbles with the condom.

Now his dick is inside me. Suddenly Gideon's coming towards us. He grabs Steve's shoulders and pulls him off me. The two men stagger together across the room, Gideon swinging punches at Steve as they crash from one piece of furniture to another. And for once in my life I do the tactful thing: I pass out.

◉

Sliding another vicious punch aimed straight for his eyes, the Captain slipped it with a quick side step and easy duck over his shoulder. Then he jerked back square on both feet. At the same second his left contacted with a thud on the big fellow's short ribs, and a sickening smack that could be heard all over the bar landed beautifully on the point of the square, brutal jaw.

—*Jonathan Wild, Old-Time "Ace" Receiver.* An English gangster, who, two hundred years ago, had perfected the methods and technique that were supposed to have been originated by Al Capone and his friends in the USA. By Edwin T. Woodhall, author of *Jack Sheppard, Claude Duval, Jack the Ripper, Spies of the Great War,* etc., etc. (1937)

I'm so hung over the next morning that once we reach the haven of the train, I stumble to the toilet and throw up. I splash water on my face, but I'm sick twice more as the train pulls out of the station. When I emerge into the carriage, we're already at Berwick-upon-Tweed. It would have been quicker to fly, but Gideon's slightly claustrophobic and prefers the train, where he can get up and stretch his legs.

Beneath my hangover, however, I have a paradoxical sense of physical well-being. I feel as though I have just had an extremely invigorating facial. The throbbing bruises on my shoulders and hips must have come after I blacked out. I have no idea how Gideon got me down the stairs and into the cab the night before. Sleepy and nauseous, I huddle in the corner, Gideon's arm around me. We are traveling like a real couple.

"Why don't you and Miranda just adopt a baby?" I ask him shortly after the train leaves York.

Gideon laughs. "Evolutionary biology has shown pretty conclusively why it is that stepfathers kill their children at a higher rate than natural fathers. You simply don't feel the same towards a child that's not your own."

I hate the argument based on feeling. It leaves no place for choice: the freedom to make a family for yourself, in your own way.

"Real fathers have been known to kill their children as well," I say.

Gideon shrugs.

As we approach London, my spirits sink. Gideon's mind is already on what awaits him at work. In the station, we separate. Gideon presses money into my hand for a cab.

"Dinner on Tuesday?" he says.

"Good," I say.

"I'll pick you up at seven."

As he gets into the taxi, he looks back for a minute. "I love you," he says.

I sleep for a few hours before I get around to unpacking my bag. I realize almost at once that I've lost one of my earrings. I tear apart my luggage. It's not there. Finally I talk myself into a state of submission. The art of losing's not too hard to master. I never wear jewelry. Anyway, you shouldn't own anything you'd miss if it were gone.

◉

Gideon arrives at my place on Tuesday exactly when he said he would. We're going out to dinner. As he lets himself into the room with the set of keys I've given him, I stand in front of the mirror to put on some lipstick.

"Ready in a second," I say.

I turn to pick up my bag and only now do I see that Gideon is visibly distressed. He walks over to the window. He hasn't even looked at me.

"I can't do supper this evening after all," he says, fiddling with the curtains.

I flinch. Then I shrug. "Whatever," I say. "I'll see you another time." In other words, I'm completely cold.

Gideon looks hurt. After a minute I relent and join him by the window. "Is everything OK?" I say.

"May I have a cigarette?" he says.

Gideon never smokes. I light a cigarette for him and pass it over, then light another for myself. The air is already stale with smoke.

"What's wrong?" I say.

"I can only stay for five minutes," he says.

"Is something up?"

"You remember my secretary?" he asks.

"Mrs. Beardsley," I say, remembering the mnemonic. (Whiskers.) "You did a baby for her daughter."

"The baby died last night," he says. "Cot death. Sudden infant death syndrome, they call it in the States."

I say nothing.

"Mrs. Beardsley called to tell me this morning. She's absolutely shattered, of course. I've got a temp in at the office. I told her to take as much time as she needs. Her daughter has a history of depression and I think she's a bit of a suicide risk, they'll have to keep a close watch on her for the next few weeks. Apparently she wouldn't give the baby up to the ambulance men, just kept rocking it in her arms and insisting it was perfectly fine.

"Sorry," he adds. "I didn't mean to unload all this on you. It's just that Miranda and I are the baby's godparents. I broke the news to her as soon as I heard but she's terribly upset. I've got to go home and make sure she's all right."

"Don't worry about dinner," I say. "Go home. Do what you need to do."

"Thanks, darling," he says.
He stubs out his cigarette in the ashtray.
At the door, he kisses the top of my head.
"I'll call you tomorrow," he says.
I go to the window and lean out to watch him walk away down the street.

◉

The next time I see him is at the office. A pathological addiction to work traditionally hurts a man's wife more than his mistress. It's up to me to mobilize Gideon's job in my favor.

First of all he makes me indemnify him. The temp has printed out a contract of several pages. I read through it carefully and sign at the bottom. He signs his name below mine.

"We'll have to do without a witness," he says.

I run the original through the fax machine and keep a copy for myself.

It's three days after the end of my last period. Gideon is going to stimulate my ovaries to produce multiple follicles. First he checks my hormone levels and gives me a baseline ultrasound.

"I'll stop by your place around seven," he says.

I spend the afternoon at the library reading accounts of Jonathan Wild's gang-busting in the final years of his career. It's almost impossible to keep track of all the players, yet while everything seems equivocal, you get the sense that Wild must have seen himself as being always firmly on the side of the law. It's the moral ambiguity that's so appealing.

At seven the intercom buzzes.

I buzz Gideon in.

When he makes it upstairs, he finds me lying on my stomach on the bed. I've just taken a bath. I'm completely naked.

Gideon's wearing his banker's suit, as usual. He starts to unbuckle his belt.

"Leave your clothes on," I say.

He kneels by the side of the bed and opens a small surgical case. He takes out two ampoules of Pergonal and gives me an intramuscular injection in the right buttock.

"You look sexy," he says.

"I'm hot for your cock," I say.

Gideon pulls off his shoes and drops his pants. He's in too much of a hurry to remove his socks. He takes me from behind, thrusting his prick into me again and again. He withdraws his penis just before he's about to come and ejaculates instead all over my back. Gobs of warm jizz land on my skin.

"The money shot," I say.

"What?" He rolls over to look at me.

"In porn flicks the guy always comes all over the place. It's more visual, I guess."

"Tell me about some of the pornographic films you've watched," Gideon says. He runs one finger down my ribcage towards my hips, lingering near the tiny mole to the left of my navel. He bends to kiss it.

"Another time," I say.

As we lie in bed together, I take Gideon's hand and ask him a stupid question. "Gideon, how did you feel when your father died?"

He's taken aback. "Why do you ask?" he says.

"No reason," I say.

"It's almost fifteen years ago now," he says slowly, not answering the question directly. "Before I went to America, at any rate. He died in a car crash, no long lingering illness or anything like that."

"Do you think about him often?"

Gideon stops to consider. "I think about him when I think about my mother, I suppose, and how little he appreciated her. Frankly, we didn't have much in common. We were never close, and I found his womanizing completely repulsive. Hard to forgive."

Because he's staring at the ceiling, he misses my double-take at his credulity-straining lack of self-awareness.

"Do you miss him?" I ask.

Gideon's silent. "Yes," he says then, the admission raw and painful.

We have sex again before he goes. I drift off to sleep afterwards and wake up at two in the morning, heart racing and teeth clenched tight. I am absolutely sure that someone else is in the room. I jump out of bed and turn on the light. Nobody's there. I leave the light on when I get back into bed. Dawn arrives before I sleep again.

◉

I test my blood samples daily.

Two days before I'm due to ovulate, I go back to the office for another transvaginal ultrasound. Gideon will evaluate the quality, quantity and maturity of the egg follicles.

The eggs are almost mature. Gideon will harvest them in thirty-six hours. The procedure takes less than fifteen minutes.

He injects me now with human chorionic gonadotropics to trigger the release of the eggs and keep my uterus primed and receptive.

I ovulate thirty-six hours later.

Gideon is very good at retrieving eggs, which he calls oocyte pickup. He gives me an intravenous sedative before starting the needle aspiration procedure. First he introduces the ultrasound transducer into my vagina. Everything looks OK, and he harvests the eggs with the hollow needle attached to the scanner. I can see the image on the video monitor: nine bubble-like follicles, each with its own egg. The nurse takes the aspirated fluid down the hall to the embryo culture lab, where my eggs will be combined with Gideon's sperm (labeled with Jonathan Wild's name, at my request) in a petri dish.

I don't want to sound ungrateful, but I'm far more excited about the other part of the plan.

In spite of the unfortunate outcome of our evening together, Steve has come through in spades. He has reconstructed Jonathan Wild's DNA and express-mailed Gideon a styrofoam box, the vials packed inside in dry ice. He has also included a supply of fertilized cow eggs whose own DNA has been deactivated. This is the really tricky part. Gideon will try to inject the DNA into the egg cytoplasm and prompt the things to grow.

"Oh," Gideon says casually, as if it's an afterthought, "he's put in an envelope for you."

I open it up. There's no note. Just the earring. For a moment I think I'm going to put it straight into my mouth and swallow it like a pill so that I won't ever lose it again. I resist the urge.

Meanwhile my own eggs will be left to develop for forty hours in a petri dish. Each embryo will double from two cells to four, from four to eight, from eight to sixteen. It's a slow process.

I go home to wait it out.

Two days later.

"Nine for nine," Gideon says.

He has grown me nine viable preembryos.

He has also grown three clones.

He's done blastomere biopsies to detect genetic abnormalities. There are no evident abnormalities, he says, in either set of embryos.

"We'll transfer two normal embryos and freeze the other seven," he says. "Then we'll put in one of the clones."

"OK," I say.

He uses a catheter to transfer the embryos from the petri dish to the uterine cavity. It's not that different from a regular pelvic exam, except for the narrow plastic catheter he has passed through my cervix.

I lie still for several hours. Gideon sits beside me and tells school-boy jokes, forgetting most of the punch-lines. I don't mind. It's Sunday and nobody else is in the office.

"Go home now," he says, "and move as little as possible for the next forty-eight hours."

"Do you think it will work?" I say.

"I don't know," says Gideon. "Only about twenty percent of the embryos I grow transfer properly. And after that, less than a fifth of all IVF pregnancies end in live births. The odds aren't terrific. The embryos may spontaneously abort. On the other hand, you may end up pregnant with twins. You're younger than many of my patients, which gives us a better chance, and I thought your eggs looked fantastic."

"What are the odds of twins?"

"Twelve, fifteen percent."

"And triplets?"

Gideon laughs. "Don't push your luck."

◉

That night I have nothing to drink (just for a change) and I fall asleep at a reasonable hour, only to find myself dreaming so vividly I can't believe I'm sleeping.

I am extremely pregnant. My ankles are swollen. My belly is big and round. I am the size of a small car: a Mini Metro, say, or a Volkswagen Beetle.

It is a sunny afternoon in Central Park. I sit by the boating pond watching the middle-aged perverts remote-control their expensive motorized boats across the surface of the water.

I rest my hands on my hard round belly.

Now I look down and see a puddle of fluid between my feet.

Suddenly my underpants are sodden.

I sit in a lake of water.

My waters have broken.

I'm lying now on a table in the surgical theater in back of the primate house at the Central Park Zoo. The baby insinuates its way along the birth canal. I feel no pain.

A man appears beside me.

"I work with primates," he says. "I've never delivered a human baby before."

"The principle must be the same," I say.

I lie on the delivery table.

A nurse holds my hand. The primate doctor appears again in a white coat and gloves.

"It's time," he says.

He puts his hands below my vagina.

I push hard.

The baby pops out.

Faint cries shrill through the air.

A nurse takes the baby from the doctor and bundles it into a blue fleecy blanket. They no longer clean off the blood right when babies are born, the coat of muck protects them against infection.

"It's a beautiful baby boy," says the nurse.

I struggle to sit up in bed.

"Give him to me," I say.

I reach out my arms.

She hands me the bundle.

I look into the baby's face.

Supple grayish-green scales cover its long pointed iguana-head. Translucent membranes lid the black beads of its eyes. Its small ears lie flat along the sides of its narrow skull. As I watch, the lizard boy flicks a pink forked tongue out of his mouth.

The last thought before I wake up nauseous, my mouth dry:

The baby looks exactly like my father.

Gideon calls me every day.

"Look," he says on Friday morning, "I'm dying to see you, but I'm needed at home. Any chance you could make your way to Hampstead for tea tomorrow afternoon? Miranda could use the distraction. I'll run you home afterwards and we'll have a chat in the car."

"What time should I come?" I ask.

"Three or so?"

"OK," I say. "I'll see you then."

I spend Friday evening at my local drinking rounds of Guinness with the two Irish guys who work on the construction site opposite my building. They think I'm hilarious. They go for my deadpan delivery in a big way. I can barely understand a word they say, but I'm happy to hang out with them anyway.

I wake up at noon on Saturday feeling something that I flatter myself may be morning sickness but that is indistinguishable from a regular hangover. I force myself to write a few pages before getting ready to go to Gideon and Miranda's. I haven't written any travel guide copy for a week.

I take the Northern line to Hampstead (Robyn Hitchcock, "Fifty-Two Stations. . ."). It's a hot day and none of the trains are air-conditioned. My jeans stick to my thighs. I walk slowly from the station to Gideon's house. I pick up a bunch of yellow freesias at the greengrocer's before ringing the doorbell, flowers in hand.

Miranda answers the door. She looks pretty awful. I give her the flowers.

"Oh, don't they smell lovely," she says, cupping the blooms in her hand and pressing them to her face. "I'll just find something to put them in. Why don't you go through to the garden? It's such a beautiful afternoon, I thought we might as well have our tea outside, though the pollen's been giving me terrible hay fever."

I follow her through the house, leaving her in the kitchen to get the tea ready and put the flowers in water. I offer to help, but she insists on doing it herself.

In the garden, I find Gideon's mother basking in a lounge chair. Gideon's kneeling by one of the flower-beds, a small pile of weeds beside him on the grass.

He stands when he sees me and comes over to kiss me. "I'm so glad you could come," he says, taking off his gardening gloves and squeezing my hand. "Mother, do you remember Elizabeth?"

The old lady looks at me, half frowning. "Good afternoon, my dear," she says.

"Tell me your name again?"

"Elizabeth," I say.

She nods. "I thought so," she says.

Miranda appears with an impressive tray of tea things and Gideon moves the weathered wooden table to a place beside his mother's chair. The tea is lapsang souchong, smoky like really expensive bacon. There are plates of cucumber sandwiches, tiny iced cakes, bourbon biscuits, custard creams. I'm still too queasy to eat anything, but I drink a few cups of tea and soak up the sun.

"How's the novel?" Miranda asks.

"All right," I say. In fact, what I have is little more than a dossier on Jonathan Wild. My transcription of his wife's narrative, a range of eighteenth-century documents. I'm not sure what I'll do with them.

"Don't tell me you're writing a novel?" Gideon says.

"I thought I'd mentioned it," I say. I catch his eye. I know perfectly well that I haven't said a word. Gideon looks upset.

Miranda pours me another cup of tea. The food's more or less untouched. Gideon's mother has a little plate with a few cakes and a sandwich or two, but she's pulling apart the sandwiches and throwing bits of bread to the sparrows.

Miranda now notices what she's doing.

"Really, mother," she says, "what a waste of perfectly nice food. I'll get you some breadcrumbs, if you like, but don't spoil those lovely sandwiches."

Gideon's mother looks at her. "These sandwiches are mine," she says, "mine to do what I like with."

Holding Miranda's gaze, she deliberately drops another piece of bread onto the ground. Her hands are knobby with arthritis. I'm struggling to hold in an uncontrollable fit of giggles.

Now Clara looks at me. "I like my son to have such pretty friends," she says.

My heart sinks. Trust the old lady to sniff out the sex. Will Miranda read anything into this? I look quickly across at her. She too is shredding a sandwich, her long fingers pinching and rolling balls of brown bread. In the state she's in now, I think, she doesn't give a damn that Gideon's been cheating on her. All she wants is a baby.

"Do you remember," Gideon says to his mother, "how you used to take me to Regent's Park when I was little? We used to throw bread to the ducks."

He's obviously hoping to distract her.

Gideon's mother looks at him. "You were a funny-looking little boy," she says. "Luckily you seem to have grown out of it."

"I don't know how you can describe your own son as a funny-looking little boy," Miranda says. She's sitting straight up in her chair. Her knuckles show white as she grips the handle of her teacup. She takes an aggressive sip, then slams the cup back down onto the saucer. The tray rattles. "I think Gideon looks lovely in those old photos."

"I dare say you'd think a monkey handsome enough if he were your own child," says Gideon's mother, with unpleasant emphasis. "You're no judge of children's looks. You haven't any of your own, have you? Children, that is, not looks. Looks to sink a battleship, but where will that get you? I was a beauty in my day. Look at me now."

Miranda stands. She's shaking all over, pale beneath her tan. I'm surprised the garden's so quiet. In my mind's ear, I can hear the crash of china on the pavement.

"Gideon," Miranda says, "you'll take Elizabeth home, won't you? I'm afraid I've got a terrible headache, I think I'll go upstairs and lie down for a bit."

She looks at me. "Sorry we're not more jolly today," she says. "I'll give you a ring next week and take you out for lunch, I'd love to see you again properly before you go."

By this time the tears are running down her face. She rubs her hand across her nose and smears the mucus across her mouth. She stumbles across the paved area and feels her way up the stairs and into the house.

Gideon gives his mother a stern talking-to.

"Mother," he says, "you mustn't go on at Miranda about children, it's rather a sore point just now."

"I didn't mean to upset her," she says submissively. She gives me an oblique look. "I think you have already been lucky enough, my dear," she adds quietly, speaking in my direction though she gestures towards Gideon, "to know what it is to find a really first-rate doctor."

"Look," Gideon says to me, "can you make it home on your own?"

"Of course," I say. "I'll call you at the beginning of the week."

"Do that," says Gideon. "I'll look forward to it. And I'll see you Thursday at the office, right?"

He goes inside to find Miranda and I stop by Gideon's mother's chair and bend from behind to kiss her goodbye.

I linger by her for a minute, looking out over her shoulder at the domestic landscape of hedges and back gardens. Pinned to the washing-line in the next garden is a row of children's t-shirts, graduated according to size. I find the sight of the smallest ones curiously touching.

"It's a beautiful day, isn't it?" I say, resting my hand on Clara's shoulder, reluctant to leave.

She reaches up and takes my hand. "Lovely, Fanny," she says absent-mindedly. "We must go again to Kew Gardens one of these days."

I've been to Kew Gardens, but never with Gideon's mother. Fanny—my accent must have misled her. Can Clara think that I'm her doctor's secretary, the American Fanny Ravish? For some reason I like the idea of this impersonation.

"Gideon is so much like his father," Clara says, still holding my hand. "Doesn't he remind you of Dr. Foster in his young days? Josef never understood the boy. They were out of sympathy with one another. But Dr. Foster followed his progress at school and university with such fondness, such concern. You know, it meant so much to him that Gideon decided to follow in his footsteps and become a doctor."

I've been keeping quiet out of curiosity, but I'm now struck dumb with surprise. Is Gideon, then, not his father's son? Can he be the child of Dr. Foster, Clara's faithful attendant—and lover?

I let myself out of the house. The sun's shining still and I don't know what to do with myself. I pass the tube station and decide to walk instead.

Averse to sex with her husband, Clara seems to have had an unexpectedly intimate relationship with Dr. Foster. I know I won't say anything to Gideon. What's to tell? Even in her dementia, Gideon's mother is capable of strategic concealment. All I can think is that this revelation puts a whole new twist on Gideon's commitment to heredity. Or perhaps not: in another sense, it's simply a depressing confirmation of the point he has insisted on all along, that it's impossible to escape our genetic inheritance—that our fates are knitted into our DNA. He believes that he chose medicine of his own volition. In fact, medicine chose him. Yet somehow I can't suppress a sneaking feeling that the joke's on me.

◉

The final copy-batch due to my editor is supposed to cover the British Museum.

I have been at the Museum almost every day for the last month. I sit in the library reading room and scan accounts of criminal trials, true histories of the life and adventures of Jonathan Wild, satirical broadsheets attacking Wild, nineteenth-century melodramas in which Wild figures as stage villain.

I've also been skulking around hoping I won't run into Allan Menzies, whose last two calls I haven't returned. I want the rest of the pages without ever having to talk to him again, though I'm well aware that I'm being both unreasonable and ungrateful.

I know the Museum too well. I can hardly face writing about the place itself. I get hold of some old guidebooks and a history or two. There's the way you write about a place you've never been, and there's the way you write about a place you know well. There's nothing to stop you from writing about the place you know well as though you've never been there before in your life.

What I do is think in lists.

The nucleus of the original British Museum lies in the collection of Sir Hans Sloane, the famous physician who brought back his first treasures from a voyage in the West Indies and continued to accumulate curiosities for the rest of his life.

Insects carefully preserved in worm-proof boxes of wood and glass, human skeletons displaying various deformities, agate carved into teacups, saucers, snuff-boxes, scent-bottles, mirrors, caskets, spoons and ladles, hummingbirds in their nests, a stuffed camel, the eighteen-foot head of a whale.

Roman urns, lamps, gems and inscriptions, Etruscan bronzes, Egyptian and Assyrian antiquities, the Gray's Inn paleolith, an astrolabe, a bronze trumpet, Chinese woodcuts and Peruvian ethnographic material, Dürer's drawings of the proportions of the human body, eighteen highly life-like wax portraits by Abraham Simon, Holbein's drawing of Sir Thomas More.

People came to Sloane with curiosities and he spent a fortune acquiring them: a fire-proof asbestos purse from Benjamin Franklin, for instance. After Sloane died, Parliament voted to purchase his things for the nation. They acquired a grand establishment to hold the collection, Montagu House in Bloomsbury, designed and built for the first Duke of Montagu. (The original house was destroyed by fire less than ten years after it was put up and subsequently rebuilt at great expense to a new design. The Duke got the money to rebuild by persuading the second Duchess of Albemarle to marry him; she was an immensely wealthy lunatic who had vowed to marry none but a Crowned Head of Europe, whereupon Montagu's friends told her that he was the Emperor of China and she settled.)

The collection continued to grow.

David Garrick left the museum his library of plays and the Roubiliac statue of Shakespeare that had adorned the octagonal temple in the garden of his Hampton villa.

Captain Cook donated the artifacts he found in the Pacific, including a pearl-shell Tahitian mourner's dress and the first kangaroo ever seen in Europe.

The Museum's Book of Presents lists a hornet's nest, an Egyptian mummy, pieces of electrical apparatus, the vertebra and other bones of a monstrous sea animal, the web of a silk-worm wrought in the form of a ribbon, a tree-trunk gnawed by a beaver, the ear and tail of an African elephant, a piece of lace made from Queen Elizabeth's hair, a Chinese bowl disfigured in the fire occasioned by the earthquake at Lisbon and discovered two years afterwards in the city's ruins, a dried thumb dug up in the foundations of St. James's Coffee-house, a chicken with two heads, a monstrous pig from Chalfont St. Giles, a live North American tortoise.

In 1807 the best of Sloane's medical and anatomical specimens were transferred to the Hunterian Collection. The Museum retained a hippopotamus, a llama, a musk ox, a polar bear, an antelope, a Siberian elk and three giraffes. The rest of the zoological material was buried or burned after several Bloomsbury residents threatened to take legal action against the Museum for introducing moth into the neighborhood.

George III donated the Rosetta Stone, key to the hieroglyphic script of dynastic Egypt, discovered by the scholarly expedition accompanying Napoleon's invasion of Egypt and confiscated by the British Crown under the Treaty of Alexandria.

The Museum acquired the Elgin Marbles and the Egyptian antiquities collected by Henry Salt, Consul General in Egypt, and his agent Giovanni Belzoni, a former circus strong-man and hydraulic specialist.

Other countries were plundered and their national treasures shipped back to England.

And so the museum came into being.

I stand in an alcove before a medieval reliquary, a saint's femur encased in silver. The air here is damp and close. Beads of sweat break out on my brow. I feel sick to my stomach.

I stagger to the nearest bathroom and fall into an empty stall. I push the door shut behind me and slide the lock across.

The floor is clean enough.

I kneel before the toilet and balance my elbows on the seat. I rest my forehead on my hands.

I take a deep breath.

Then I heave into the porcelain bowl.

After a minute, I feel better.

I stand and leave the stall. I dampen a paper towel at the sink and wipe my face clean. Then I wash my hands.

I catch sight of my face in the mirror.

I look like shit. I haven't had a drink for five days.

"I'm having Jonathan Wild's baby."

I have never been so happy in my life.

In the lobby I take out my mobile and call Gideon at his office. He'll want to hear this news immediately.

"I'm definitely pregnant," I say.

I'm beaming.

"How do you feel?" Gideon asks.

"Unbelievably good," I say, "if you don't count the throwing up."

I catch myself thinking that I will have to put a bucket by the side of my bed so that I don't have to run down the hall to the toilet. But it's too early to worry yet about domestic arrangements.

"Stop by the office tomorrow," Gideon says, "and we'll do a test to make sure."

"I can't drink coffee any more," I say. "It turns my stomach."

"Drink tea," Gideon says.

"Tea is so watery," I say.

"Best stuff in the world," says Gideon.

"Did you know," I say, "that in 1668, the Duchess of Monmouth sent a pound of tea to some friends in Scotland? They had no idea what it was. They boiled the leaves, poured away the water and ate what was left as a vegetable."

"How revolting," Gideon says. "Is that one of the curious new facts you've dug up for the guidebook?"

Someone taps me on the shoulder. It's Robert Forsyth.

"Hi there," he says.

"Look, I have to go now," I tell Gideon. "Call me later."

Rob and I drift out together onto the steps for the inevitable cigarette. Something about him has the effect on me of a magnet. I don't like him, but it's hard to stay away.

"The tarte tatin," he says, "was absolutely delicious."

"My loss," I say. "Anyway, I'm going back to New York."

"Drop me an e-mail when you get home," he says. "I pass through New York occasionally."

We continue to smoke our cigarettes.

"I knew you wouldn't stay that first time," he says after a minute. "Why aren't you willing to take a chance on me?"

I am saved from having to answer by the otherwise inopportune appearance of Allan Menzies, whose face lights up when he sees me. He heads towards us, waving a stiff brown envelope in his hand.

"I've got some more pages for you," he pants out as he arrives at the foot of the stairs. "What a lucky thing that I should happen to bump into you like this. I've been thinking about you all morning."

I introduce the two men and enjoy watching them eye one another with extreme suspicion. I am not sure why the British Library should have become the hub for my romantic encounters.

"Good luck with your work," I tell Rob. I'm eager to get rid of him.

He takes the hint and crushes his cigarette beneath his heel.

"Allan," I say, steeling myself, "I can't thank you enough for your help with the manuscript. It's everything I hoped for."

"This is almost all of it," he says, bouncing up and down like a Labrador puppy. "The last few pages were in particularly bad shape. I'll have to post you the photographic reproductions in another day or so; they were held up at the lab when we found that the lighting for the first set was too dim."

"OK, don't overwhelm me with technical detail. I'll be in touch, anyway, about what's going to happen to the original manuscript."

"Lovely. I'll look forward to hearing from you soon, then."

There's an awkward silence.

"If you'll excuse me," I say. "I'm desperate to get home and read this next installment."

He steps back and lets me go. I refuse to look back, but once I'm outside the gates of the courtyard in front of the museum, I can't stop myself from looking over my shoulder.

He's still there.

I despise myself.

In January of this year Mr. Wild heard there was a warrant out for his arrest, but was too proud to keep himself private and evade the constables, instead showing himself in public whenever he could. In the wake of Blueskin's attempt on his life, though he had recovered better from the injury than anyone expected, his affairs had fallen all to pieces. In the end I believe my aunt had a hand in his downfall after all, on account of a new grudge she held against Mr. Wild for having her lover thrown into gaol. I know now what I was too young to understand before, that half her animosity towards my husband was for him having chosen the niece over the aunt. Mr. Wild went about his business as usual, then, but he saw enemies all about him, and even argued with Mendez, who nobody could say did not have Mr. Wild's best interests at heart. Mr. Wild would no longer lie with me at all; and when I told him that he still owed me a child, he simply looked at me with the coldest eyes I ever saw, and turned away.

The day they came to arrest my husband I was downstairs in the kitchen overseeing a spring-cleaning the likes of which you've rarely seen, prompted I dare say by my uneasiness at the goings-on I have described. I grumbled when the boy came to ask for a cold plate of meat and cheese for Mr. Wild's visitors, for I did not understand why the high constable of Holborn and his two assistants should be treated so well, and I resented the interruption. And Mr. Thomas Jones was indeed here to charge Mr. Wild with assisting a friend to make his escape the day before from a constable at Bow, near Stratford in Middlesex. The authority of the constables had been challenged, and the law wanted blood.

Mr. Wild asked for half-an-hour to settle his affairs, and Jones allowed him all the time he wished, for the charge seemed then a trivial one that would be easily dismissed. Jones and his men had been our guests on happier occasions, and the high constable was hardly at ease in his present task.

Mr. Wild called for me next from his office, and when I came in, sleeves rolled up to my shoulders and hands covered with suds, he told me that he'd be away for a week or two, but that I was not to worry my head about it.

"Are you sure?" says I.

"As sure as can be," says he. He talked very gravely, though, and I feared his mind was more disturbed than he wished me to know.

When they took him out into the street, the people crowded round as though they had never seen such a spectacle. They spat and called him names, cursing him for hanging their darling Jack Sheppard.

Mr. Wild then made a speech to them, one so very much to the point as to make me wonder whether he'd seen this day coming and prepared a few words against it. He was always ready with his tongue, though, and I suppose he may have made the words up on the spot. He was limping badly that day, due to the gout, and I was astonished to see that he could scarcely stand without the assistance of the constables.

"I wonder, good people, what it is you would see?" says he, with them clamoring all around him. A rotten piece of fruit hit him full in the chest and he staggered back a little, before beginning to speak again. "I am a poor honest man, who have done all I could do to serve people when they have had the misfortune to lose their goods at the hands of thieves. I have contributed more than any man living to bring the most daring and notorious malefactors to justice, yet now, by the malice of my enemies, I am in custody. Why should you therefore insult me? I don't know that I ever injured any of you—let me entreat you, therefore, as you see me lame in body and afflicted in mind, not to make me more uneasy than I can bear. If I have offended against the law, it will punish me, but it gives you no right to use me ill, unheard and unconvicted."

He would doubtless have continued longer in this vein, but Jones becoming impatient, ordered the constables to lay into the crowd with their staves, and thus they carried him off in a coach to Sir John Fryer's house, where Mr. Wild was examined and thence committed to Newgate.

On the evening following Mr. Wild's arrest, I served up a good dinner as usual: chicken, venison, ham, pudding and beans, with apricots and walnuts to follow. Though none of us had much appetite, I saw no reason why the household should grind to a halt in what would surely be a brief absence on the part of its master.

Arnold could not stop talking about his mother's late illness, though she was a hale and hearty old lady who showed every sign of living well into her eighth decade. While she had turned yellow as the yolk of an egg the month before, it did not seem to stop her from meeting her cronies at the fruiterer's stall in the market and gossiping with them half the day.

"Your mother may cure her jaundice," says I at last to Quilt Arnold, "by hard-boiling an egg in her own urine, then pricking it with a pin and burying it in an anthill. As the egg wastes away, so will the disease. So let us hear no more of this sad stuff; I want to see you put away the rest of the food on your plate, for waste I do not hold with."

Arnold used the tip of his knife to flick over the cutlet he was meant to be eating. It looked no better that way up, and he sat back, sighing.

"A pity Arnold can't write," snaps Mendez; "he'll forget what you've told him as soon as you're gone."

I turned on him and scolded him for his cruel reflection, but the long and short of it was that we were all desperately afraid of what would happen next. Business went on in many ways as usual, of course, as Mr. Wild continued to see his clients in the suite of rooms he'd taken at Newgate. People do not stop wanting their things back just because the thief-taker is laboring under a temporary inconvenience, and trade was as good as ever, Mr. Wild even gaining a certain cachet with his customers by the environs in which he found himself; and he was treated like a king by the other prisoners, as well as by the prison staff.

Even when his reputation was at its very nadir, the world never charged Mr. Wild with being himself a highwayman or robber. All were in agreement that his house was an office of intelligence for inquiries about lost property. He corresponded with the gangs of thieves who plagued honest men of business, as he would be the first to admit; but he did so only to support the public good, in taking and apprehending the most notorious criminals and by procuring and restoring goods to their right owners. He was always mighty forward to detect the villainies of these people.

But the warrant of detainer that came down in February listed many reasons why Mr. Wild must be kept in custody: as head of a corporation of thieves, it said, he had concealed his criminal activities under pretense of being an officer of the law (down to the short silver staff he carried as a badge of his authority). It would be foolish to say there was no truth whatsoever in these charges, but the warrant put the most sinister complexion upon the matter, and as for the whole, it was a serious misrepresentation of my husband's business—he did no different than others, though he had more success at it on account of his abilities, and thus their envy prompted them to charge him, thinking to put him out of the business and have all opportunities for themselves.

Needless to say, Mr. Wild declared himself innocent of all the charges, and was sent back to Newgate to await trial, but I could tell the house was about to fall down on our heads. They took Quilt Arnold the same day the court heard the warrant of detainer, and half-a-dozen others over the week that followed. The worst was when they decided to arrest Mendez, who was committed at once to New Prison by Justice Street, on a charge of receiving stolen goods.

Mr. Wild sent for me the day after the departure of Mendez, and I went to him that night, awaiting with fear and trembling whatever news he might have of our fortunes.

"Mary," says he, when I was let in at last to see him, "I have asked someone to come to town, and when I introduce him you will receive him in the house as if he were your own flesh and blood."

"I will receive anyone you ask, and with a good grace," says I, inwardly assigning this guest to the worst bedchamber, with its roof-leak and infestation of mice; "and who may he be?"

"My son," says Mr. Wild, me goggling at him all the while, for though I knew he had a son at Wolverhampton, I had hardly thought of him putting in an appearance here, as none of us had ever seen hide nor hair of him.

The boy came forward then, and I was astonished. It was as though Mr. Wild himself had regained all his lost youth and health and looks. I looked at the boy's downy fair skin, and the dark locks curling about his shoulders, and shook my head in wonder.

I took the boy home, cleaned him up, fed him a good meal or two, and before the week was out had taken him as my lover. It was like having Mr. Wild as Elizabeth Mann must have had him, or indeed others long before her. The boy was all mine, and I found such very great satisfaction with him that I did not catch on as quick as I should have to the new catastrophe that threatened.

In all the years I had spent with Mr. Wild, I never thought once about the expense of keeping up the establishment; indeed, I sometimes liked to make little economies, for I prided myself on being a thrifty housewife, but I never inquired into the exact sources of our income, or the relationship between income and expenses. And then the first of the bailiffs showed up. He was most courteous, or so the maid told me when she came upstairs to ask if I'd see him, but when she went back down to tell him I was not at home, he sat himself down on the sofa in Mr. Wild's front parlor and said he'd not leave till I agreed to meet him. There he sat, whistling away and refusing all refreshment, the housemaids cleaning their way around him, until after dark, when I took pity on him at last and descended from my bedroom, where I had been dallying all the afternoon with Mr. Wild's son.

He stood to greet me when I came in, and made me some pretty compliments, but the long and the short was that Mr. Wild owed him a matter of five hundred pounds, and that he did not mean to leave without his money, or an assurance that he'd get it before the month was out.

I was able to persuade him to return the next day, in part because I sincerely believed the money would be easily found. Meanwhile it was my job to discover where Mr. Wild kept his money, for he had not had time to explain everything to me before he was taken away. I had the keys to his desk, however, and made free now of the ledgers, with the idea of taking over the management of Mr. Wild's money matters and doing him a good turn.

But money there was none. As I perused the accounts, I began to feel sicker and sicker; indeed, when I got to the end of the last column of figures, I really thought I was going to vomit, and only my not having eaten anything since breakfast stopped me from spilling my guts out on the carpet.

How could it be, that in such prosperity, with such very great takings, Mr. Wild should have amassed such extraordinary debt? As I went back through the books, I began to see how it was. Mr. Wild had lost a deal of money in the Bubble, I learned, but that was not the half of it. The case was this. Our establishment had always involved significant expenses, not just for running the household, but for paying the network of assistants, informers and so on, supporting scores of dependents left without means, etc. And Mr. Wild had become so preoccupied with taking scores of gang-members, rousting out vermin and making the roads in and about London safe for all travelers that he'd lost sight of the fact that he was running a business. Moreover, he had been so concerned to ingratiate himself with the people of quality, that even when he got back for them things of great value, often at considerable expense to himself, he'd not accepted a penny from half the ladies and gentlemen he'd helped.

It was when I realized that should Mr. Wild die as a consequence of his present imprisonment, I'd be left a pauper or, worse, with thousands of pounds of debt I had no means of discharging, that I think I began to hate him.

I said nothing of this to Mr. Wild, of course. And the money had to be found to keep up appearances, for poverty would only further prejudice the town against him. The expense of keeping Mr. Wild alone exceeded two hundred pounds a week, for as my aunt said, an uncomfortable bed at Newgate had always cost more than the best accommodations in Mayfair.

Mr. Wild's counsel was adamant during this time that they must charge him in a specific fact or else let him loose, which forced the law's hand. And what did they charge Mr. Wild with in the end but the silliest business you ever heard of! I thought till the very last minute they'd have to dismiss the case, it was so ludicrous: as though the same thing did not happen a dozen times every day, with the full knowledge and assistance of the law.

At the April sessions, counsel moved that the trial might be deferred till the next sessions, and the court granted the postponement. Only then did we learn the particulars of the case they were building against Mr. Wild.

"My dear, do you remember the old blind lace-seller on Holborn Bridge?" says Mr. Wild to me one afternoon towards the end of the month, I having brought him a hamper of food and a set of clean linen. He looked a sad, nay, even a grotesque figure in his room at Newgate, though everything was as fine as money could make it, and we had furnished it almost as well as his parlor at home (for he continued to see clients there, and it was essential to keep up the show of wealth—he assured everyone who came that it was a foolish plot against him by a parcel of rash magistrates, but that they would shortly come to an accommodation and restore him to liberty). Mr. Wild still thought that we had all the money in the world; he did not understand it was all gone, and I supposed I might as well keep the worst of it from him.

Perhaps it was the contrast to his son that now made Mr. Wild's physical decay so marked. Underneath the callimanco headcloth he always wore, his shaved head bore any number of scars, in addition to two silver plates where the skull had been fractured. I had counted once, in the early days of our marriage, and found that he had seventeen wounds in various parts of his body (from daggers, swords, gun-shots, truncheons). I made sure now that he had a warming-pan in his bed each night, a necessity on account of the stiffness from his gout and the dank cold of Newgate.

I idly wondered what Mr. Wild would say if, instead of listening so obediently to his woes, I told him frankly that his son had been rogering me these three weeks, and that I had an inkling, though it was too soon to know for sure, that I might already be with child by him. But I knew I'd say nothing. Even in his present state, Mr. Wild was greatly to be feared.

"Mrs. Stetham?" says I, coming to myself and dragging my eyes off my husband's encroaching decrepitude. "What does she have to do with it?"

"Nothing, but that my life is in her hands," says Mr. Wild with a bitter sneer.

I wrenched my mind back, as he asked, to the January afternoon when I had sat in the parlor at the Old Bailey. We had two visitors that day, an Irishman called Henry Kelly and his friend Margaret Murphy, who brought me a pretty present of a pair of brocaded shoes. They had come over from Ireland together in one of Mr. Wild's own ships, and it was the captain's wife (then a lodger under our roof) who made the suggestion that the Irish couple should go to the shop of an old blind bitch called Stetham on Holborn Bridge, to speak with a box or two of lace.

Kelly and Murphy went there together, and Mr. Wild happened to show them the direction, as he was going that way himself and thought he might as well take pity on a pair of ignorant lumps come so recently from overseas. Mr. Wild showed them the door and left them there, thinking—I can assure you this is the extent of it—that they meant to buy a piece of lace, perhaps as a present for me. He had no idea what they contemplated, not having been in the room when the topic was raised by Captain Johnson's better half; would he have involved himself in such a plot while carrying the silver staff that served as the symbol of his authority? Unfortunately his figure was all too easily recognized, as it later emerged, a number of witnesses placing him at the scene just before the theft took place.

Kelly and Murphy looked at several parcels of lace, turned over a piece or two, found fault with everything and made Mrs. Stetham reach down a tin box or two of lace that she'd not meant to bring out. She was almost blind and in the hurry of business they found no trouble in concealing several goodly pieces of lace about their persons. They left the shop as soon as they could, and returned straight to the Old Bailey.

Mr. Wild came home a half-hour after them, and they went to him at once to ask what he'd give them for the lace. He did not conspire in the theft, you see; he only wanted the goods restored to the woman who'd lost them.

"If you will have your reward in ready money," says he, "I can give you no more than three guineas and four broad pieces between you."

"No more?" says Kelly. You could see he did not mean to hand over all the pieces until he had milked my husband of every last penny.

"No," says Mr. Wild, with the horse-sense for which he was famous; "for Mrs. Stetham, the lady from whom you took the lace, is a hard-mouthed old bitch, and it will be tricky to get so much as ten guineas from her for the return of her lost goods, though they be worth five times as much."

Indeed, she'd just left our house the day the constables came to take Mr. Wild to gaol, doing little to conceal her impatience to have her things again and her conviction that if Mr. Wild could not get them back at once, he was a blackguard and a villain himself—and so she fell straight into the hands of the law.

During this time, any thief who was taken tried to get a pardon on the grounds that he or she could make great discoveries of the dark transactions of Jonathan Wild. Kelly and Murphy were bound to appear against Mr. Wild on pain of imprisonment, and Mrs. Stetham and her daughter also bound on recognizances of fifty pounds apiece.

The case came on at the beginning of the May sessions. As I stood and watched, I remembered the day of my uncle's death, and the tens of times I'd stood here looking on.

It was not merely the criminal prosecution that weighed heavily on my mind, nor my bitter regret at not having thought to lay up goods and money against the day when I should have nothing but what I had kept for myself. What was I to do about the fact that I now knew myself, by all the usual signs, to be certainly pregnant? Mr. Wild's son stood at my right as we waited for the case to come on, and I put my hand into his—for this intimacy might be allowed a mother-in-law—and felt him squeeze it a little.

It was a very great comfort to have him there, too, though I hardly knew what the boy was thinking. Taking someone into your bed does not make his mind open up to you; on the contrary, it is often harder to know what your lover is thinking, than to intuit the thoughts of a stranger. I reckon besides he must have been a silent young man at the best of times. I lavished as much attention on him as I could spare, but I was very much occupied with fending off the bailiffs, frantically converting what I could into money and hiding it where they could not get it, and visiting Mr. Wild in prison. I scarcely know what the boy did with himself during the days when I was about my business.

He was indeed a kind of cipher. How would you feel if your acknowledged father had abandoned you in the country while he made his fortune in London and then, when he had come to grief, asked you to come to see him in London, granted you a single audience, then banned you from visiting him again? For Mr. Wild had not let his son come again after that first time, and the boy understandably resented it. I could tell the boy as often as I liked that it was affection and remorse that prompted Mr. Wild to show himself so cold to his young relation, but I could not make him believe it; and god only knew what tincture of love and hatred the boy must feel for his father.

On the morning of that first day, at any rate, Mr. Wild handed round to the men of the jury a printed paper naming all the felons he'd captured, but the prosecution took it amiss, charging him with taking the credit off the king's witnesses and attempting to prepossess and influence the jury. The judge informed Mr. Wild that whatever he might hope for from this indirect management, it was far from making his cause appear in a more favorable light.

The testimony of Kelly and Murphy was very much as I could have predicted. The court gave them credence because they were testifying against a man the law had determined to bring down, but they were unprepossessing characters, hard to credit with even common honesty. On the other hand, the jury warmed to Mrs. Stetham at once. As she took the stand, we saw before us a brisk respectable businesswoman so short-sighted that she could hardly see six inches in front of her face, but her blindness did not stop her remembering the thieves, that she missed the lace shortly after they left, and valued the lost box at fifty pounds.

The first indictment against Mr. Wild was sloppily phrased by the prosecution, the jury taking only half an hour to acquit him. Mr. Wild celebrated by sending wine and brandy all round, though I could tell that several of the great men present thought him not cowed enough by the gravity of the proceedings. His friends (those left to him, that is) crowded around him and clapped him on the back. Mendez was not there, being in custody still at the New Prison.

The second indictment came under the Jonathan Wild Act, which the judge ordered the clerk to read aloud in court. Mrs. Stetham then took the stand again and told of her course of action subsequent to missing the lace. She went to Wild's house the very same night the box was stolen; he was not at home, so she advertised the lace she'd lost with a reward of fifteen guineas, no questions asked.

Hearing nothing of it, she went to Wild's house again and met with him. Calling several days later, she was told that he'd heard something of the lace; a man came in while they were talking and had a word aside with Wild, who then told Mrs. Stetham that he thought one Henry Kelly was concerned in the fact. Mrs. Stetham came back the same day Mr. Wild was arrested, as I have said already, just before the constables arrived. She told him she'd give more than the reward she'd advertised, and my husband told her not to be in such a hurry, as he thought he could get the box back for less.

Mrs. Stetham's next contact with Mr. Wild was in March, when she received a message telling her to come to him in Newgate with ten guineas in her pocket. She came to the prison, was admitted to see him and was told by him to call a porter. She pleading her blindness as an excuse, Mr. Wild sent one of his men for a ticket-porter. Mrs. Stetham gave the porter ten guineas and my husband's instructions about the lace. The man returned an hour later with the box she'd lost, and only one piece gone from it, so that she had almost all of it back.

"What must I give you for your trouble?" she then asked Mr. Wild.

His response—and I swear this is what he said to her, word for word: "Not a farthing, madam, not a single farthing. You know I don't do these things for worldly interest, but for the benefit of poor people who have met with misfortunes. As for the piece of lace that is missing, do not be uneasy; I hope to get it for you before long, and I don't know but that in a little time, I may help you not only to your ten guineas but to the thieves as well. As you are a widow and a good Christian, I desire nothing of you but your prayers. I have a great many enemies, and god knows what may be the consequence of this imprisonment."

After Mrs. Stetham's testimony, Mr. Wild asked for the earlier witnesses to be recalled. He tried unsuccessfully to examine them himself, but the judge forbade him to propose questions directly to the witnesses. Mr. Wild was trying to demonstrate one of those points of law by which lawyers get men off, hoping to escape the second indictment on the grounds that as the thieves had sworn Mr. Wild *himself* guilty of a felony, in being concerned with those that stole the goods (because he stood outside the door of the shop), the act under which he was indicted could not be meant to affect him. The act having as its target only such persons as were not felons themselves, but who merely held a correspondence with felons (or so Mr. Wild's lawyer argued on his behalf), it could hardly apply to one who was himself supposed to be a felon in his own person.

The judge asked the clerk to read the relevant passage of the Act again to the court. For the defense, Mr. Kettleby observed that the law would imply that Jonathan Wild should have caused himself to be apprehended and given evidence against himself, and that this made a nonsense of the indictment.

The prosecutor proceeded to pull apart the argument for the defense, one piece at a time. He pointed out that Mr. Wild had accomplices in the fact, that he did not discover them to the law and that this was all that mattered. The judge agreed, emphasizing that Mr. Wild's case came within almost every provision of the act: he had secret acquaintance with felons, he made it his business to help people to stolen goods, etc. etc.

The jury was out for some time. When they came back in, the foreman handed a sheet of paper across to the judge, who read the sentence to the court. Mr. Wild was acquitted on the first indictment and found guilty on the second. He was returned to custody to await sentencing.

The boy stood beside me all the while, never saying a word although the day in court had been long indeed. When I asked him if he'd come back with me now and eat some supper, he turned on me and hit me, telling me that his father deserved better than to have married a whore, and that I was not to expect him home that night, for he had a duty to find a way to help his father.

Well, thought I as he hurried away from me, who would have thought the boy had so much of his father in him? I had more to worry about than when I'd see him again, and I put him out of my mind.

On the last evening of the sessions, Mr. Wild and the other prisoners were brought back to the bar to be sentenced. I could see that my husband was much dejected. I was nearly as disordered myself, as Mr. Wild's son had not yet come home, and I had heard that he was making a great nuisance of himself about town, telling everyone he met with of the very great injustice about to be perpetrated against his father, begging for their assistance, and threatening to raise a posse himself to ride out and rescue Mr. Wild on the way to Tyburn.

"What have you to say why judgment of death should not pass upon you?" the judge asked Mr. Wild before the sentencing.

"My lord," Mr. Wild said, consulting a scrap of paper as he spoke, which was most unlike him, and a sign of the disorder into which his mind had been cast, "I hope that even in the sad condition in which I stand, I may pretend to some little merit in respect to the service I have done to my country. I have delivered the nation from some of the greatest pests with which it was ever troubled. I have brought many bold and daring malefactors to justice, even at the hazard of my own life, and my body is covered with the scars I received in these undertakings. I presume to say I have done merit, because at the time these things were done, they were esteemed meritorious by the government. I submit myself wholly to His Majesty's mercy."

The judge said nothing in response to Mr. Wild's plea. It was very noticeable that Mr. Wild had been placed directly beside the common felons: Robert

Harpham, William Sperry, Robert Standford, John Plant. Now the hangman tied their thumbs together with whipcord. The Recorder pronounced death on each of them, one at a time. When he came to my husband, he stopped. After recounting Mr. Wild's crimes and recalling the warnings he'd been given, he said one more thing that made even my blood run cold.

"Make the most of the time left to you," says the recorder, "that time which the tenderness of the law allows English sinners for their repentance. You may depend on justice. Do not hope for anything more."

When I visited the prison straight after Mr. Wild's name had appeared in the Dead Warrant, I found him raging about his rooms like a madman. He could not credit the course of events. "At Wolverhampton," he told me furiously, "I know several persons that would have proved my friends, had I thought my case so dangerous that I need apply to them. I have carried on the same practice above a dozen years; how shall I suffer at last, for what has so long gone unpunished?"

I had brought him a few of the broadsheets that were selling out all over town, and he leafed through them with a curiosity that soon turned to disgust.

"It is strange," says he, "that a man's life should be made a romance before his face, while he's still alive to contradict it."

"And after you're dead?" says I.

He made me no answer. Instead his fingers stroked the barely healed gash along his throat where Blueskin had tried to kill him six months before.

All the while I sat still as a mouse, for I feared his mood would soon change, and I was right. He looked at me then, and seemed to notice something different about me, though I hardly know what could have aroused his suspicions.

"You have played me false, haven't you?" says he.

"False?" says I, entirely the innocent. I could not prevent my hands coming up to my belly, though, and as Mr. Wild's eyes followed I knew all was lost.

"You bitch, you're pregnant," Mr. Wild roared, coming at me then across the room, and the scene that followed was more brutal than I can rightly tell. I will not say I had not contemplated seducing Mr. Wild during this time, particularly once I knew I was with child; for if he should be reprieved, how would I explain away my growing belly? The disease was an obstacle, but not an impossible one. This encounter, however, hardly proceeded as I had imagined. It was not a seduction. It was a rape. Mr. Wild threw me against the wall and thrust himself into me. I was dry as a bone, and could not stop retching as he moved in and out. He was not able to ejaculate, and at last he pushed me from him, and told me to get out, and that if I was lucky, he'd forget the whole thing.

A few days after I felt an unaccustomed pain in my private parts. Examining myself more closely with the help of a hand-mirror, I discovered a nasty red rash, and knew that I had become infected with whatever it was had plagued Mr. Wild so long. I applied a salve to the affected parts, but I feared it would do little good.

That was when I tried to hang myself.

My husband sentenced to die on the gallows—to lose one husband in such a way, I could hear my aunt saying, might augur simple bad luck, but to lose a second could only be sheer wanton carelessness—all the furniture in the house under an execution, and more bailiffs camping out downstairs with each day that passed—Mr. Wild's son still away, and no father for the child quickening in me—now this last affront to health and sanity.

I was reduced very low indeed, in short, and I had a rope among my things. I rigged a simple noose and hung it over a large hook above the door. I put the noose about my neck and climbed up on a chair I had pulled over to the corner. I kicked aside the chair. My sight went dark.

I came to myself some time after. My throat was extremely sore, and when I put my hand to my neck I felt the abrasions and bruising.

My woman Mrs. Betty sat beside me. "Quilt Arnold coming into the room accidentally, found you and cut you down," she said into my ear.

"Reprieved against my will!" I cried. My voice came out as a hoarse whisper, cracked and rough.

All I could think was that Mr. Wild would give anything to be allowed to live. And yet I had something to live for myself, if I could only remember it, thought I then with remorse, and put my hand once again to my belly, though it was too early to feel anything like a flutter of life. Seized with guilt, I struck my head with my fist and beat myself about the face to remind myself that another life now depended on mine, and that I had not the right to deprive the child of its chance to come into the world whole, nor indeed would I have the inclination to do such when I was properly myself again. My sore neck would meanwhile serve to remind me I meant to live.

Meanwhile the Dead Warrants came down, and Mr. Wild was not yet reprieved. All the money in the world would not keep him much longer out of the condemned hold. Fifty sheriff's officers and as many more from the Compter had been ordered to attend at Newgate on Monday morning to convey the prisoners safely to Tyburn.

Safely! So much concern for getting them there, and then to turn them off like wringing so many chickens' necks. Mr. Wild's son came home at last, after failing to find anyone bold enough to assist him in the rescue he projected. Now he wanted to leave the country, because he was unable to bear the reflections that would be cast on him on account of his unfortunate father, but I told him it would show a lack of confidence in his parent, and besides, he must wait till I was ready to go with him. He made no objections—after all, he was young and impressionable enough to do as I asked.

The next time I came, I learned that Mr. Wild had been fasting upward of four days. The keepers complained to me that he wouldn't go to chapel, pleading his fast, his lameness and his illness to get off.

"You have no concern for his soul," I said to my friend the turnkey Tom Silas, who seemed to expect me to persuade my husband to go to the chapel at once. "You are simply afraid to disappoint the visitors who have paid eightpence a head to be admitted to the chapel to see Mr. Wild. No man should be carried to chapel against his will, as to pray to God without attention or regard is worse than not to pray at all."

Indeed, they were destined never to receive satisfaction. Mr. Wild did not show his face again in chapel after he received the sentence of death. The last time he had gone, his enemies among the crowd interrupted his prayers by pointing and whispering. If they had dared, they would have insulted him openly and raised a tumult, but that his name still carried some little authority.

The saddest thing I saw in those last few days was that Mr. Wild was no longer able to keep the other malefactors in order and regularity. He sat penned up in his rooms, afraid to venture out even into the yard, and the officers and clergymen about the prison continued to exert themselves to persuade Mr. Wild to come to chapel. The most effectual threat they could make, was to withhold from him the sacrament, which Mr. Wild—never before a pious man—had come to believe was essential to the future state.

"You cannot refuse the sacrament to a dying man!" cried my husband, after they had turned him down three or four times.

The ordinary shook him off. "Only if you repent, Mr. Wild," he said.

"I will not go to the chapel to pray," Mr. Wild said. "I am lame from the gout, and the crowds and disorders of the people discompose me. Moreover, certain enemies of mine among the crowd will insult me, and raise a mob if they are able."

Even from his rooms on the master's side of the prison we could hear the jeers and catcalls from outside, the rabble mocking him by calling out the name of Thief-Taker General of Great Britain and Ireland.

"You ought to have taken warning when you were first of all committed prisoner in the Compter," Mr. Wild was told by one of the reverend gentlemen who haunted the prison. "You should have observed the misery of vicious people instead of learning their ways, and endeavoring to understand them and their practices, and afterwards associating with them."

"My business is doing good in recovering lost property," said Mr. Wild, hanging on to what he knew, though his senses were much disordered by this time. He struggled up out of his chair then and pulled up his shirt, brandishing his chest at his interrogator. "I have apprehended the greatest and most pernicious robbers that ever molested the nation. See the wounds and scars still remaining in my head and my body."

But the conversation that happened the time after is the one I remember best. Mr. Wild had become as stubborn as a two-year-old child. He seemed to have shrunk into himself, smaller by far in his body than when he'd gone to prison in the middle of February.

"I want to receive the sacrament," he insisted, staring at the parson. He had hardly noticed my arrival, being so taken up in the matter of life after death; and indeed we had exchanged few words since the rape, though I had relented enough to promise him whatever he needed to ease his last days.

"Repent of your sins, and read and study the passion of Christ," said the hard-hearted cleric. "Then I will administer the sacrament."

At last Mr. Wild mumbled a prayer or two, and at this sign of repentance, the clergyman relented. He spent the evening there, and they conversed about many things of great import. I attended closely, for I knew I'd see him only once or twice more and whatever he said to the clergyman was meant in part for me.

"I have a question," said Mr. Wild, some time into their discourse, and I pricked up my ears, for I thought he pitched his voice most strangely in my direction. "How did the noble Greeks and Romans who killed themselves come to be so glorious in history, if self-murder be a crime?"

"Even the most learned among the heathens called self-murder cowardice," was the answer he got, one designed to shut down the topic at once. "We are meant to sustain the misfortunes that providence lays upon us, and moreover, Christianity comes out expressly against suicide."

I took my leave not long thereafter, and as I bent to kiss my husband on the cheek, I heard him whisper the word laudanum. I did not need to ask what he wanted it for, and I resolved to do as he bid.

On my way out I was accosted by the writer Defoe, a spare middle-sized man about sixty years old, a meddler and a trouble-maker, hook-nosed and sharp-chinned, with a large mole near his mouth. He looked a bedraggled old dandy in his heavy old-fashioned wig (he'd have pawned it if it were worth more, I knew his kind) and a pinkie-ring whose stone had long since been replaced with paste.

"May I have a word?" says he.

I looked him up and down, not much liking what I saw, but agreed to join him for a glass of gin, knowing he might still serve my husband if he so chose. Mr. Defoe had already done my husband the dubious kindness of causing *Applebee's Weekly Journal* (the Tory paper that currently employed this devious fellow) to print a list of all the men returned from transportation whom Mr. Wild had captured and convicted; he did it in such a way, however, as to show very clearly that it had been printed only to comply with the wishes of a man whose life was in jeopardy.

"What do you want?" says I at last, as we took our seats in an alehouse two streets away from the prison.

"I refuse to take things upon the credit of common fame," he says, "or to supply by invention the particulars of Jonathan's life. I would like to hear the truth, as it were from the horse's mouth."

It was hardly the most complimentary way of putting it, thought I; and could he not have the courtesy to call my husband by his proper name?

"My husband is an honest man," says I.

"He had the reputation of an honest man," says Defoe correcting me, "until the public began to apprehend the truth of the business."

"He served the public."

"He served the public when he detected criminals," snaps out the writer, "but he abused it when he assumed the power to protect others. Moreover, he believed that his being useful in the first instance would prevent his being considered criminal in the last; in which supposition, he was sorely mistaken. How could he have hoped to maintain such intimacy among the gangs and societies of thieves, without gaining the reputation of being in some sort a party to their management?"

"Reputation, aye; but it was only the malice of his enemies that brought him to his present pass."

Defoe looked at me then and sneered. "Why so loyal?" asks he. "You owe the man little."

"I am his wife," says I, drawing myself up and fixing him with my stare.

"Out of all the women he ever took to wife," says Defoe, "he only loved Elizabeth Mann."

"Not so," says I. "She was a whore."

Defoe shakes his head. "She was the most sensible and agreeable person he ever met," says he, "and he says he'll be buried beside her in St. Pancras Churchyard. He told me so not two hours since, and that the next time you came he would entreat you to make it so; he did not trust you to keep the information to yourself, had he told you any sooner."

I had a long night of it and a long day following, thinking of what the writer had said and what it meant for me. I swore then that if Mr. Wild indeed made the request at which Defoe had intimated, I'd make him pay for it in every way I could. I came at the hour I'd promised, though, for this was the very last time I'd be allowed to see him before he met his end, and in the basket I'd brought for him, among a dozen more innocent things, was the bottle of liquid laudanum he'd asked for at the end of my last visit. That I had not the heart to withhold from him, no matter what else I might have in mind.

"Could my son not have come to see his father one last time?" was the question he opened with, when I was let into the room to see him. It was the condemned hold now, not the comfortable suite of rooms to which I had become accustomed, and I shuddered at the cold dank air and the low company; indeed, I found myself in the utmost horror of soul, not just at his fast-approaching death, but at the revenge I had begun to contemplate.

"The magistrates thought it proper to confine the boy this week," I told him, which was the truth, he being of so turbulent a disposition that they feared he would cause some mischief among the mob.

"Will you care for him, as though you were his own mother?" says Mr. Wild feebly.

"Yes," swore I, and meant it too, though not in exactly the sense that Mr. Wild thought.

"What's a-clock?" he asks me then.

Checking my watch, I assured him that we had another hour before my visit must conclude; but the hour of his doom was rapidly approaching, and naught either of us could do to avert it.

"I swore once," says he then, looking at me entreatingly, and I braced myself for what was to come, "that I would be buried close to the grave of my last wife, Elizabeth Mann. I have such an impression of her sanctity and goodness, that I can contemplate no other resting place. Will you take care to see this performed? She lies in the churchyard of St. Pancras-in-the-Fields, and if you promise to see my body laid there in secret, it will be a very great weight off my mind. You must do everything you can to prevent the surgeons learning my whereabouts. When the day of judgment comes, there will be little hope for mercy if my body does not lie there in one piece."

It may seem like a little thing, but the words about his other wife struck the mortal blow to my affections, attenuated already by circumstance, withered by old dissatisfactions and new penury, dissolved now by this final insult.

I made an inventory in my head of the slights and degradations I had endured, a reckoning I should have made years before.

I knew then what I'd do.

Jonathan Wild Thief-Taker General of Great Britain & Ireland. To all the Thieves, Whores, Pick-pockets, Family Fellons & co. in *Great Brittain & Ireland. Gentlemen & Ladies.* You are hereby desir'd to accompany yr worthy friend ye Pious Mr. I—- W—d from his Seat at Whittington's Colledge to ye Tripple Tree, where he's to make his last Exit on 24 May 1725, and his Corps to be Carry'd from thence to be decently Interr'd amongst his Ancestors. Pray bring this Ticket with you.

I arrive at Gideon's office just after six.

"Hello, dear," Mrs. Beardsley says.

She looks just as she always does, whiskers and all. She's putting together her things in a mechanical fashion. She is about to leave for the afternoon.

"Would you like a cup of tea?" she asks.

"No, thanks," I say.

She draws the curtains, turns off her computer and locks the desk drawer.

"Goodbye, dear," she says.

"I'm sorry about the baby," I say.

She nods.

"Is your daughter all right?" I ask.

"Not too bad," she says, her words routine.

Gideon emerges as she leaves. Once the door closes, he comes over and kisses me.

"I've only got half an hour," he says. "Miranda needs me to take some clients of hers to the opera."

"Do you have time to do the test?" I say.

"Of course," he says.

I pee in a cup.

He takes a small blood sample.

"Still having morning sickness?" he asks.

"Yes," I say.

"You're almost certainly pregnant, but we'll do the test just to be sure. If I come round tomorrow at eight, will you be at home?"

"All right," I say.

He looks up at me.

"Anything else?"

I wrinkle my nose.

"Thanks," I say.

"Not at all," says Gideon.

He brushes his hand across my face.

"I love you," he says again. "Take care of yourself, will you?"

◉

I'm having Jonathan Wild's clone, I say to myself. I can't be sure, of course, but my gut tells me it's Jonathan Wild. I'm riding the tube back into central London after a morning at Hampton Court. Jonathan Wild has been dead for a quarter of a millennium.

On a poster across from me I read the words of a poem by Thomas Hardy, a poem called "Heredity" that is part of the high-minded project to put poetry on the Underground. I have seen this verse before, on other trains:

I am the family face;
Flesh perishes, I live on,
Projecting trait and trace
Through time to times anon,
And leaping from place to place
Over oblivion.

Oblivion. The word's easy enough to define. The state or fact of forgetting; forgetfulness. Intentional overlooking, especially of political offenses, as when amnesty is provided by an act of oblivion. The state or condition of being forgotten.

I am determined to forget.

I do not want to be forgotten.

There is no record of Mary Wild's trip to the Americas, though I have been able to discover that Jonathan Wild's son went to Maryland as an indentured servant not long after his father's death. I imagine them traveling together as a married couple. I can picture their descendants spread out all over the country, running used-car dealerships and protection rackets, prisons and police departments, body shops and a constellation of other rackets. Even if Mary Wild took her revenge by betraying her husband in more ways than one, they're undoubtedly Jonathan's descendants too. Two hundred years later, what difference does it make?

Sir Hans Sloane's herbarium still fills three hundred and thirty-seven folios in the Department of Botany at the British Museum. In the middle of the nineteenth century, when the Keeper of Botany sowed fourteen seeds of *Nelumbo nucifera* from the herbarium, he obtained twelve seedlings. In 1941 a bomb attack on the Museum caused a fire. They extinguished the fire with water that wet some of the collections and Dr. John Ramsbottom later observed an outgrowth over an inch long from one of Sloane's seeds.

There's every reason to believe the seeds remain viable.

My return ticket to New York bears a date two days from now.

I have not called to change the flight.

I do not know whether I will be on the plane.

Gideon arrives promptly at eight. Gideon is often unavailable but he is never late.

He bears flowers and a bottle of champagne. He's also picked up my mail from the table in the hall downstairs. I recognize one of Allan's trademark brown envelopes. But it can wait till later.

"God, you look beautiful," he says.

I am wearing a short black chiffon dress, a garter-belt, stockings and heels. My hair's slicked back and I've done my makeup properly. I look like a grown-up.

Gideon is happier than I have ever seen him.

He puts the champagne and flowers in the sink and holds out his arms.

"Come here," he says.

I go to him and he hugs me, lifting me off my feet and whirling me around.

When we come back down to earth, Gideon asks me whether I want the good news or the bad news.

"Good news first," I say. He wouldn't have brought champagne if the bad news was really bad.

"Wild certainly didn't have syphilis. I got the results back from the lab. Forensic scientists do this kind of work quite often on historical figures, and there's a high level of accuracy when you look at the bone."

"That's good news," I say. "What's the bad news?"

"Well, it's not exactly bad. In fact, it's not bad at all. I'm fairly sure that only one of the embryos has implanted in the uterus. You must know that it's—"

"Don't tell me!" I shout.

Gideon's taken aback.

"I won't know for some time," I say now, adopting a calmer voice in a half-hearted attempt to persuade him that pregnancy has not destroyed the last shreds of my sanity. "I hope I'll never know. It's not like the Jonathan Wild clone's going to pop out speaking in eighteenth-century thieves' cant and selling stolen rattles back to the other babies in the nursery. In the twenty-first century, Jonathan Wild could do anything: he could be an investment banker, or the director of a big research lab, or a movie producer. He could enter any one out of hundreds of cool and disreputable professions."

Gideon laughs. Then he puts his arm around me and kisses me on the lips, a long lingering open-mouthed kiss.

"I can't wait to be a father," he says softly.

I pull away from him.

"What's wrong?" he says.

"You're not necessarily the father of this baby," I say. "I'm going back to New York the day after tomorrow."

He stares at me in amazement.

"You can't do that," he says. "It's my child too."

"Only in the sense that you helped make it," I say.

"So I should hope," says Gideon, beginning to laugh.

"Make it in the most technical sense, I mean," I say. "It's mine, really."

Gideon laughs even harder.

"Give it up, Elizabeth," he says. "We both know I'm the baby's father."

"What?"

"The Jonathan Wild embryos all died in the lab," he says. "They were never viable, not even the one I showed you. I implanted it along with the two real embryos—I'm not a liar, and I told you I'd do it; besides, it couldn't make any real difference—but it's impossible that this so-called 'clone' should grow beyond the preembryo stage. Frankly, it's a miracle the thing got so far. All the sheep Steve's tried this on have spontaneously aborted within a few weeks of conception."

I am aghast.

"We implanted two viable embryos made from your eggs and my sperm. I put in the third just to humor you. All that DNA business was just a game. It's not yet technically feasible, of course. As you know perfectly well."

I say nothing.

"You're unbelievably sexy when you trot out the clinical jargon," he says, pulling me towards him and stroking my hair. "I'm really blown away by it. It's a waste, really, if you don't go to medical school one of these days. You're so capable."

'Blown away' is one of my own phrases. I've never heard Gideon use it before.

"You're a scientist's daughter, for god's sake," says Gideon. "As I say, it was a miracle Steve got so far with the stuff in the first place."

"But this is assisted reproduction," I say bitterly. "Miracles happen all the time."

Gideon laughs.

"I didn't want your baby," I mutter. "I only ever wanted Jonathan Wild."

"How could I have known you didn't want my child?" he asks. "You've been sleeping with me without any contraception."

"My tubes were tied," I say. I am outraged.

"Not much security in that," he says. "It often spontaneously reverses, especially in younger women. Eggs slip through and so on."

"Oh god," I say. "I'm definitely going to have your baby?"

We stand there and stare at each other.

"Miranda and I will adopt the baby if you don't want to keep it," Gideon says calmly. "We've been looking to adopt for some time. We can't have children. I met her when she came in to see me as a patient. I sent her to one of my colleagues instead and asked her out to dinner; I am actually au fait with standard medical ethics, believe it or not. But her infertility hasn't responded to treatment.

"Also," he adds, "I've got a low sperm count."

This admission clearly costs him something.

The ludicrous aspect of the situation suddenly strikes me. I start to giggle. Soon I'm laughing hysterically and Gideon slaps my face.

I fall silent.

"Have you told your father?" he says now.

"No."

"Why not?"

"I can't deal with him."

"When did this start?"

"Do you really want to know?"

"Of course."

I pause.

"I hate my father," I say.

Gideon raises an eyebrow. "Surely a rather banal sentiment," he says.

"When I was sixteen," I say, "I got pregnant."

He's taken aback. Whatever he expected to hear, it wasn't this. "What did you do?" he asks.

"I went to my father and told him I'd slept with a guy and got pregnant."

"And?"

"He hit me."

Gideon stays quiet.

"He slapped my face and called me a slut. He told me that he'd abort the fetus in his office the next day. After hours and off the books, so there wouldn't be any evidence in my medical records."

Gideon looks confused.

"He figured I might want to run for political office someday. He thought an abortion might hurt my career. He did a physical right there in his study. You remember the study. That leather couch, the one covered with a single seamless cowhide—he always made sure everybody knew it cost twice as much as the one with the seam. He made me take off my clothes and lie down on the couch. He put on a pair of latex gloves and thrust his hand into my vagina and pressed down from above with his other hand onto my ovaries and uterus. He didn't use any lubrication."

"Why didn't you say something?"

"Like what? The last thing I wanted was to be pregnant. What was I supposed to say? I met him at his office the next evening. The whole place was dark. He'd sent home the nurse and the receptionist and the blinds were pulled down over the doors and windows. He was terrified someone would see us."

"How did he terminate the fetus?"

"A standard D&C. It was horrible. And then he tied my tubes."

"He what?"

"He tied my tubes," I say again.

"He performed a tubal ligation without your consent? You were only sixteen?"

I nod.

Gideon does not know whether to believe me.

"If that's true," he says finally, "he ought to be struck off. Banned from practicing medicine, I mean."

I shrug.

"Believe it or not," I say. "It's all the same to me."

There's a long pause. A stand-off.

"You still have to tell him," says Gideon then. "You must tell him you're pregnant. It'll be different this time, you'll see."

The bile rises in my throat. I cough and light another cigarette.

"You certainly shouldn't be smoking," Gideon says, taking the cigarette from me and grinding it out in the ashtray.

"Don't be so fucking sensible," I mutter.

"Your father will be delighted to have a grandchild, I'm sure. You should be over the moon, Elizabeth. You've got exactly what you wanted."

"I only wanted a child that would have nothing of myself in it."

Gideon throws up his hands in a theatrical gesture deeply at odds with his usual affect.

"I love you," he says.

"Get out," I say.

For once I am stone cold sober. I can't drink because of the baby.

"I'll call you later," he says. "Will you be all right?"

I can't believe I have been so stupid.

"Get out," I say again.

I slam the door after him.

After a while I take off my nice clothes and put on a gray ribbed t-shirt, black biking shorts and Adidas sneakers. I'm too wired to go for a run. I don't know what to do with myself. As soon as the razor's in my hand, though, I know what's the right thing to do, the thing I've been waiting to do all day, the thing I've been waiting to do since I left home.

Without further ado I roll up my sleeve. I fill my lungs with air and then I slice deep into the shoulder, one long slash over the old marks, and another. Then another. The blood wells up in trenches and I feel the sense of release that nothing else gives me: it's like shooting up and finishing a marathon and having a screaming orgasm all in one smooth flood of feeling. Half an hour later, the bleeding has slowed down. I clamp a towel to my shoulder and get into bed with the envelope from Allan. Inside is a single sheet of photographic paper, the writing so small I have to squint to read it.

I hardly know what we talked of that last hour in the hold. To tell the truth, I was greatly relieved when the attendant told me I must go. I went home and took to my bed, though I slept not a wink, knowing what was to come the next morning. Afterwards I was able to get a full account of what passed. In the condemned hold the keepers watched Mr. Wild as narrowly as they could, to prevent any violence he might offer himself. About two o'clock in the morning, when they had dozed off, he drank the laudanum. The ordinary was there for it all, and gossiped about it the next day to anyone who would listen, which is how I came to know the particulars. Mr. Wild soon grew so drowsy that he could not hold up his head or keep his eyes open at prayers. Harpham and Sperry perceived his disorder and endeavored to rouse him, taking him by the arms and persuading to stand up and walk a little, for both the crowds and the law would have gone mad with rage had Mr. Wild successfully eluded them at the last.

The motion awakened him somewhat, it now being about six o'clock in the morning. He began to sweat violently and then grew exceeding faint and sick. After vomiting up the greatest part of the laudanum, he remained drowsy and hardly sensible of what he said or did.

The next he knew, the officers were putting them all into the cart, having refused Mr. Wild's request to be carried to the gallows in a closed coach, though they allowed him to have his hands untied.

Meanwhile I had much business to conduct, and rose from my bed at dawn. I did not yet know the laudanum had failed Mr. Wild. I went to the stables first and paid for the coach and horses (which meant clearing the debt we owed there, a fact I greatly resented, but could not think how to get around it without very great inconvenience), and half-a-dozen men to guard it down to the Cardigan's Head near Charing Cross. Then I retained a sexton and gravedigger to meet the coach secretly at night and lay Mr. Wild's body in what was supposed to be its final resting-place at St. Pancras Church-yard, though I did not tell them the exact place.

After that, knowing that by now my husband was beyond making any reprisals, and being myself desperately short of ready money, I had one more visit to pay. I dressed myself in an old pair of pattens and a shabby chip hat whose wide brim would conceal my face. I put an old cloak over my clothes, so as to travel incognito, although the dress beneath was the best one left in my wardrobe. I took a sedan chair, even though it cost a shilling a mile and I could scarce spare the money, for I thought I could get a better price from the man I went to meet if I did not seem desperate for what he had to offer.

I had always thought of the surgeons as devils incarnate, but the man I saw that day was an ordinary-looking fellow who you would never have looked at twice on the street. Our transaction was quickly concluded; he gave me fifty pounds as a tender of his being in earnest, with another hundred to follow the successful exhumation. Had I not offered for the money myself, the hundred pounds the surgeon paid me would have doubtless gone to one of the men who drove the coach, and why should he have had it instead of me?

And so, having paid out a mint of money to prevent the surgeons getting their hands on Mr. Wild's body, I had secretly taken steps to render all of those precautions ineffectual. His skin and entrails would be left to rot on the common shore of the parish.

I saw the rest with my own eyes, riding along in a closed coach ready to take away my husband's corpse as soon as the hangman had done his work. I had converted as many possessions into cash as I could, keeping only the few clothes and jewels I could not bear to part with. I had been alarmed at the great outlay involved in this enterprise: four men to take the body, after all, and two more to guard the coach with a blunderbuss, in addition to the expense of the burial itself. But it would not have done to make it known in the most public manner that I had betrayed my husband's trust, and the expense could not be avoided. The fifty pounds given me by the surgeon was almost all I had in money, and I depended on his next installment to secure my future in the Americas, where I would begin a new life.

Mr. Wild sat directly between Sperry and Stanford. Someone had put him into a callimanco night-gown and shoved a prayer-book into his hand. His head was bare.

I can hardly bear to remember with what roughness he was treated by the mob. Unlike the signs of pity they always showed when common criminals went to execution, they reviled and cursed him, and pelted him continually with stones and dirt. I had never before heard such loud shouts and huzzahs on the day of a hanging. The mob cried out the names of Blueskin and Jack Sheppard and a hundred other malefactors Mr. Wild had brought to justice. They called for his blood.

All the train of prisoners and their attendants stopped at the Griffin Tavern near Gray's Inn Gate to drink a glass of wine. I descended from the coach myself and pressed through the throng of people to try to reach my husband for one last word—I believe I thought of telling him of the real arrangements I'd made, gasping at my own boldness and shivering a little in the fear he'd somehow find a way to punish me from beyond the grave—but I could not get through to him, though I was close enough to overhear his words to a man standing beside him. "What a strange rig they run on me," was what he said, mumbling still from the laudanum and not seeming to know what he was about.

Ahead of us, the coaches of the quality and gentry almost blocked the road, the officers having to stop several times to clear the way. In Holborn, Mr. Wild's head was broken open by a stone thrown from a window, and thereafter the blood ran down his face unchecked.

They stopped again at the White Lion in St. Giles, where I saw Mr. Wild fumble for coins in his pocket and give money to one of the officers to pay for wine, and again at James Figg the prize-fighter's house at the Oxford Arms.

Mr. Wild drank another glass of wine at Figg's house, and I could see that he had begun to come to his senses again, at the very worst time. Was it a kind of joy I felt at the thought that he would be in his right mind at the moment of death? Tyburn loomed before him, and the spectators ushered him to his death with cries of jubilation.

I ordered the coachman to pull up as close as he could to the gallows, then clambered on top of the coach when we had come to a standstill. From there, I could see everything that transpired.

Now the other malefactors were ready to be turned off.

The executioner was Mr. Richard Arnet, once a guest at our own wedding. I saw Mr. Wild hand him something, and I knew that he was making him a present of his gold watch—I caught myself thinking that I could have used the money the watch would bring.

Arnet told Mr. Wild that he might take any reasonable amount of time to prepare himself—or so the newspapers reported the next day—and hanged the others. Mr. Wild continued sitting in the cart a little while longer. The mob called for Arnet to do his office. "We will knock you on the head if you do not perform it," they cried out, pelting the platform with stones and rubbish.

At last Mr. Wild stood up in the cart and Arnet put his neck into the halter.

"Ready, Mr. Wild?" he asks.

"Aye," says my husband, and even across the way I see him nod.

So Arnet strings him up. As he yanks the rope Mr. Wild catches hold of the arm of the corpse that hangs beside him, and the rope slackening as the crowd roars, Arnet pulls it tight.

◉

Eighteen hours later I'm still huddled under the duvet.

I have put Gideon's champagne in the fridge and Gideon's flowers in a jar of water.

My plane ticket and passport are sitting on the counter.

I can't decide what to do. I read somewhere once that people who don't respond to stimuli with the appropriate emotions turn out to be catastrophically bad decision-makers. Patients with frontal-lobe damage, for instance, experience incapacitating indecisiveness. It seems that even the most insignificant choices—which tie to wear, what to eat for lunch—depend on emotional cues. These individuals are flooded with information that the intellect is simply incapable of processing on its own. Without emotions, it's impossible to make up your mind.

I hear a voice in the street outside.

I cover my head with a pillow to drown out the sound.

"Elizabeth," I hear again. "Elizabeth."

Finally I drag myself from sleep. My charcoal-gray t-shirt is glued to my skin, dark enough to conceal it from the eye but stiff with dried blood.

I stumble out of bed and buzz him in.

The doorbell must be out of order.

"Thank god you're here," he says.

He is out of breath from the stairs.

"Are you all right?" he asks. "I've been trying to call you all morning."

"I turned off the phone," I mumble. "I can't seem to get enough sleep."

"Didn't you hear me outside?"

I shrug.

"I was sound asleep," I say.

I head for the bed.

I am too tired to be upset.

"Did your stepmother reach you yet?" he asks.

I come to a dead stop in the middle of the room. I have not spoken to my stepmother for five years.

"She called my office this morning," Gideon says. "She's going out of her mind trying to track you down. She'd called a few other old colleagues of your father's in London, then she remembered my name and phoned on the off chance that I might know where you were.

"She got my number from your father's Palm Pilot," he adds.

I fall into bed and pull the covers up to my chin.

"Elizabeth, I've got some rather terrible news for you," Gideon says.

I turn towards the wall.

He sits down on the side of the bed and begins to stroke my hair.

"Your father's quite ill," he says. "He had a heart attack on Tuesday, a bad one, and they rushed him to intensive care. He was actually dead for a couple of minutes, but they managed to resuscitate him. His condition's been upgraded from critical to stable, and there's every reason to believe he'll be all right, but I do think you've got to get there as soon as you can."

I lie still as he caresses my hair.

"Can I book a flight for you?" he says. He runs a finger along the lower lid of his right eye to catch a few tears. I don't know why he's crying.

"No," I say.

"Do you want me to come with you to the hospital?"

"Go away," I say.

He waits fifteen minutes, half an hour, an hour.

I will not speak.

Finally he goes away.

"Call me if you need anything," he says at the door.

I don't answer. If I had, I'd have told him that I need nothing. I need nothing at all.

In the end I do the only sensible thing. I call Dahlia. The buzzer rings twenty-five minutes later and I stumble out of bed to let her in. But it's not Dahlia. It's a delivery man with a huge vase of flowers, a fancy arrangement that makes me sneeze just looking at it.

I tip him and open the card. With love and condolences from Miranda and Gideon. The florist's address is right next to Miranda's office. Why couldn't Gideon have made the fucking call himself? I know this is Miranda's work.

When Dahlia arrives five minutes later I'm retching into a plastic bucket. She looks at the card that came with the flowers. Then, calm as ever, she takes the vase over to the window, opens it wide and tips the whole thing out. We hear the smash a second later in the courtyard below.

"I can't believe you did that," I say. Suddenly I don't feel so nauseous.

Dahlia snorts and starts packing. I go back to bed, pulling the covers over my head. When she taps me on the shoulder I don't respond at first. Finally I uncover my head and look at what she holds in her hand. It's the other letter, the one that Gideon brought upstairs along with Allan's last packet.

"Congratulations," she says. "You've been admitted off the wait list to Columbia Medical School."

"I'm not going to medical school," I say. "I'm pregnant."

Dahlia ignores me. She picks up my mobile and dials the international calling code, then the number for the Columbia registrar. She tells the registrar that I will accept the place they have offered me.

"You'll manage," she says when I protest. "The fact that Gideon and your father both wanted you to do it doesn't mean it's an inherently bad idea."

"I don't want to see my father," I say.

Dahlia gives me a long but not unsympathetic look. "As far as I can see," she says, "it is most straightforward. You tell me after reading these moldy old pages of Jonathan Wild that in the past the wife rejected the father for the son. Now you must do the opposite. As the daughter you will reject the son and embrace the father."

There's something both muddled and banal about this oracular sentence, but I see the logic behind her pronouncement. Half of me thinks it's a perfectly ridiculous thing to say. The other half knows she's completely right.

"Go to Connecticut," Dahlia adds, in case I haven't already gotten the point. "Go to medical school. Go home."

I give in and get up to help her pack. I can't stay in bed forever. It's time for me to go home.

It takes surprisingly little time to pack all my possessions into the duffel bag. An hour later, the only thing left that I care about is the box that held Mary Wild's narrative. I open the top and run my fingers one last time around the interior. Underneath the paper that lines the bottom of the box I find one final scrap of newsprint, a clipping that Mary Wild hadn't the heart to paste into her account. Even before I unfold the clipping, I know what it will say. The paragraph comes from the *Daily Journal* of 15 June 1725:

> Last Sunday Morning there was found upon Whitehall Shore, in St. Margaret's Parish, the Skin, Flesh and Entrails (without any Bones) of a Human Body: the Coroner & Jury that sat upon it, ordered it to be bury'd, which was done on Tuesday last, in the Burying Ground for the Poor, and the Surgeon who attended, gave it as his Opinion, that it could be no other than the Remains of a dissected Body. It was observ'd, that the Skin of the Breast was hairy, from whence People conjecture it to be part of the renowned Jonathan Wild.

ACKNOWLEDGMENTS

Over the course of writing *Heredity,* I consulted so many books that it would be impossible to name them all individually, but I am especially indebted to the following: Rob De Salle and David Lindley, *The Science of Jurassic Park and the Lost World, or, How to Build a Dinosaur* (1997); Robert R. Franklin and Dorothy Kay Brockman, *In Pursuit of Fertility,* 2d ed. (1995); Gina Kolata, *Clone: The Road to Dolly and the Path Ahead* (1998); Julian Litten, *The English Way of Death: The Common Funeral Since 1450* (1991); Ruth Richardson, *Death, Dissection and the Destitute* (1987); and Lee Silver, *Remaking Eden: Cloning and Beyond in a Brave New World* (1997). I could not have written the novel at all without the meticulous research and the compelling narrative of Gerald Howson's *Thief-Taker General: The Rise and Fall of Jonathan Wild* (1971), and I have also poached shamelessly from the writings of Jonathan Swift, Daniel Defoe and several other early eighteenth-century writers, including the anonymous compilers of *Select Trials at the Sessions House in the Old Bailey.* Thanks are due to the staff of the British Library, the Widener Memorial Library at Harvard University, the Sterling Memorial Library at Yale University and Butler Library at Columbia University, and to Ms. Elizabeth Allen, curator of the Hunterian Museum at the Royal College of Surgeons in London; I hope she will forgive the liberties I have taken here with her person and place of work.

I would like to thank the following people for reading partial or whole drafts, offering ideas or simply providing moral support: Idit Alphandary, Tina Bennett, Louise Bernard, Alejandro Bilbao-Guerra, David Bromwich, Stephen Burt, Seeta Chaganti, Partha Chattoraj, Radiclani Clytus, J. M. Coetzee, Sarah Cole, Imraan Coovadia, Julie Crawford, Alun David, Luke Dawson, LeeAnn Deemer, Joy de Menil, Jason Furman, Martha Glasserman, James Griffiths, Sean Gullette, Sloan Harris, John Hollander, Hellin Kay, Eve Keller, Ticky Kennedy, Karen Kenyon, Paul Kiel, Wayne Koestenbaum, Adam Lehner, David Liss, Bruno Maddox, Vijai Maheshwari, Michael Mallick, Dan Mandel, Michele Martinez, Joyce Carol Oates, Patrick Pearsall, Caryl Phillips, Nick Raposo, Claude Rawson, Marco Roth, Arielle Saiber, Miguel Sancho, Elaine Scarry, Simon Schama, Tanya Selvaratnam, Troy Selvaratnam, Natasha Shapiro, Joey Slaughter, Emily Steiner, Sara Suleri Goodyear, Ed Tilson, Naomi Wainer, Emily Wilson and Kevin Young. I am also grateful to my many students at Yale and Columbia who expressed interest in this project and encouraged me to keep writing, particularly the students in English 120 and Daily Themes at Yale.

A number of people deserve particular thanks. I am grateful for the financial generosity of Jay Furman and Jane Stevens, as well as for the extraordinarily kind and longstanding support of Gail Furman, who has been my benefactor in every sense of the word. Four friends have read multiple drafts and/or offered comments that had a significant impact on the final shape of the book: Elizabeth Teare, Carra Leah Hood, Jane Yeh and Amy Tübke-Davidson. Lisa Hamilton served briefly as my agent and has helped me at every turn. My family have also been immensely supportive: I would especially like to thank Ian Davidson, Caroline Davidson, Jonathan Davidson, Michael Davidson, Barbara Richards and Denis Richards. Finally, thanks to everyone at Soft Skull for making this possible, including David Janik, Tennessee Jones and (especially) Richard Eoin Nash.

ABOUT THE AUTHOR

Jenny Davidson was born in London in 1971 and grew up in Philadelphia, where she attended Germantown Friends School. She has degrees from Harvard and Yale and currently teaches eighteenth-century British literature and culture in the Department of English and Comparative Literature at Columbia University.